I0630204

ENCHANTING FATE
FAIRY TALES OF GALLIA BOOK ONE
ASHLEY EVERCOTT

Star Glass Publishing

This is a work of fiction. Names, characters, places, and incidents either are the product of the author's imagination or are used fictitiously. Any resemblance to actual persons, living or dead, business establishments, events, or locales is entirely coincidental.

Enchanting Fate

Copyright © 2022 by Ashley Evercott

Cover Design by: Miblart

Published by: Star Glass Publishing

All rights reserved. No part of this book may be used or reproduced in any manner whatsoever without written permission of the author except in the case of brief quotations embodied in critical articles or reviews.

Trade Paperback ISBN 979-8-9854115-0-8

Digital ISBN B09PLP75XT

www.ashleyevercott.wordpress.com

To my seven-year-old self who dreamed of becoming an author.
We did it.

1

Henri

Henri supposed he should feel sad as he stared at his father's corpse. Dozens of roses surrounded the body in a crimson halo, and floral arrangements hung around the wake room. They were sent by those who respected the man, but no amount of floral perfume and oils could mask the faint stench of death. His eyes roamed over the sutures keeping the corpse's mouth closed and down to the purplish blotches decorating the clasped hands over a fitted jacket. With no life to animate the body, his father was nothing but an empty shell.

A father who allowed his only son to live a life of solitude. Who allowed his stepmother and half-sisters to ignore his existence and leave servants to care for him. A *father* who saw him on rare occasions and only when his stepmother's eyes weren't watching.

Forgotten and alone.

No, perhaps the dead man was not much of a father at all.

Henri's grip tightened over the edge of the casket. Several eyes watched him. He felt them boring through his back, waiting for him to complete the custom expected of him.

Soft, meticulous footsteps clicked against the floor before a shadow fell over his face. A black veil covered his stepmother's face. However, her silvery eyes dulled whatever beauty she possessed, for they held nothing but disdain. The delicate folds of ribbon and lace upon her head gave her height, but not enough to tower over his tall frame as she used to when he was a boy.

"Please don't make us wait any longer," she said, soft like the rose petals around her husband and sharp enough to prick. He clamped down the urge to shudder at her closeness. It was the first time she had ever uttered the word "please" in his ear, and if he were not any wiser, he would have thought the death of her husband had softened the shriveled coal of her heart.

The white of his knuckles stretched into transparency while he stared at her retreating form. Her black dress swept like a sea of starless night behind her. Her three daughters sniffled in chairs, each wearing similar black gowns, and each glared at him until he turned his head back toward the corpse.

As the last one to view the body, they, along with all those who attended, waited on him before they could close the casket and transport it to the burial site. The religious tradition would ensure peace for his father while his soul traveled to the Inbetween, the realm between the Heavens and Hells, to be judged by Kyros, the God of Judgement. Henri was unsure if the Gods he was taught to believe in existed, if both Heavens and Hells were real, but if they were, he could only pray for his father to be judged accordingly.

Now, he was expected to lay his lips on his father's cold brow to show his respect, but his stomach churned at the thought of placing any part of his body on the corpse.

With clenched teeth, his fingernails screamed as he dug them further into the expensive wood. The smell of decay grew stronger, clouding his senses when he leaned closer toward the waxy face. It was too late to take a deep breath and hold it in to keep the smell at bay. He was already too close, but his stomach constricted as his lips ghosted over the space between its brows.

This was ludicrous.

There was no reason to keep up with the act any longer—to put on a show for those who wished he could trade places with his father.

He retreated and abandoned the custom. He felt his stepmother's acidic scowl through her veil, but for the first time in his life, he ignored the daggers aimed at his shame and walked away. She would have to do better if she wanted to scare him.

Henri tugged at his red cravat—a flippant burst of color in an ocean of ebony—while several pairs of eyes followed his retreating form. A large man with a round nose peered down at him and murmured, "Byblow," as he passed, but he didn't flinch at the insult. It was a title he bore and a title he continued to hear hurled in his direction while he weaved through the crowd.

He ignored them and the piercing eyes from the portraits of his father with his stepmother and half-sisters. Despite being his eldest, and only son, he was absent from all the paintings. No one wanted the memory of an illegitimate son, so the only memory of his face in these halls was his reflection in the mirrors between the portraits. But those reflections disappeared when he took one last glance before fleeing the hall altogether.

Mourning guests loitered in the foyer near the grand stairs, and a golden chandelier shimmered above them. Footsteps pursued him, clicking fast, but he reached the door first, opening it and rattling the hanging, sloping crystals.

Taking a deep breath, Henri allowed the fresh air to purify the miasmic smell of death out of his lungs and headed toward a carriage and four wagons. Each was prepped with luggage bags, furniture, hand-picked servants, and horses pawing the ground. Yet, he could not help but scan through each wagon to ensure *she* was there as he commanded. Finally, he spotted her sitting with another maid, but even when she glanced away and refused to look at him, he sighed in relief.

Isa.

No matter how much she despised him, he couldn't do this without her.

"What is the meaning of all this?" his stepmother asked. "When did you arrange this?"

Henri kept his stride, never once looking behind him. "Open the door, Claude."

The sandy blond valet opened the carriage door, but his eyes darted toward Henri's pursuer.

"Where do you think you are going?" his stepmother demanded.

A hand grabbed his shoulder, and he brushed it off with a swift shrug. Everything screamed at him to ignore the woman. To get in the carriage and never see her again, but her touch undid him.

Henri twisted on his heel so fast that his stepmother stumbled backward over the gravel. "I am leaving this place."

She gaped up at him. "Leaving? Your father has not yet been buried, and you're leaving already? Have you no shame?"

Shame. An emotion he felt all his life just by existing in her precious home. He composed himself and ground his teeth. "Ironic you should accuse me of such a thing when you are an expert of having little shame yourself."

"How—"

"How dare I?" he finished for her. "How dare you. I know what you tried to do with the will, to erase my name, and how you attempted to bribe the lawyer in secret. But little did you know," he reached into his inner coat pocket and withdrew a folded piece of parchment, "you have no power to do so."

"What is this?" She snatched the paper from his hands and unfolded it. She scanned the words, and all her smooth, angled features fell like axed timber. "This is not possible. Thierry assured me your name would never be in these papers."

He plucked the estate documents from her grasp and signed in the early hours of this morning in front of the clerk. "Apparently, my father had declared you no longer fertile to produce any male heirs and left me as the only viable option."

"I had an heir. His name should be on these documents—not yours."

Ah. The stillborn, the one hope she had of usurping him once and for all. "It's a shame he is dead, then."

"You little byblow," she hissed and raised a hand to strike him, but he caught it with ease. She struggled, twisting like a snake, but he refused to let go, clutching tighter until she screamed. Gasps and whispers filled the air as guests from the funeral filtered out to see the commotion. His stepmother's cheeks puffed, her eyes glinting with the intent to scratch his eyes out before three girls flew at them.

"Mama!" Georgette cried, pushing through the crowd and coming to her mother's side.

"Let her go, you horrid monster," Elayne, his oldest half-sister, demanded. Her black wavy curls she and her sisters inherited from Father, which matched his own, bounced in her marching footsteps. She charged like a fearless warrior in battle, hatred burning in her silvery eyes from her mother, and his heart leaped in fear at the sight of her. She had never voluntarily come this close in all her eighteen years, two years younger than himself.

After the shock of her approach wore off, hurt spread where fear had clutched him. It pained him to admit he still longed for his sisters' friendships—a respectful acquaintance at the very least—but his stepmother succeeded in poisoning them against him.

He unhooked his fingers from his stepmother's wrist and stepped back.

His youngest half-sister Francine came to her other side, and his stepmother cradled her hand to her chest. "Are you alright, Mama?" she asked her mother while taking the hand and inspecting the red indents of his fingers painted on her skin.

"I am fine, girls," his stepmother said before piercing him with a dark look. "But our estate will not be. Not in his hands."

"You are lucky then that I have no plans to stay and run this estate."

"What?" his stepmother said, her jaw slackening. "Where else would you go? This is where your *inheritance* is."

"It's not all. There's still one place: the Chateau d'Alarie. The place my great-great-grandfather built."

All three of his half-sisters stared at him with large, rounded eyes. His stepmother scoffed. "Are you mad? Your grandfather abandoned the chateau for a reason. It's not operable, let alone livable, in those woods."

"It's haunted," Francine whispered. Of course, as a girl of eleven, she would still believe in such fairytales—of sacred magic lurking within forests. Such tales and superstition drove out his ancestors, but he believed in no such thing. Even the scriptures claimed magic had been revoked from the face of Gallia.

"If it's far from you all, it will do," he responded coolly.

Someone in the half-circle crowd around them tutted their dismay, and his stepmother's cheeks flushed under her veil, no doubt humiliated in front of their audience. Whispers curled like shadows through the crowd until her face sharpened into steel. "You ungrateful little wretch! We housed you, clothed you, and fed you. You wouldn't be alive if it weren't for us! You don't deserve your father's title." His stepmother took a step forward and pointed a finger in his face. Although he was taller than she, he shrank at her sudden proximity.

The muscles in his back stiffened at the memory of her riding crop against his back when he was ten years old. All for running into the right wing of the estate—her domain. It was the first and last time the crop bit into his skin, but it was enough to know she would never accept him as her son. His fists curled by his side. "If you believe I will grovel at your feet for providing the basic necessities, you would be sorely mistaken."

His stepmother swept her arms out in a dramatic gesture. "Of course, you wouldn't be grateful. I allowed a byblow under my roof. I suppose you plan to leave us all penniless and ruined of our reputations, then? Prove yourself a monster. Go on, do it!"

"Oh, I certainly shall." He pulled out a second document signed by the same clerk that morning. "As master and Count of my father's property, I have already sold this estate. However, I corresponded with Mr. Jacques, a second cousin of yours if you recall, and he said he'd be happy to marry you and adopt your daughters.

Of course, your title of Countess will be stripped from you, but I suppose being homeless is a worse fate." He paused to revel in the horror in her eyes. "Is that monstrous enough for you, *Mother*?"

For once, she and her daughters were speechless and dared not breathe lest they draw life into their new circumstance.

"A Baroness is still a fitting title," he said in response to their silence. "Did you hope for more? He is not so bad on the eyes. Perhaps a little older for your tastes."

"See here, now—" a voice said, one he recognized as his step-mother's brother, Mr. Tremblay. The tall, wiry man stepped forward, but Henri turned his back on them.

"Everything I have not already packed with me is yours to sell," he said over his shoulder toward his stepmother. Tears slid past her veil, and she held a hand to cover her trembling mouth. "You should leave with a small fortune if you sell all those pretty portraits. It could be worse."

A ragged sob escaped her lips. Another cry from Francine followed, but he masked any twinge of guilt, pulling at his conscience over his young sister's tears. A heavy hand fell on his shoulder, twisting him back around.

"You have gone too far, Henri," Mr. Tremblay said, his hand squeezing over the muscle there painfully.

"It's *Mr.* Alarie to you." Henri jerked from the man. "You would be wise to never lay a hand on a Count again."

Mr. Tremblay did not reach out or strike him, although the intent lay clear in his eyes. Good. Mr. Tremblay understood his place, as so should everyone here. No longer could they have power over him for as long as he lived.

His stepmother's cries erupted into a chorus of wails, and his half-sisters clung to one another. Mr. Tremblay went toward her side, and she threw herself into his arms. The man whispered something in her ear, raising his gaze to direct another malicious glare toward him.

"You will regret this, *Mr.* Alarie," Mr. Tremblay said.

"No." Henri fished around his pocket to retrieve a coin. "I don't think I shall. Here." He tossed it up in the air, and it bounced, clanging against the cobbled ground until it rolled to a stop at his stepmother's feet.

They all looked at him, their fear and loathing palpable.

"For your troubles," he said, eyeing their ugly, tear-stained faces.

This was it. This was the last image he would have of the woman he so desperately wished could have been a mother to him. Instead, his very existence disgusted her. She manipulated her daughters against him, and they punished him for daring to be born.

He should feel sorry for them, especially his half-sisters, who were all under the age of nineteen, but he searched through his heart and found he didn't care. They would continue living a comfortable life in the city of Avilon if their mother accepted Mr. Jacques' proposal. The Baron was an elderly widower, lonely, but kind, even if his table manners were atrocious. And, although his half-sisters might be the center of gossip for years to come, they were pretty enough to snag a wealthy husband, with or without a title. They would be fine.

It was time to leave.

He turned his back on them for the last time and took his place inside the carriage. Without another glance, he rapped on the carriage ceiling, and it took off with a lurch. As the wheels rumbled down the road, the estate, the prison of his childhood, became nothing but a distant speck on the horizon.

2

Marguerite

"I don't have a good feeling about this, miss, not one bit."

Marguerite glanced behind her to see Sophie purse her lips together. Her maid's cheeks flushed red as she shuffled to catch up with her pace. Marguerite's face felt warm from exertion, and her lungs ached under her stays, but she waved a hand forward.

"I must try, Sophie. For all our sakes, I must," she said.

Puddles gathered from the rain, pooled from yesterday's downpour, but she skipped over them, attempting to keep her hem clean. A gentleman and lady gave her curious stares as she hustled past them in a whirl of skirts and petticoats. She knew she was gathering unwanted attention speeding along, but there was no time for 'proper' strolls. She would have taken a carriage and horse if given a choice, but preparing both would have taken too much time. It would be faster to walk, and, although her ankles ached against the satin of her shoes, she could not afford to slow down now. She must catch Mr. Bellanger before his audience with Mr. and Mrs. Paquet.

Turning another corner, she stepped onto a muddy street before a carriage rushed in front of her. Murky rainwater splashed up her face and down the front of her floral gown, leaving her no time to scream. It stained the blue material a dubious brown and painted her chest in icy cold rivulets.

"Miss Dupont!" Sophie cried, claiming her soaked arm between her warm hands, and pulled her away from the road. "Oh, you should know better than to run out into the street before looking. Are you alright, miss?"

Marguerite's cheeks flushed with embarrassment. Indeed, she knew better than to cross a busy street, but determination clouded her judgment. After a moment, she nodded. Then, wiping her eyes, she flicked the rainwater and mud away and reached for her hair. When she felt soaking wet tendrils, her heart dropped. "I am fine, Sophie, don't mind me."

"Oh, I knew this was a bad idea, miss. You will catch a downright cold if we don't fix you right up. Come on, let's get you back home, now."

"No." She resisted her maid's tugging. "There won't be a home if I don't do this. I must continue."

"But your appearance—"

"Will have to do." She brushed the sludge from her neck. "I don't have a choice."

"There is always a choice, miss. You know that. You don't have to do this at all."

"If only it were that simple. My family needs me—they depend on me to do this."

"What about your sister? That Mr. Laroux chap was planning on proposing to her, right? And she likes the fellow well enough to accept the offer. You don't need to put yourself through this."

"Mr. Laroux has changed his mind." Her jaw clenched at the thought of the thin man with an under-bite rivaling a bulldog's. He seemed to be a pleasant gentleman until she overheard him mocking her family's misfortunes two days prior on his daily stroll, and more infuriatingly, he had made obscene comments about her sister.

Marguerite had been sorely tempted to march out of the jewelry shop and slap him in front of those animals he called friends, but she refrained. The action would have only tarnished her family's little reputation, so she stood there and heard their vulgar speech while everyone in the shop listened on as she exchanged her pearls for money. No one intervened, no gentleman defended her sister's honor—no one dared to when her family had nothing left to their name.

It was more reason to press on and confront Mr. Bellanger once and for all.

"Even so, miss," Sophie said, cutting through her thoughts. "Must you sacrifice what you want so dearly for your family? Isn't there another way?"

Marguerite looked down at her muddy hands, which had painted hundreds of portraits and ached to paint hundreds more. If not for the storm that claimed her father's merchant ships, she would have been meeting Sir Jean-Pierre Deschamps by now, discussing an artist apprenticeship despite her mother's chagrin, but Sophie was right. If she approached Mr. Bellanger, and he accepted her proposition, she knew she would never be able to pursue the artist career she dreamed of, for he was the kind of man who would never allow his wife the *privilege*.

Yet, even if she did not meet Mr. Bellanger and turned around and abandoned her pursuit as Sophie advised, she could not afford such dreams anyhow.

"What I want doesn't matter, not anymore." She looked at Sophie, whose face crumpled with sympathy. She was a good friend—better than she deserved—but she must ignore her words lest she be tempted to act on them. "I must hurry," she said, looking both ways before rushing across the road. Sophie's protests were lost in the commotion of passing carriages and clomping horses, but she kept up, huffing behind her.

A row of white estates decorated by trimmed hedges lined the street three blocks further. Mr. Bellanger lived in the fourth house on the left, and her heart picked up speed as she advanced upon the black door. Before she or Sophie could convince her that her plan was pure madness, she lifted the golden door knocker and rapped three times.

She patted her dress and tucked the stray, dripping hairs out of her face before a woman with sagging jowls opened the door. It only took one cursory glance over her figure, and the woman began shutting the door back in her face, but Marguerite quickly wedged her foot in.

"Please, tell Mr. Bellanger that Miss Dupont is here to see him."

The woman's mouth pinched together. "Miss Dupont, you say?" She glanced at Sophie to confirm her claim but returned to scrutinize her dress. "Does the miss have an appointment?"

"No, but please, tell him who I am, and he'll allow me in."

The woman harrumphed, muttering something about the state Marguerite was in before telling her to wait and shut the door. It opened again after a few minutes, and the handsome face of Mr. Bellanger followed. The surprise in his eyes dissolved into horror upon looking her up and down, taking in the mud and soaking hair.

"By the Gods, what happened to you?"

His response was not the greeting she had hoped for when she first set out this morning, but it was better than having the door slam in her face.

"I was unfortunate enough to have been splashed by a passing carriage," she said. "A little rainwater is all."

"A little? You look absolutely miserable."

She pursed her lips at his tact. "May I come in? I would like to speak with you, please."

His eyes strayed behind her to the muddy trail and her dripping hair. "Of course, but first, a towel. I would rather not have the floors dirtied. I had them polished this morning."

He left her with a smile, too wide above his strong jaw. When he returned, a servant gave her a towel, and she dried herself as best she could before entering the parlor with Sophie. Cream walls detailed with gold piping glimmered in the sun, and a set of blue chaises sat beneath a golden, gilded mirror. Upon seeing her reflection, she blanched.

All the brunette curls Sophie heated and pinned limped to the back of her head, and the fashionable curl down her neck had unwound and sat on her skin like a soggy rat. The rainwater left crusty dirt stains down her jaw, neck, and chest, and her favorite blue gown was beyond repair. No amount of washing would be able to get rid of the sludge clinging to her whole front.

Mud did not belong in such an opulent room. She was out of place—a dirty mark against the cream walls. She was sure to bring more humiliation to her mother if she was spotted entering and departing from Mr. Bellanger's home in this state of dress.

Unfortunately, she had no choice.

Tearing her eyes away from her reflection, she forced herself to swallow down her apprehension when she looked at Mr. Bellanger, who sat lounging beneath the mirror. It was a calculated move, she thought, with his eyes filling with mirth while he dissected her bedraggled appearance. He wanted her to see how she looked before him.

No matter, she held her head high and remained standing to not soil his couch despite being tempted to do so. It would certainly wipe the smug smile off his perfect, square chin.

"Mr. Bellanger," she said, folding her hands in front of her stained dress.

"Miss Dupont. How may I entreat you this lovely morning? I don't mean to be hasty, but I have guests coming in a quarter-hour."

"I understand, and I will be quick then. I have come on behalf of your proposal."

One thick brow curled upward. "Oh? And what proposal are you speaking of?"

He was playing coy as usual, but she refused to play along. "The one you asked of me just a fortnight ago. At the gala, if you recall."

"Ah." He leaned forward and raised a finger in a gesture of remembrance. "I remember now. The one *you* rejected, where you left me standing alone on the balcony? Is this the same proposal you speak of?"

She did not break her gaze. "Indeed it is."

"Well, what makes you believe there is still a proposal to speak about?"

It took all her willpower to school her features and reign the nervous emotions banging against her heartbeat. If the circumstances were different, she would have had more tact, but desperation called for tactless measures. "I believe you were sincere in your offer, and I have come to claim it."

"Did you, now?" His dark brows shot up before he stood, blocking her view of the mirror. Mr. Bellanger stood taller than her by one head, but she did not feel intimidated by his height. Instead, she squared her shoulders and stared into his dark, brown eyes. The white wig he wore was tied at the nape of his neck, and the curls framed his chiseled face without a hair out of place. If his character had matched his exterior, she would have accepted his proposal the first time he had asked. Now, she prayed to the Gods, to Erus of the Heavens especially, that he would stand by his offer.

"Yes, I accept your proposal, Mr. Bellanger." She forced the words out as pleasantly as she could manage. "I will gladly become your wife."

"Oh, no doubt you would." He pointed a finger in front of her face and then to her maid behind her. "No doubt you have come crawling back to me—to accept my offer once your dear father's business is devastated, hmm?"

She feigned a sweet smile. "My father's business has nothing to do with this."

"Bold you are, but a liar you are not, my dear. Pray, do tell, did he send you here? Did he send his daughter to beg for my hand in marriage in his stead?"

Stiffening, the rounds of accusations slapped her across the face. She could only open her mouth to deny him.

He wouldn't let her. Instead, he continued his tirade, "I don't blame him. I wouldn't want to show my face to anyone after the travesty he called a business. I imagine he wants me to swoop in and save him," he sneered, and heat inflamed her cheeks. "If so, he sorely underestimated your powers of persuasion. Especially in the hideous state you're in."

She bit her tongue to suppress how she really felt about him in return. If she had her way, she would have struck his cheek, but she clenched her hand by her side instead.

"If you marry me and revive his business, you would be made head of the business and our estate. All of it could be yours."

"You truly are persuasive, aren't you?" He laughed and strode toward a small table with a champagne bottle and glass goblets. Uncorking it, he poured himself a drink and raised it toward her in a mock toast.

"If you invested—"

"If *I* invested. That's quite a bargain, isn't it? What if all my investments don't pay out? What then?"

"Everything we have would be yours to keep, to sell, to do whatever you please."

"Ah, I wonder how much I could get out of those cheap pearls your mother wears?" He sipped the drink and shook his head with another laugh.

Her hands clamped over her silken dress at her sides. Every muscle stiffened, ready to pounce on the insufferable man. Never had she been insulted so thoroughly by a gentleman, but she took a deep breath.

Perhaps Sophie was right. She shouldn't be here. "I was mistaken to believe your offer still stood, then. Good day, sir." Turning on her heel, she waved for Sophie to follow and marched toward the doors.

"Wait, come now, Marguerite, don't go, not yet."

She swiveled around but did not inch from the door. "I don't believe I gave you permission to use my given name."

"On the contrary." He sauntered toward her, the champagne in his glass swirling in his hand. "You did the moment you begged me to marry you."

Her eyes tapered into a glare. "I did not beg. I only came to accept your offer, which is clearly off the table."

"I never said such a thing."

"You certainly made your intentions known, sir. You clearly don't wish to marry me, so I will be on my way—" She turned to open the door until he pressed his hand against it, right above her head.

"Sir!" Sophie interjected.

"Thank you," Marguerite said quietly to her maid before straightening herself to meet his gaze. "Have you reconsidered then?"

"To be clear, it was you who reconsidered."

"Well." She held back another biting comment. "Are you taking my reconsideration seriously?"

"Of course." A roguish smirk spread across his mouth. He leaned toward her, studying her face. "I am now."

"Shall we speak more civilly then? If we are to finish this conversation, I would rather us proceed without your churlish remarks."

His smile widened, and he released his hand from the door. "Of course, just come away from there."

"Very well." She walked back toward her previous spot in front of the mirror. He sat down, making himself comfortable once more.

"Mr. Bellanger," she started.

"Come now. We are past that. Call me Gustave."

She said nothing in return but nodded to acknowledge the comment.

"I underestimated you, Marguerite," he said to break the silence, sipping elegantly from the crystal glass. "You are more spirited than I took you for. I like that. Cunning too. I don't know how you heard of my next appointment with the Paquets but, I admire your tenacity. You beat them to it."

Her lips pursed. Cunning was an underhanded description, one she did not care for, but she would not reveal how she sent a servant to retrieve the information. It was not cunning if her family was in need.

"They are offering me their daughter in marriage, as you know. A match that would certainly benefit me but my father, sick as he is, still has a soft spot in his heart for yours."

His eyes narrowed, disgusted, but Marguerite's heart took flight with hope. It was true that his father, the Senior Mr. Bellanger, and her father had been good friends since childhood. Both men had conspired to marry her to Gustave Bellanger despite her dislike for the man. She had only interacted with Gustave three times in her life due to his studies abroad, but all three times left a bitter taste in her mouth.

"I pray your father has a speedy recovery," she said.

"Ah, well, the old fool will make it. A bout of pneumonia won't stop him if he has anything to say about it. He might be sick but won't shut up about your family. It's all I hear about."

Good. There was more than hope for her family if the Senior Bellanger had a say in his son's affairs.

"Was he the reason why you proposed to me?" she dared to ask. "The night at the gala?"

"Yes, and no. It might be unbelievable in the state you're in now, but you are a beautiful woman. I thought you were fair and the least annoying of your father's daughters. I didn't mind the match my father suggested until you opened your mouth to refuse me."

He took another sip, his mouth pinching as he swallowed. The clock on the mantle ticked in time with the frustration boiling within her, but she let out another long exhale.

She prayed to the Gods for strength and forgiveness for the dignity she was about to sacrifice. "I apologize for refusing you, Gustave. But I am here before you now to accept your proposal. Will you reconsider?"

A devilish grin shadowed his features, and her gut twisted with fear.

3

Henri

H enri sat alone. Golden candelabras glimmered, their flames waving gently on the table set with steaming, delicate dishes, but none inspired hunger. He eyed one of the silver dishwares and frowned upon seeing his appearance in the shiny metal. His dark hair curled neatly down to his collarbone, and even in the distorted, makeshift mirror, his nose still appeared straight above his small mouth.

An exact replica of his father.

Memories of the dead man resurfaced in waves, stealing what little appetite he had. It had been three weeks since his passing, but he could still feel the man's disapproval as he sat at his ancestral table.

"*A table and home you do not deserve after what you have done,*" Henri imagined his father saying. No doubt the man would have been appalled at how he left his stepmother and half-sisters.

The platters were put aside before Claude, his valet, dipped down to replace his napkin. A second course was laid out before him, and he speared the turkey with his knife. When he forced himself to raise it to his mouth, a rapid knock startled him, and the morsel and the knife clattered on his plate.

The dining room door swung open before a figure appeared. A young man of eighteen averted his eyes to the ground. "Mr. Alarie?"

"Do you really wish to disturb my evening meal, Joseph?" Henri clipped, retrieving the knife and pointing it at the boy.

"No, Mr. Alarie, but the door."

He stilled. Who in all of Gallia could be at his doorstep at this time of night, let alone in the middle of the woods? Perhaps his stepmother sent someone to kill him or set his abode aflame? Although both actions were implausible, he did not put it past the woman to seek revenge somehow.

"Who is it?"

"An old beggar man refuses to leave until he speaks to you," the doorman said.

A deep crevice carved between Henri's brow before he glared at the young man. "What incompetent imbecile let him past the gates?" he demanded.

"I...I do not know, sir, but he has insisted, and I cannot sway him."

"Then grab him and forcibly remove him. Call more servants if you must. Are you so stupid that you cannot even manage that?" His hands swung with gusto, the knife glistened dangerously, and the boy swallowed.

"I have tried, sir, but no one will touch him. I didn't want to disturb you, sir, and did everything I could, but—he...he has a strange air about him, and they are afraid—I am afraid too. Oh, sir, *please.*"

He stood suddenly. The delicate silver and China spread on the table rumbled at the movement.

"Do you realize what you all have done? How could you have even allowed a stranger on the premises? You will be dealt with *after* I do your job."

"Sir," Claude, his valet, called out, but he ignored him and kept the sharp knife in his hand. If this were some vengeful ploy from his stepmother, she would be sorry.

Henri's black, polished heels clacked across the parquet floors while another set of footsteps followed close. "Sir, this is not necessary. Please, let someone else handle this," Claude pleaded behind him.

"How can I trust these idiots if a mere *beggar* can show up at my doorstep?" he said, rounding a corner and finding the entrance. Three servants huddled together by the closed doors, their backs facing him. "Cowards!"

They snapped to attention but averted their gaze shamefully. "Sir," they said, bowing their heads.

"Give me a light," he snapped at them. Jeanette quickly grabbed a lit lantern from the door's hook and handed it to him. They parted for him, and he threw the doors open. He raised the lantern, turning left and right with a sneer.

"Where is the wretch?"

From beside him, Claude pointed, his arm outstretched but shaking. Henri followed his hand and spotted him. In the darkness of the night stood a man leaning on a tall, wooden staff.

"Leave this place," Henri commanded.

The man shuffled closer, hunched and limping; the light from his lantern slowly revealed his features. He was old and feeble, with deep wrinkles stretched across his skin. White hair hung limp and greasy around his mottled, balding head. One of his eyes had been gouged out, an old wound judging by the way the skin had healed, leaving a gaping hole in his socket, and the flesh there had been stretched so thin, the bone could be seen through its transparency. The other eye was a round, bulging orb that assessed him with strange, rapid movements.

Henri's nose scrunched at the smell of manure clinging to the old man when he stepped closer. Instinctively, Henri took a step back when the beggar took one forward. Something carnal, the drive forcing humans to survive, whispered that danger was approaching.

"Stop. I said leave," he said, but his voice cracked. Who knew if the man carried a plague? Perhaps this was his stepmother's scheme after all: to send a diseased man into his home in the hopes of killing him and everyone inside.

"I have been asking to see you," the old man said, his voice warbled with age.

"What do you want? Did my stepmother send you?"

"My daughter is sick, and her children are starving. Could you not spare alms for a poor, old man?" His knobby hand reached out and nearly touched him. It was covered in open sores with pus and oozing blood. Raised scabs and scars crawled up his arms like a spiderweb. Henri flinched while striking the offending, diseased-looking hand away with the lantern. The metal hitting the beggar's skin made an audible cracking sound. The old man cried out, grunting, and cradled the proffered hand with the other.

"Don't touch me. How dare you trespass my lands and come begging at my door? I will not ask again. Leave, or I will be forced to throw you out myself."

The injured hand was brought up to the man's heart in a fist with his wandering yellow eye assessing him. "You...you would deny an old man the crumbs from your table?"

"I will happily deny you. Return to the scum from whence you came." He spat toward his feet. "I have warned you already, old man, and you did not heed me. You three," he called to the servants peeking through the open doorway. "Take him away from my sight. Be sure he remembers never to step foot here again."

There was no sound of purposeful footsteps, and after standing there for several moments, his smug expression fell as he turned to them. They had not taken a single step toward the offender but looked at the old man in fright—their wide eyes suggested they saw a ghost rather than a weak invalid.

They failed him again.

Rankled, he gestured to the old man. "Are you deaf or simply stupid? I told you—" he gripped the knife tighter and grabbed one of the male servant's arms, "—to get rid of him!"

Henri pushed the servant toward the beggar, and the servant wobbled at the sudden force, but as soon as he found his balance, he stood there, staring at the elderly man like he was hypnotized by a swinging pendulum. The three remaining servants, including

Claude, also stood their ground. Henri looked into the eerie eye and felt his rage pound behind his own, painting his vision red.

"I am surrounded by idiots. Will no one listen to me?" He swung the knife around with little regard, sweeping it toward every face behind and in front of him.

"Sir, please, let me handle it then," Claude said and approached his master with his hands up in a gesture of surrender.

Henri laughed at the irony of the situation. "My dog is braver than these scared rats."

Relief was evident in his valet's expression, but he despised the look on his face—the look of a man who thought his master was unhinged.

"Don't interfere. Know your place. I will deal with this myself!" Henri yelled before spinning the weapon toward the old man in a deranged sweep. "You have lost your chance, and my patience has run thin," he said, pointing the metal's tip to the beggar's stomach.

The old man did not recoil at the threat. His wandering eye ceased to shift around like a buzzing hummingbird and became still on him. Henri's skin prickled at the clear and quiet focus in the man's eye as his infected hands came up and clasped the knife between his palms. His brows furrowed, and he attempted to understand what it meant before the metal shattered. The shards rattled around his boots, and his bottom hit the ground hard, but his hands continued to scurry his weight backward, away from the old man.

"Witchcraft!" Henri whispered.

The old man's feet lifted like he was suspended by strings, and his hands stretched out beside him before a burst of light consumed him. Henri shielded his eyes, peeking through his fingers, and gasped at the sight.

The beggar had transformed. The wrinkles disappeared, revealing smooth, luminous, light blue skin with eyes glowed like two firefly brimstones. Gone were the limp, white locks replaced by long onyx hair pulled into a band behind his nape. The power exuding from him was palpable. A strange energy he had never experienced pulsed from the floating figure's white staff. His heavy robes, trimmed with gold and silver threading, rippled around him like he was floating underwater.

"Centuries ago, your kind named me Gaël," it said. The resounding voice demanded respect and wonder. "I am an Enchanter, Count Henri d'Alarie."

He knows my name! he thought, but the words would not form over his mouth.

This was impossible. Enchanters and all magical beings didn't exist—they hadn't for over two hundred years. The priests of his youth told how most magical creatures disappeared from their world, Gallia, and the Enchanters returned to Erus, the God of the Heavens, never to be seen again.

But, he sat, trembling before the staff, which burst into swirling, emerald flames. "I warned your ancestors never to step foot in this sacred place again," the Enchanter said. "This forest is protected by my master, Erus of the Heavens, and I have been appointed to keep it safe. I have been sworn to keep humans like you from destroying and building upon the sacred wood the Goddess Ghiana created. But here you are, less than a hundred years later, and you trespass again."

Warm liquid trickled down Henri's breeches and his socks. He willed himself to move, speak, and do anything to escape, but his limbs froze.

"Moreover, I have seen your selfishness, your cruelty," the Enchanter continued. "You treat your servants like animals."

The floating Enchanter drew closer, so close he could see the molten gold swirling in his green eyes. But fear won and drove him to stumble back on his hands, twisting and finding the strength to stand. He shoved a servant toward the Enchanter and sprinted inside the safety of his home.

Blood pumped wildly under his skin, clawing for an escape. His footsteps squelched from the urine trailing down his legs, and his eyes throbbed, searching, pleading, and desperate for the back door—an exit. Finally, after turning down several hallways, relief filled him like a sweet embrace.

Throwing the doors open, they crashed hard against the walls, glass shattering everywhere. Stumbling over the scattered shards, he ran through the cobbled path until his coat pulled, springing him backward. He looked down to find sharp thorns from a rose bush embedded in the material. Whimpering and shaking, he unhooked his arm from one of the sleeves to free himself.

He froze.

The Enchanter loomed above him; he could sense the unsettling power emanating from his floating form. He could no longer run. He was trapped. He must accept his fate. Turning, Henri sank to his knees with his hands clasped together.

"Please spare my life," he begged.

Gaël chuckled something dark and deep. "I think you misunderstand. You will not die."

"Oh, thank you, bless you," Henri sobbed, pressing his forehead to the dirt.

"No, you will not meet death this day, no. You will be cursed instead and may wish for death soon enough."

Henri's head shot up; his eyes widened as the realization flooded his mind like a drowning man. "No," he whispered. "No, I beg you. Don't curse me. I...I will do anything. Anything!" he insisted, reaching up to touch the glowing robes but flinched when the material burned him.

"The Gods have spoken, and it shall be done. I am happy to oblige them." The tip of the staff blazed like hot embers and was lifted toward the starry night.

"No, no! Listen to me. Please don't do this. I beg of you!" he hollered. Gaël ignored him.

> *"From the ashes of the dead*
> *to the sky,*
> *let the powers of Gallia hear*
> *my cry.*

Lend me your powers and
gifts,
let all know that justice was
swift."

Gaël pointed his staff toward him, and he could see the fiery swirl crackle green. He hollered obscenities, attempting to flail and escape, but some force beyond his control held his tongue and rooted him to the ground.

"I curse you, Count Henri
d'Alarie
that you may know your
crimes and savagery.
Reveal your true form
Let your bones crack and be
reborn."

Excruciating pain shot through his entire body like a shock of lightning. Tendons, muscles, and insides were aflame, and he screamed in agony. Every fiber of his being was breaking, melting, growing, and shrinking. The shouting grew hoarse in his throat, but the sound of them distorted into a howl—a beastly, animalistic cry that frightened him amidst the pain.

"Let this be a lesson of hu-
mility
To overcome all of your
anger and hostility.
A woman fate shall send.
She is the key to the curse's
end.
Only by learning to love and

be loved in return,
may you break this curse
and find what your heart
truly yearns."

To his horror, the muscles in his arms began to lengthen, muscle growing where he had none. The clothes on his back pulled and stretched like young tree sap before they ripped into pieces. The hair on his arms grew long and coarse, the teeth in his mouth shifted in his gums and sharpened against his tongue.

"Break the spell before your
garden wilts.
Only then can your life be
rebuilt."

A flash of light consumed him before his body convulsed into agonizing spasms. Another howl reverberated from his chest before the darkness embraced him.

4

Marguerite

The carriage rumbled, swaying Marguerite and her family down the road. Tears pooled down her cheeks as she craned to watch Avilon, the bustling capital of Varis, and the city she was born and raised in, disappear along the horizon. Everything her family owned was discarded or sold off to the highest bidder that morning. An ache buried itself beneath her ribcage at the thought of all her paintings being thrown into the "non-valuables" pile to be incinerated later.

An order given by her mother. *"They aren't worth much any-way,"* her mother had said. Marguerite had not shed tears then, not when her heart soared with gratitude when Sophie had saved some portraits from the pile and promised she would keep them safe for her.

Oh, how she'd miss her.

Now, the carriage meant for four persons, cramped with heat with the five occupants. The May sunshine beat through the open windows, the navy curtains drawn aside to allow air to flow through the muggy space. The small bench had little cushioning, and her shoulders bumped against her brother's strong arm every time the wheels creaked over the uneven dirt road.

No one spoke. Their eyes were also trained on the disappearing city skyline.

"I had hoped you could have secured a better arrangement with Mr. Bellanger."

Marguerite jolted and glanced at her mother, who broke the heavy silence. Mr. Bellanger accepted Marguerite's proposal but would not marry her and save them from poverty until his return from his Navy tour. He hadn't said it, but she knew he was enacting revenge for how she rejected his proposal at the Gala.

"Mama, I tried. I really—"

"If you had seduced him properly, we would not be in this mess." The whites of her mother's eyes burned red, and her words clawed around Marguerite's insides.

"I did the best I could—"

"Your brother and sister could have kept their engagements, and we would not be on our way to live like horrible peasants."

"Now, now. It will be alright, my love," Papa said, his voice gentle but weary.

"It's easy for you to say. You have always wanted to live like pigs. Out...out in the *country*." Her mother spat the word like a curse while snatching her hand away. "Now we are forced out of our home. If she had done her job, Mr. Bellanger would have been more charitable toward us. We would not have to sell our home or wait for his return to help us."

Marguerite resisted the urge to burst into more tears and opened her fan to hide her crumpling expression. It was wise to keep her mouth shut and take the abuse when her mother was in such a state.

"Dear, we will work things out," Papa said.

"Says the man who invested *everything* we had—even *my* dowry—into the business. I told you it was a bad idea. I told you."

"What use does harping on Marguerite or Father do for us?" Phillipe, her older brother, said, looking up from picking at his nails to her right. The fact he could speak openly to their mother in this way made her jealous, but she was glad he could speak reason on her behalf when she could not.

"Mother is right, though," Rosalie, her younger sister, said from across them, sitting next to Mother. The fan in her hands whipped open, and her dog, Bonbon, looked up from her lap. "If she had not rejected him the first time, we wouldn't be on our way to live in the country like some paupers."

"We have already discussed the matter, so bringing it up again does little to solve it," Phillipe said.

"Well, I had a life here. I was supposed to have a proper engagement, unlike Marguerite."

Father waved his hands down. "Please, can we lower our voices—"

"Oh, my poor daughter—my son." Her mother burst into tears and pressed her hands into her face, smudging her powdered makeup. "They'll never marry well after this!"

"Mr. Laroux is a pig," Phillipe said, ignoring their mother's cries.

"I don't care," Rosalie sneered. "His inheritance would have allowed me and all of us to live more than comfortably. Why aren't you more upset anyhow? Catherine wants nothing to do with you now that we have nothing."

Guilt nestled around Marguerite's heart, and she could not help but look to her brother. By the tightening of his lips, she knew he was holding back the hurt from his sweetheart's rejection.

"I will not blame my father nor my sister for Miss Aubert's decision," he said, his eyes narrowing.

"Well, I certainly can."

Marguerite snapped her fan shut, unable to keep her emotions at bay. "What more do you want from me? Did you expect me to throw my dignity out the window? Besides, you are only seventeen. You are far too young to be getting married."

"And you're too old," her sister said, rolling her eyes. "You are twenty, and yet most of my friends are married, and they are only a year older than I. I think you're jealous because Mr. Laroux still wants me."

Thoughts of Mr. Laroux's braying laughter outside the jewelry shop surfaced in her mind, and her grip tightened over her fan. "He is a horrid man; you should not be pining after him."

"Pining? I am not in love with him. Is that what this is about? Are you upset because Mr. Bellanger did not love you enough to save us from poverty?"

Heat flashed through Marguerite's veins. Her sister had no idea what kind of man she had bound herself to—the sacrifice she would make for all of them. "Mr. Bellanger has given me, and all of us, his word. We must wait a few months, and then we can return to living as we were."

"To what home? We already lost ours. It won't be the same," Rosalie shot back.

"Mr. Bellanger will help us find a new one. Besides, I do not see your Mr. Laroux bending the knee either. Where is he?"

"Enough!" their father shouted above them. Her sister looked like she wanted to retort something, but she refrained. The sharpness of Papa's voice indicated the fight was over.

Papa sighed. "This is not an ideal situation, I know, but Marguerite has done us all a great favor. Without her, we would have no hope of ever returning here. All I hope is that in time you will forgive your father and find happiness in our temporary home." The reassuring smile did not reach his eyes. It was apparent he felt the loss of his business the most.

Marguerite reached forward to pat his knee. "It's alright, Papa. It's not your fault."

Papa looked away to peer into his wife's face, but Mother attempted to put as much space as possible from him. Frowning, he reached for the hand Marguerite placed on his knee and squeezed it gently.

"I just want to do right by you all," Papa said.

"And you are Papa, you are," she said, smiling at him.

"You really are," Phillipe echoed. Rosalie hmphed, fanning herself faster while looking out the window.

Mother continued weeping, but her cries eventually subsided into little hiccups before sitting with numb resignation. After a few hours, the sun began to dip in the cloudy sky, and rows of farming fields became more abundant. Instead of going through the village, they went around it. From the distance, she took in the thatched rooftops, the wooden planked walls of shops, and the many stalls and carts being packed away for the day.

They continued down another mile before thunder rumbled and rain fell in sheets. A crack of lightning lit the sky and illuminated a small cottage with a thatched, gray roof. A dirt path carved between the patchy grass and unkempt garden and a pond filled with cattails sat behind the cottage, creating a barrier between them and a forest.

The forest was so dense she could not see beyond the thicket of gnarled trunks and branches. Yet, it appeared untouched. No ax or saw had disturbed the perfect line of trees behind the cottage. Perhaps it was how the trees swayed and shivered in the rain, but something felt unnatural about the forest. Something whispered *danger* in her mind.

"This place is frightening," Rosalie shuddered across from her, echoing her thoughts. "You don't think ghosts or wolves are in there, do you?"

"No, but perhaps the fae will come to whisk you away," Phillipe said, snickering when their sister opened her mouth in horror.

Marguerite shook her head at her brother despite the grin tempting her lips. "There's no need to worry. They don't exist anymore," she reassured her sister. "There's no more magic."

"What is this?" their mother demanded, swerving in her seat to swat at their father.

"We-well, this is our new home—"

"You stupid, stupid man. Why did you not tell me we would live next to some horrid woods?"

"I was assured it was safe, dear."

"I cannot believe you. We will die before Mr. Bellanger retrieves us!" she wailed.

The wheels groaned as the carriage came to a stop, and Clarence, their driver, climbed down to open their door. "We have arrived," he said.

"Very well," Father said, attempting to smile. "Come on, dear, let's get out, shall we?"

Marguerite was closest to the door, and she pulled up her red hood before stepping out first into the rain and mud. The rest of her family followed, including Rosalie's little dog, and Mother pulled out her parasol with a sour expression.

"Let us start unpacking," Papa said, and Clarence nodded, stepping up and retrieving the little belongings they had left sitting on top of the black carriage.

They quickly unpacked their belongings, racing the last of the daylight. Thunder rumbled, but the rain had eased and sprinkled light specks across their cloaks. After the task, they all stood in the dim light and bid Clarence, their last servant, goodbye as he took their carriage and horse with them. Her mother burst into tears again while they watched the little luxury they had left rolling down the path and disappearing around the bend. Their father touched her mother's shoulder, but she shrugged it off before running inside the cottage.

Papa heaved a sigh and followed their mother, and Marguerite and her brother shared a knowing look.

Rosalie sniffed, keeping her tears at bay, and scooped down to pick up Bonbon. However, something rustled beyond the woods, and within a blink of an eye, the dog transformed into a maddened, barking beast, squirming and then jumping out of her arms.

"Bonbon!" Rosalie cried, and she dashed from the door. Marguerite did not think. She ran after her with her brother at her heels. Wet dandelions exploded against their legs as they ran, but the dog evaded them, sprinting around the pond and into the thickness of the forest.

"Rosalie, no!" she cried, but her sister ran after her dog toward the woods. "Phillipe!"

"Already on it," he said. It did not take long for him to catch up to her, and soon he wrapped his arms around her waist, dragging her away from the trees. Rosalie screamed.

"Let him go. I promise he will come back to you," he said, attempting to dodge her flinging arms. Marguerite caught up to them, gasping and putting her hands on her hips to steady herself.

"What if there are wolves? I have to go to him." Rosalie struggled against him, but his arm barred her from freedom.

"He'll come back. You don't know what's in there. I don't want you getting lost or hurt."

"Please, he means the world to me," her sister said, and the unspoken words were there: *he is all I have left of our life*.

"I know, I know. But please, let's look for him in the morning when there's more light. And who knows? Bonbon might come back before then."

"He is right," Marguerite said, finally catching her breath. "I know he means a lot to you, but he'll be okay."

Tears pooled in their sister's eyes before she flung her arms around her brother. Her sobs were trapped under his cravat, and he gently patted her back. Marguerite also put a reassuring hand on her sister's arm, hoping it would soothe her but it was quickly shrugged off.

Sighing, Marguerite looked toward the creaking trees. The swaying of the leaves whispered strange things to her, and for a moment, she thought she saw two green embers burning bright within the darkness. She stepped back with a gasp.

"What is it?" Rosalie asked and then looked in the direction she had seen the eerie glow, but there was nothing but darkness. "Do you see him? Is it Bonbon?"

"No." She shook her head. "It was nothing."

She must have been convincing because her sister continued weeping, but no matter how much she tried to reassure herself of the same sentiment, she could not stop the goosebumps from pricking her arms.

5

Marguerite

"That'll be one copper, please." A burly arm extended toward Marguerite and she reached for her coin purse within her skirt pockets. After rummaging around to find the copper, the man sighed. "Well, don't flash all your pretty coins at me. That's not smart, miss."

Her head snapped up, and a blush painted her cheeks. "Oh, I didn't mean to—"

"No, but if you fancy, Avilon folk don't learn quickly someone will take advantage of you. Mark my words," the baker said and shook his head. "City folk don't mix with village folk so well."

She tensed and quickly gave him the coin he asked for. In return, he gave her a loaf of bread for her basket. The crisp baguette sat snugly with the other vegetables she bought earlier that day. The heat of the brick ovens behind the counter warmed the small, empty shop, making her perspire under her arms. She eyed the rows of flaky croissants lined behind the wooden counter and the stack of warm baguettes, sourdough, and soda bread clustered in baskets. She wished she could take a bite from a tempting cheese croissant, but she didn't have enough coins to i.

She made to leave, but his gruff voice stopped her in her tracks. "You all safe out there by that forest?"

She frowned as she turned to face him. "We are," she said, hesitant. "But is there something we should be worried about?"

Her thoughts strayed to the two glowing green lights she'd seen in the darkness of the woods, and a chill threaded down her spine.

"Ah," he said as if her remark revealed a secret she was not privy to. "So, no one's warned you yet?"

She clutched her basket tighter. "Warned us of what, sir?" The emptiness of the shop had not bothered her until now, but its walls closed in on her as he beckoned for her to come closer. Although he seemed friendly enough, she was unsure if his intentions were pure, but she obliged with tentative steps.

When she came to the counter, he cupped his large hand around his mouth and whispered, "The forest is haunted, see? Be sure never to enter it. Anyone who sets foot there will be cursed."

"Cursed?" she echoed with rounded eyes.

He nodded solemnly. "Didn't your priests out there in Avilon tell ye the tales?" When she shook her head, he heaved another sigh. "Figures. The stories get muddy in some places. But I'll tell you. When the Goddess made all of Gallia, she created some sacred forests for herself and the other Gods. Strange magic still lives there. Be careful, miss. And tell your family to stay away. Most folks don't come out once they enter."

The seriousness in his voice, the way his mouth twisted into a grim line under his burly beard, inspired a shudder to run down her spine. Talk of magic was ludicrous, but she would heed his warning. Magic or no, the forest may have other dangers not worth discovering.

Including the lights.

She exited the shop as swiftly but as politely as she could manage, but her heart beat like a drum when the doors shut behind her. Light specks of rain fell across her red hood when she pulled it up. Storm clouds sat angry and gray in the sky, chasing away the sunshine since her family's arrival.

Green vines crawled over brick shops, their leaves damp and shiny from the rain. A few wooden stalls lined the space, and the vendors stared at her, eyeing her dress made of expensive silk.

Ducking her head, she closed her cloak closer around her and hurried down the road toward the path leading to the cottage.

The next morning, thunder and the creak of the door woke her from her sleep. Her sister's bed was empty, and Marguerite quickly donned a house dress before tiptoeing out of her room.

Upon seeing a familiar figure, she hissed, "What are you doing up so early? Come inside before you catch a cold. You don't want to soil your pretty nightgown, do you?"

The silhouette in the back doorway turned to Marguerite. Her sister moved listlessly like a despairing apparition as rain sprinkled inside the cottage. Thunder rumbled but could not deafen Rosalie's hiccups. The pool of tears in her dark brown eyes glittered in the dim light.

"I cannot bear it." The dam broke as tears spilled down Rosalie's cheeks. "I cannot bear thinking he is cold and alone. He is probably starving or worse—eaten by wolves!"

"I think he'll be fine. It hasn't been too long—"

"It's been long enough," Rosalie snapped, her mood swinging, and Marguerite knew she must tread carefully.

"Well, we can look for him later. It's cold; let's go back to bed."

"Fine." Rosalie shut the door without warning, jolting Marguerite and the windows from the force. "He could be dead, and it's all your fault!"

"Oh, Rosalie," she said, reaching out to her, but her sister stomped away and slammed their bedroom door.

Sighing, she turned to the small living space and pulled a rocking chair by the fireplace closer to the window. The embers had died, and nothing was left but soot and ashes. Despite the chill, she was content to watch how the tree branches swayed in the wind—a rare sight in the bustling city of Avilon.

However, she would be lying to herself if she said she didn't miss Avilon. Mama was not the only one who yearned for the life they once had. Although it had not been long, she missed the bustle of carriages that clacked over cobbled streets, the leisurely walks near shops of perfumes and ribbons, and the salons she and her brother would visit together to listen in on enlightened conversation.

Most of all, she missed her dear friend Sophie. Without the woman's shadow chasing her everywhere she went, keeping her company, the days grew longer and lonelier.

But to admit all of this now would only grieve her father more. Mama was devastated enough. She hardly looked at food and stayed in bed since their arrival. Papa had more to worry about than how she felt about the situation.

It was only temporary, after all. Wasn't it? Unless Mr. Bellanger punished them all and left them here. She shuddered at the thought.

Thunder roared above her, and a crack of lightning flashed, spilling light into the room. Yelping, she covered the offending noise with a shaky hand while the other clutched her beating heart. Perhaps she had waited long enough.

She stood, hugging herself while the rocking chair swayed beneath her. As she made to leave, something caught her eye—something white. Her slippers padded across the dirt floor as she drew closer to the window. The darkness of the night had slowly morphed into a diffused gray sky swirling with purple and orange hues of the morning. The soft glow was enough for her to distinctly make out a shape that bent through the cattails of their small pond. She blinked and rubbed her eyes and looked out again.

Yet, there he was, sniffing innocently through tufts of wet grass. Grabbing her red cloak from the hook, she wrapped it around herself and opened the back door. The thunder rumbled above, but thankfully the rain eased into a drizzle against her hood. The same could not be said for her slippers. They squelched across the grass, soaked as soon as she raced toward the dog.

"Bonbon," she called. He looked up, his bat-like ears quivering—either from nerves or the cold, she could not tell—but he looked at her like she was a stranger.

"Bonbon, come here. Come here!" She patted her knees, but his large, brown eyes stared at her dumbly before he turned around and scampered toward the forest.

"Oh, not again," she muttered. Her cloak billowed behind her as she spurred herself to run, but it was too late. He leaped like a graceful doe into the forest and then stopped, turned, and sat as though he were waiting for her to cross the threshold.

She slid to a stop, waving her arms for balance before she used one of the tree trunks for support. A strange tingling shot up her arm, and she wrenched her hand away. Bonbon tilted his brown ears at her as she rubbed her arm and glanced up, hypnotized by the perfect line of trees she dared not cross.

He was right there. All she had to do was take two steps into the woods and pick him up. She could do it in less than five seconds. Yet, this situation was too strange—like the dog was purposefully luring her in.

She shook her head. Bonbon was a little dog. He was not even smart enough to do something so illogical.

Despite her logic battering her brain, confusion and fear continued to paralyze her. Not only did the baker's warning echo around her thoughts, but the strange aura she had felt on their arrival pulsated tenfold. It was tangible, like invisible tendrils of power reaching toward her, but she was just out of reach. She recoiled, but the beckoning sensation refused to relent.

Breath quickening, she turned on her heel and began marching away from the woods. She didn't have the curiosity or courage to find out whatever it was in there. But, after a few steps, she stopped and peered over her shoulder at Bonbon, who continued to sit patiently for her. He hadn't moved.

The memory of Rosalie's tears, her heartache, nestled by her fear. This was her chance to do something for her sister, even if Rosalie wouldn't have done the same for her. If she turned back empty-handed, she wouldn't be able to forgive herself.

She approached the line of trees once more and took in their looming heights. Their branches whipped in the wind, cracking and creaking above her. If something happened to her by stepping past the tree trunks—no. She shook her head to rid the thought. Nothing would happen. She was overreacting, and her racing pulse was deceiving her. It was one step to reach the dog. Nothing would happen.

Finally, she summoned the last dregs of her courage and stepped past the line between safety and the unknown. When her two feet hit the forest floor, she instinctively winced and closed her eyes, expecting some strange wind to whirl around her or a wolf to jump out of the bushes and gobble her up. Neither happened.

Relief flooded her, and she exhaled. She had been frightened over nothing.

Bonbon sat, doe-eyed and wagging his tail, but his charms would not work on her, and she glared back at him before scooping him up.

"Oh, you reek!" she said, holding him away. He smelled just as he looked: a wet dog. "You will be the death of me," she grumbled, turning around.

Every muscle in her body stiffened.

"Wha—"

The word was lost in the back of her throat.

There was no cottage or pond. There was nothing but dense brush and trees as far as she could see. It was as though she took one giant leap in the middle of the woods rather than a timid step, and there was no path toward where she had come from.

Staggering backward, fat drops of rain splashed across her skin and cloak. The wind blew the flurry against her face like it was coaxing her to turn around and walk the path behind her, but her feet were rooted.

Perhaps she was dreaming.

But the chattering of her teeth and shivering felt all too real. It was too cold, colder than her dreams or fantasies could ever conjure.

Bonbon whimpered in her ear and squirmed. The movement woke her from her trance, and she held him tighter, determined not to lose him. He bucked and placed a muddy paw on her face, and the cold, slimy texture surprised her. He leaped out of her arms and turned toward the thicket, barking.

"What in all heavens are you—"

She was too afraid to make another sound. The air grew bitter, and every hair on her arms raised to attention. There, in the darkness and chaos of whipping branches, was a set of glowing green eyes.

The lights!

They stared at her high above the ground—too tall to be man or wolf, yet a face with blue skin and midnight hair appeared from the shadows. A thin, white staff glowed, and the creature pointed it toward her. A chill seized her, clawing down her spine, killing any scream wanting to burst from her throat. Power radiated around the creature in waves as he floated above her.

"Go."

The thought was unequivocally someone else's, a distinctive male voice, injected within her mind. There was no time to think—no time to wonder what in Erus' name she was looking at. The demand was clear, and she did not hesitate to obey.

Marguerite spun on her heel and ran down the path. Bonbon raced beside her, barking as she leaped over fallen branches and rocky protrusions. Her heart clawed its way up her throat. Fire crackled in her lungs. Heat prickled over her wet skin. Sweat mingled with rain. Bushes snagged her cloak, but she continued forward, shoving branches out of her way.

All her muscles trembled in an inferno she had never felt before. If this path went on any longer, she would collapse. But the path curved into a bend, and pent-up tears sprung in her eyes as she came around the corner.

A large chateau sat behind a tall iron gate.

Hope spurred her forward and gave her the strength to reach the gate. All that mattered was escaping those eyes.

She was so close—so awfully close.

Before she crashed into the black gates, they swung when a powerful gust of wind forced them open. No obstacle stood in her way. She kept her pace, ignoring the crunch of the rocky gravel beneath her thin soles. The flurry of rain chased her back, egging her onward, and she bent to its will.

At last, she flew up the marble steps and fell against white, oak doors. Bonbon slid to a stop and barked madly, and she knew then that the eyes were upon her. She could feel the power from the being right behind her, but she dared not look.

"Let me in, please, I beg you!"

She slammed her fists against the wood before trying the latch, and the door creaked open. A strangled sob of relief caught in her throat.

"Come on, Bonbon," she said, and she rushed inside with the dog. Slamming the door shut, she refused to stop—she must put as much distance between her and the creature.

She did not get far.

Pain exploded in her skull as she crashed into a figure, head on. The momentum sent her sprawling to the ground with wet skirts flailing up in a heap. Cradling her head, she screwed her eyes shut to ease the stars dancing across her vision.

"Ah, Erus, that hurt!" a masculine voice groaned in pain.

Had she not already been on the ground, she might have collapsed when she assessed the stranger. Fine blond hairs covered his face until it grew thicker and coarser around his jaw and up his temples. Tufts of sandy-colored fur matched his hair and jutted from pointed ears that lay on the sides of his head. A flattened down nose sat on his face, and the tip was round, black, and wet like a dog's. Hairy hands with claws instead of fingernails cradled his head.

Behind him, other creatures, not quite human but not quite animal, stopped and stared at her. She was surrounded by monsters.

She opened her mouth and—

6

Claude

The woman's screams echoed across the foyer. Claude's pointed ears flattened on his head as he backed away. The door prevented her from going further, but she stood, her hands coming up in shaking fists.

"Come any closer, and I-I won't hold back," she said, and her eyes darted to a decorative vase beside her. Grabbing it, she raised it as a weapon. "I am not afraid to use this!"

Pain throbbed in his head from where they collided, but his thoughts stuttered as he attempted to piece together the image of the strange woman who had barged into his master's abode. Never in all his twenty-five years of living and service as a valet had a guest made an entrance as she did.

Soaking, wind-swept hair stuck like a haphazard web across her face. A rain-spattered red cloak hung over a brown dress of strange making. He did not linger on the fashion for too long and looked back up into her wild eyes full of fear. Her chest heaved, but she clutched the vase tighter as a threat.

A high-pitched yap sounded, and he jumped when a dog pawed at his leg. The little thing bounced up and down, shifting toward his rear to get a sniff.

"Stay back, Bonbon," she screeched.

"Ah." He gently removed himself from the dog, undoubtedly drawn to him due to his dog-like transformation. "It's alright, miss. I'm not going to hurt you."

He stepped away and held his hands in surrender, but she raised the vase higher. "I said stay back. All of you!"

Whispers surrounded them, and he glanced back to see his friends coming closer to look at their new guest.

He turned to them. "Let's give her some room."

"Is she the one?" Joseph asked, his long, white floppy ears quivering.

Isa, his raven-feathered friend, touched Joseph's shoulder and raised a finger to her lips.

Claude faced the new woman once more, but she was gone. From the corner of his eye, a blur of red bolted toward the hallway to their right, straight toward the left wing.

"Curses." He looked at those who had gathered behind him. "I will go after her but spread the word that she is our guest and is not to be approached suddenly," he said, emphasizing the last word. They nodded and grimaced at the reminder of her screams.

He pursued the cloaked woman down the hall. Her scent of rain with subtle floral hints was not far ahead. He followed it up a flight of stairs and caught up to her at a dead-end. She whirled to face him, her eyes wide like a mouse backed into a corner. The little dog barked happily.

Without another word, she threw the vase at his head, and he ducked just in time. It shattered against the wall, and she used the distraction to charge forward.

"Wait, please, miss, hear me out," he pleaded, reaching for her hand.

"Get away from me!"

He ran after her down the stairs while she took two steps at a time and glanced over her shoulder. The sight must have frightened her because she stumbled and tripped. With horror, Claude watched the young woman roll and crumple at the bottom of the stairs. He bounded down and skidded to a stop near her limp form.

His heart thundered in his ears as he crouched down and felt for her face to see if there were any injuries there. A red mark marred her forehead, and her eyes did not flutter. He reached for her wrist to check her pulse. Her heartbeat thudded under his grip, but she was otherwise unconscious.

His eyes wandered over her face to check for more injuries. Under the grime, her wet, tangled hair was pale, with smooth skin and rosy cheeks. A long nose and high cheekbones sat gracefully on her oval face. His gaze traveled to her parted, defined lips and paused over them.

She was beautiful.

Shaking himself from such thoughts, Claude did not allow himself to linger on her appearance. Instead, he sobered at the situation and frowned.

"Oh, miss, I am so sorry."

The sight of him—of all of them must be so terrifying. But, if they were a horror to behold, he dreaded to know what she would think of his master.

Grimacing, he murmured another apology before he dipped his arms around her and lifted her. "We'll take care of you, rest assured," he whispered to the top of her head as the little dog trotted beside him.

Marguerite

With a jolt, Marguerite sat up with a throbbing head. Golden comforters dwarfed her body, and a ruby canopy curtained the bedposts. A white marble fireplace sat on the far-left end of the room with a fire crackling over wood, casting a warm glow in the dim light. Above the mantle were hooks left in the wall as though someone had removed a portrait or a mirror, and a floral settee sat near a wooden table with matching chairs.

The last thing she remembered was the dog-looking creature pursuing her down a flight of stairs. But, as she searched further into her memory, a tremor ran through her at the pair of eyes staring from the darkness of the woods. The floating figure. Its eyes glowed like green candles and whispered a command that compelled her to obey.

Hopefully, the eyes, the blue face, had not followed her here. The reason why she was in this mess abruptly came to mind.

Where was Bonbon?

A knock startled her, and she threw herself from the bed. Thankfully, her clothes had been untouched but were damp from the rain, sticking to her skin like sap. When the door slowly swung open without invitation, she grabbed the nearest object, a porcelain bowl for hand washing. The figure stepped into the room with his hands raised in surrender.

The same dog man who chased her down the stairs. Her captor?

As with the vase earlier, she held the bowl up like a weapon, ready to hurl it at the strange creature. He scrambled behind the door again but held it open to peer out of a small crack.

"Please, miss, don't be scared. I promise I'm not here to hurt you."

"How can I believe you?" she demanded, and her thoughts strayed to the memory of her heart drumming out of her chest as he chased her. Spotting a large wardrobe, she dashed beside it to seek refuge there.

"I suppose you have reason not to. I will stay behind the door if it makes you comfortable?"

"Yes, stay there," she said, her voice too shrill and cringed. So much for being brave. "Don't come any closer."

"Of course, of course. Anything for you, miss."

She exhaled. Images of his animalistic appearance flashed through her, and her apprehension soared. Phillipe used to scare her with tales of wolfmen who gobbled up little girls, but those stories were fiction, fables to scare young children. But now they were real, and her mind toppled dizzily at the revelation. How was any of this possible?

And how easy would it be for him to rip through her like butter with those claws?

"Are you going to eat me?" she asked with a quiver in her voice.

A quiet chuffing sound reverberated behind the door. He was laughing, she realized but could not piece together what was so humorous about the situation.

"Oh, miss, no...I am not going to eat you," he said, and she chanced a peek around the wardrobe and found him smiling. Two pointed, canine incisors gleamed in the soft light falling through the door's crack. They looked sharp enough to tear through flesh.

"Are you going to kill me?" she tried again, raising the bowl out like a weapon.

"No, I am not going to kill you," he said, frowning this time.

"Then what do you plan to do with me?"

"I know it seems unlikely considering my appearance, but I don't have any plans to harm you," he said. He did not appear to be lying, but those teeth still gleamed dangerously in the light. "I actually wanted to apologize for the way I frightened you earlier. I only meant to steer you away from harm. I'm terribly sorry you fell down those steps. I should not have pursued you as I did. Forgive me."

There was nothing but sincerity in the creature's voice, and her death grip around the bowl relaxed. The dog man—whatever he was—had not attempted to enter, but she met his gaze through the cracked door. The pleading in his eyes matched his words, but she refused to step out or grant him entry.

"How is your head? There was a nasty mark there the last I saw," he continued.

One hand instinctively moved to the soreness around her forehead, and she hissed when she brushed against a large goose egg.

"Gods, that looks painful. I apologize."

Gripping the bowl tighter, she pressed her back around the side of the wardrobe to conceal herself. She could not trust his sympathies.

"What have you done with Bonbon? Where is he?"

"Bonbon?"

"The dog, my sister's dog. Where is he?"

"Oh!" The creature backed away from the door, scuffling until a little dog waltzed through the cracked space. Bonbon stood there, tongue lolling, before he bounded toward her hiding place when he recognized her. He jumped up at her legs, and she crouched to check his fur for injuries.

"Is the name a making of your sister's?" he asked casually.

After finding no blood or twisted bones on the dog's body, her brows furrowed at his question, and she decided to humor him. "Have you not heard of bonbons before?"

"I cannot say I have. Is it a type of dog?"

How could he not know what a bonbon was? Then again, he was not entirely human. Perhaps his kind—her head reeled at the thought of there being any "kind" other than human—did not know of such things. "It's a dessert. They are quite popular. Especially at court."

"Really?" His surprise sounded genuine, and a peculiar silence washed over the room. Finally, he said, "Well, I made sure he relieved himself and gave him food and water. Please let me know if there is anything else we can get for you or your dog. I am more than happy to serve."

He spoke as though she were a guest and not a woman trapped in a place full of monsters. "Who are you, and where am I?"

"Oh, pardon my rudeness, miss. You may call me Claude. I belong to the Count d'Alarie, and it's his home where you now reside. I am pleased to make your acquaintance. May I inquire your name also?"

Would that be wise? She peered around the wardrobe and found he had not budged from behind the cracked door. He had given her space; perhaps if she played her cards right, she could play along with this conversation and find a way out.

"My name is Marguerite Dupont," she said slowly.

"Again, it's my pleasure to meet you," he said, and a pause followed. "You are probably wondering why the residents and I look as we do?"

"The thought has crossed my mind."

He chuckled, a mirthless sound. "Simply put, this place and everyone in it is cursed."

Marguerite was sure she had misheard him. "Come again?"

"Cursed," he emphasized. "We are all cursed."

"What? How—how is that possible?"

"An Enchanter, miss. He has cursed and bound us here. I know how it sounds. By all accounts, I thought every Enchanter, fae, and magical being had vanished too, but here we are."

Silence stunned her to the spot, but the image of the glowing eyes flashed before her eyes.

No, it wasn't true.

This creature—man—was mad, plain, and simple. Enchanters and Enchantresses did not exist in their world anymore. The holy texts had said they had returned to their master, Erus, in heaven, never to be seen again. None of it made sense. The magical being in the forest, this creature before her, was all ludicrous. None of it was real. She had no reason to stay and hear anymore.

Marguerite scanned the room and spotted a window on the opposite wall. If she was quick enough, perhaps she could outrun him and escape. On the count of three, she sprinted toward the window. Lifting it, she blanched upon seeing three stories worth of distance between her and the ground. She would break her ankle if she were lucky, and her neck at the very worst.

Bonbon yapped at her side, and she muttered a curse under her breath. There was no way his fragile little body would come out unscathed either. Their only exit was the door.

A hand on her shoulder startled her, and she screamed.

"Miss, please, it's not safe."

"Don't touch me!" She whirled around and brought the bowl down on whatever body part she could reach. It bounced off a sturdy shoulder and crashed into pieces around them on the floor. The sound stunned her as they locked eyes, but reason pushed her to the open door.

Without a second thought, she started for it until she winced in pain and crashed to her knees. Looking back at her foot, a shard of porcelain embedded into her bare skin. Sticky blood dripped down, and her stomach lurched.

"Oh, Erus, Kyros, Ghiana," he swore all three of their holy Gods' names so fast, they merged into one word. "Miss, please, don't move! I-I will be back. Just stay where you are—please."

His hairy hands hovered over her before he bolted to the door and shut it behind him. A click sounded, and she knew he had locked her in.

All she could do was wait.

A dull thud pulsed behind the cut as she dragged her feet forward. Luckily, her knees had come out unscathed, and the cut did not look as deep as it felt. The bowl had split into ten pieces, and she dragged one in her skirt pockets for safekeeping. She then touched the shard in her foot and held back a hiss and bubbling nausea climbing up her throat.

Maybe it would be best to leave it alone until she could manage the sight of her blood. It was a ridiculous predicament, and Rosalie would have laughed in her face for sitting on the floor as she was, afraid of her blood oozing from a slight cut. She didn't understand it, especially when she could tolerate her monthly bleeding. Fears were a peculiar thing.

As she took deep breaths, the door shut behind the creature. She took in his clothing for the first time: a dark green coat hugged his lithe form. It hung long and trim, with a low waist. The style contrasted her father's and brother's coats, which were not as narrow and were typically fully open to reveal their vests. His square-toed shoes were rather large—too large for a man—and his stockings conformed around a leg that curved, like a dog's haunches.

In his arms was an assorted cloth pile, both wet and dry. "May I?" he brought up his full arms in gesticulation. She considered her bleeding foot and then glanced up at the dog man.

"I will bind it myself," she said.

"Miss, please, I—I know how I must look to you, but I swear I am simply a man beneath this...this form. Allow me to help you."

Something about the sadness in his eyes, his frown, tugged at her heart. Now that she could assess him from this close, there was something very human about him. However, he was still a stranger, and she would remain wary.

"Alright."

"May I have your permission to touch you? I promise I will be gentle," he said.

After a moment, she relented. "You have my permission."

If he made to kill her or harm her now, she would have to strike fast. However, the shard from her foot must be removed first, and her eyes never left his when he crouched beside her. As promised, his touch was featherlight while he moved her foot. She winced when he took hold of the shard with gentle fingers and frowned.

"This might hurt."

With one swift tug, the shard was free, and spots danced across her vision at the sight of more blood dripping from the small cut. Looking away, she held a hand to her mouth to keep the bile from bursting from her stomach.

"I didn't hurt you too badly, did I?"

She took a deep breath. "No, I-I simply cannot stand—" She looked away again.

"Blood?"

"Yes, that."

"It's not a pleasant sight, that's for sure," he said gently.

She chuckled and grimaced.

"Fortunately, it's pretty shallow. I don't believe you need a stitch," he said lightly. "I'll clean this up for you and make sure no blood is in sight."

She looked to the ground as he tended to her. He gently wiped her foot with a wet cloth and bound it with a thin wrap. Knotting it into a bow, he smoothed his hands over it.

"There. I believe it's safe to look now."

True to his word, there was no blood. A smile sat on his lips, and the sight chipped at her wary resolve.

"Thank you..."

"Claude," he reminded her.

"Claude." The name rolled off her tongue in a pleasant manner. "Thank you."

"It's my pleasure." He stood and offered a large, hairy hand in her direction, and she looked at it, hesitant. A sad understanding flitted over his warm, brown eyes, but she grabbed it before he retracted his hand.

Maybe an impulse drove her to accept it, or maybe it was his kindness. Either way, a bright smile curled upward on his hairy face as he helped her.

"I'm here to tend to you when you need it," he said.

"Tend to me?" she echoed dumbly.

"Of course. Although I am my master's valet, my services are also yours. I found it prudent to introduce myself first. We didn't want to overwhelm you. I am here to make your stay comfortable."

Several questions charged through her mind, brawling for her attention until she settled for one. "Where is your master, then?"

"He has other matters to attend to," he said rather quickly as though to race over the truth behind his words.

"Is...is he..."

"Cursed? Yes, he is."

She walked to the bed and sat down, finding that her wound did not hurt so much. There was a chance all of this was a dream—a horrible dream—and she had dozed off in their new home. Maybe her brother or father would gently place their hand on her shoulder to wake her so she could prepare for the day. Rosalie would still be in a sour mood, but it would be better than this—better than being surrounded by *magic* she assumed didn't exist anymore until now. The idea of curses and magic rattled her mind and formed a headache.

What else was possible?

"Are you hungry?" Claude asked gently, but the change of subject did not go unnoticed. Moreover, the thought of food seemed frivolous when there were more important matters like a cursed man standing in her presence.

"No...not at the moment."

"Are you thirsty at all? I can fetch you some tea if you'd like?"

He seemed eager to serve her, with his eyes imploring her softly. The kind display did not warrant trust, but if she were honest, her throat did feel terribly dry. Moreover, the sooner he left her, the better. "I—umm, well, I suppose tea would be nice, thank you."

"Of course. You must be parched. I'll inform Jeanette when I leave. She will be waiting on you, but I will introduce you to her after she returns."

She nodded, too dazed to be frightened about the prospect of other creatures waiting outside her door.

He kept his distance which she appreciated. "Is there anything else I can do for you? Answer any questions? I promise I won't bite." He chuckled at his joke.

"No, not right now," she said, wishing to be alone to confront whatever this reality was. Then, with a nod, he left and locked the door behind him.

Glancing toward the bed and then to the window, a plan formed in her mind. She tore off the duvet, and the rest of the sheets followed.

She would have to work fast.

7

Isa

T he bedroom door creaked open, and Isa peered inside. The stink of wine stung her small, beak nose, and she eyed the bottles piled near the bed.

Golden curtains framed the bedposts, and a large, misshapen lump sat beneath the brocade duvet. She stepped inside and crossed the space between them to make sure the lump was breathing. She approached with soft footsteps padding over the crimson rug. A large, hairy arm and sharp claws moved and dangled from the bedside.

Good.

Henri was still breathing. She took another step, hoping he would wake, but he let out a deep snore instead.

"Mr. Alarie," she whispered.

The arm pulled back under the covers, and the shape of her master rolled over. Her mouth, untouched by the curse, screwed into a hard line before retreating and exiting the room. Henri was sound asleep, undoubtedly drunk, and it was best not to wake him lest he startle in a frightened stupor. They could wait to tell him of their guest later.

When the door thudded behind her, an invisible force clenched around her heart. She had six cursed months to build walls around her emotions to prepare herself for the one who would come and break their spell. But now that a woman was here, perhaps the fated one, hurt spread like poison in her veins.

Ignoring the pain, the way it caved her chest in, she drifted through the empty halls. Henri found solace in the east wing like he'd always had in his youth, but unlike his stepmother, he did not care for decor. A few paintings from his father's house lined the walls paired with ornate, golden candelabra sconces. Otherwise, white filled the bare, paneled spaces. It would've been an impressive dwelling if Henri had put more care into his ancestral home. Nothing was to fill the hollow emptiness except for the mysterious thrumming of power she felt when she touched the walls. She grazed a finger against it to feel the subtle tingling warming her skin. The curse's doing, no doubt.

After ascending the third floor, she found Jeanette pressing her ear against a guest bedroom door.

"Oh, Isa!" Jeanette said and backed away with her white, moth antennae twitching above her head. Instead of human eyes, Jeanette had two large, bulbous black eyes and no lids to protect them. "Claude should be out any second. Let's see what he has to say about our new guest."

Isa obeyed Jeanette's beckoning hand and came closer. The door suddenly opened, and Claude came out, locked it, and slid the key into his coat pocket. With the three of them crowded around the white oak door, the hallway felt small.

"How is the girl?" Jeanette asked.

"Scared and wary," Claude answered and sighed.

Jeanette folded her white, felt arms over her chest, and frowned. "I don't blame her. The poor thing."

"I don't either," Claude said, looking down at his clawed hands. Isa tucked her feathered hands in her apron pockets and tried not to dwell on their hideous state.

"She did have something peculiar on, no?" Jeanette said. "I have never seen such a style."

"It's a strange fashion," he agreed, but his mouth tightened. There was something he was hiding, she could sense it by his nervous hand-wringing, but before she could press him on the matter, he changed the subject. "How is Mr. Alarie faring? You checked on him, right?"

"Still asleep. Drunken as usual," she said.

"I wish that room were not enchanted to give him whatever he wanted," Jeanette tutted, tucking her soft, moth feathers to settle comfortably on her back. "I'm surprised he hasn't killed himself with his drink yet."

Isa's throat tightened, and she kept her gaze on the floor. As selfish as Henri was, the bile in her stomach rose from her throat at the thought of finding him deceased in his bed. He'd been more liberal with his drinking since the curse began, and she hoped the curse would prevent anything like that from happening. The Gods wanted him cursed, not dead.

"Either way, we must keep an eye out for him and make sure he doesn't wander out of his room before we let him know of our guest," Claude said, waving a hand for them to follow away from the door. He appeared to sense her discomfort, and she was grateful for the distraction.

"I imagine he will be very surprised and pleased. Our guest is quite pretty, don't you think?" Jeanette elbowed her, but she stiffened. "I don't doubt it will be difficult for him to fall in love with her. By how she ran, she has quite the spirit too. I think it's a good match."

A good match, Isa repeated in her mind while her gut coiled into knots. *Everything I'm not.*

No. She mustn't think of such things. She mustn't let old feelings cloud her judgment. The curse must be broken, and if this woman was fated to be with Henri, so be it. Steeling herself, she buried the emotions deep into the pits of apathy.

Claude put his hand on Jeanette's shoulder and broke the silence. "Speaking of, I told our guest you would bring her some tea. Would you mind taking care of that?"

"Oh, yes, of course. I will get it ready, don't you worry," Jeanette said, grabbing her skirt and racing ahead.

When Jeanette was out of sight, Isa exhaled in relief. "I'm glad she doesn't know."

The secret between her words sunk deep into her heart. Claude was the only one to know of her past romantic relationship with Henri when they were teenagers. The forbidden affair lasted for two years, but those two years carved themselves permanently into her memory no matter how much she wished she could forget.

"Nor should she, or anyone else for that matter," Claude agreed and brought his voice down to a whisper. "Will this be an issue for you?"

She shook her head. "The past is the past."

"Are you sure—"

"Claude." She stared at him firmly. "It won't be a problem—*I* won't be a problem. Are we clear?"

"Very well," he said, but he eyed her warily as though he could sense she was trying to convince herself more than he. "If needs be, we can always change your shift, so you don't have to interact with her."

"That will not be necessary. Jeanette and I are the only ones trained in dressing and helping guests."

"Even so."

"No, there is no question." She halted, and he stopped beside her. "I will see through to helping her. Besides, our only female staff member is Anna, but she knows her way around a kitchen more than a wardrobe. We don't want to subject our guest to that."

"You're right, but if it ever becomes too difficult—"

"It won't," she said. "Now, please stop with all of this. If it becomes too much, then I'll tell you."

His round eyes continued to assess her with concern, but he finally yielded. "Very well, I'll stop badgering you on the subject."

"Thank you."

They walked silently to the bottom of the staircase, where they met all eighteen staff members. Too many voices fought to be heard when they saw Claude.

"Claude, what is happening?"

"Is she the one?"

"Have you told Master?"

Claude waved his hands down to quiet the excitement she wished she could share equally. "Now, now, listen, everyone. If you have not already heard, we do have a guest, and her name is Marguerite Dupont—"

"Where is she?" Pierre, the badger-like butler, asked.

"In the second guest room on the third floor now—"

"Is she here to break the spell?" Joseph, the doorman, asked as his rabbit ears quivered.

"Yes," Claude said with a smile spreading across his face. A canine fang peeked through his grin. "I believe she is the one who has been sent to us."

The air buzzed with chatter, and Claude attempted to quiet them again. Isa weaved past her friends, who crowded closer around the valet. Their questions fired out like ceaseless canons and in their haste, they almost toppled the old, decorative table near the foot of the stairs—something left by Henri's ancestors when they abandoned the place. Isa put a hand to stop it from wobbling and righted the empty vase at its center. Usually, it would be filled with a full floral arrangement, but nothing was left but the rose bushes within the garden. But no one dared to pluck the living roses in fear of accelerating the curse.

When both table and vase were safe, she took her place near the back by the vertical, crescent windows. Angry rain clouds huddled across the sky, blocking any sunshine. Shadows of gray painted the view of the forest beyond the brown hedges, gravel paths, and creaky gates. A forest that wouldn't allow her to escape this nightmare.

No matter how long she ran, it always brought her back here.

It happened two weeks after they were cursed. In the middle of the night, she ran, hoping the Gods would allow her to escape and be free of the curse. She hadn't done anything wrong. Her only sin was encouraging Henri's love when they were teenagers. But, minutes grew into hours, and each path led back to the chateau.

There was no way out.

Something cream and cotton-like entered her vision. She startled, blinking until her mind could understand what she was seeing. A sheet, she realized, tapped the window, and at the end was a small bundle with a little dog's face peering out. The puppy breathed from its mouth, unaware of its danger as something or someone lowered the chain of sheets. As soon as the makeshift basket touched the ground, the dog leaped out and ran for the gardens.

A piercing whistle cut through the cacophony of voices, and Isa jumped at the noise.

"Thank you," Claude said to Paul, the head cook, and the pig man nodded in return. "Now, we must be quiet and not wake Mr. Alarie yet. We will inform him as soon as he is awake, but in the meantime—"

Isa pointed to the window, and Claude's eyes followed the gesture and widened with horror.

"In the meantime," he continued as he walked in the opposite direction to direct the crowd's eye away from the window. "Resume your duties as normal. And do not, under any circumstance, approach our guest. She is wary of our appearance. Jeanette, Isa, and I shall handle her."

He ushered them along, and Isa eyed the sheets while Marguerite slowly descended the chain.

Whoever this woman was, she begrudgingly admitted to liking her already.

8

Henri

A servant crouched on all fours and lifted the bed skirt. A six-year-old Henri stood behind him, giggling at the display, holding one shoe to his chest. His sock-covered feet wiggled impatiently. The servant, Daniel, shook his head and hummed to himself as he searched the depths beneath the bed.

"Ah, master Henri... It seems your other shoe has escaped us again. Wherever could it be?"

Henri laughed, spinning around fast so he could see all corners of the room at once. "Maybe-maybe Jeanette has hidden it from us!"

"Pah." Daniel scooted back and raised himself from the floor. "Or maybe a mischievous little fairy took it." He smiled and tapped him on the nose. Henri squealed and backed away from the man with a breathy giggle. "I wonder where it could have gone?"

"Fairies! Fairies! Fairies!" Henri sang, stomping around in a circle.

"So, you like magical creatures, do you?"

"Yes! Fairies and dragons and wizards and-and—" Henri gulped for air and found he could not breathe through his sentence, "and werewolves."

"I see. You know my son Claude? Well, guess what?" Daniel asked in a whisper, enticing him to come closer.

"What?"

The man sank to his knees again and beckoned him to his side. Henri obliged, running to him before he collided with the man's ear.

"Whoa there. Ha, well, I am glad you are eager to hear this. Because what I am about to tell you is very important. Do you think you can handle it?"

"Yes, yes, yes," Henri said, vibrating with energy.

"Alright, let me tell you." Daniel dipped down and cupped his large hand against the boy's ear. "Claude knows where to find the fairies."

Henri's eyes widened like teacup saucers before his mouth screwed into a pout. He backed away before folding his arms. "How come he knows?"

"Well, Claude is a little older and has had more time to play outside. Maybe one day you two can play together, and he can show you all the magical places he has found."

Henri's eyes lit with wonder, and he imagined all the secret corners he had yet to discover outside. If Claude knew where they were, they must be close by! Would there be dragons there to slay? His smile widened.

"Henri!"

The sound pierced him to the spot like the sinking teeth of a basilisk, sucking his enthusiasm and dissolving it into ash. His shoulders hunched when he peered up at a tall, lithe form at his open door.

"Countess," Daniel said softly before standing and retreating toward the wall, leaving him to stand and face the woman alone. A pearl necklace lay high on her throat, and a silver dress hugged her body like shimmering scales. The woman's sharp eyes cut through him like a hot knife.

"Are you ready?" she asked. Her golden walnut curls bobbed when she tilted her head to one side, caressing the bare skin across her shoulders. The question would have been innocent enough had it not been icy enough to chill his blood.

She never came to the east wing—to his room—if she didn't have to. In fact, he rarely saw or heard her at all growing up. However, today was Father's birthday, and every year, he was allowed to join in the celebration if he kept to the walls with Daniel and didn't disturb the guests.

"Yes, Countess," he said quietly despite the lone shoe he held.

She regarded it with one high-arched brow. "Are you lying to me?"

Shrinking further in himself, he looked to Daniel for comfort, but the man refused to look at him. He was abandoned. "I-um... my shoe," he said quietly as an offered explanation.

"Well," she snapped, "where is it? You know we must leave soon!"

Fear gripped his heart, but he could not stop the tears from flowing down his cheeks. Sniffling, he averted his eyes to the ground. "I-it's lost. We cannot find it—"

The planes of her face became all sharp and steel. "Stop your crying. What do you mean you cannot find your other shoe? You are doing this on purpose. You hid it, didn't you? Do you pride yourself on making us late for your father's birthday? Do you?" Her rage crackled all around her, suffocating him. His body refused to move.

"And now you force me to come to you. Come here! I said come here, you stupid little boy!"

One leg moved accordingly and the other without his permission.

"That's right. Come closer, don't be shy..." she crooned with misleading sweetness and crouched so she could be eye-level with him.

Her hands shot out as soon as he was in reach, and she grabbed his arms in a vice grip. He coughed against the noxious wine hanging over her breath. Her grip tightened when he tried to raise his hands to his face. "You are a byblow—a disobedient little monster!"

Henri woke with a cold bottle against his jaw. He bolted upright, panting, and looked around the darkness of his room. Only the vague shadows of furniture were there to comfort him.

He was utterly alone.

Unbidden tears pressed against the corners of his eyes, but he wiped them away with terse swipes.

"Curse it all."

It was just another dream. Another memory.

It had been six months since he had been cursed, and yet images of his stepmother still clung in his mind, clawing for his attention. How typical of her to haunt him even when she lived so far away. Even when he was trapped in this curse-forsaken place.

No matter how many times he had attempted to escape, to run from the nightmarish spell he always found his way back to the chateau.

Trapped.

Clenching the empty bottle by his side, he threw it with all his might. It shattered against the wall, and the sound soothed the anger storming through his veins. The red liquid rolled leisurely like blood against the walls, pooling at the green shards on the floor.

Looking down, the size of his hands, their unnatural paleness ending in black claws, made his stomach churn. He was hideous. A monster. Perhaps he deserved his gilded cage.

He wished for another bottle within his mind and it appeared beside him. At least the Enchanter allowed him to wallow properly in his misery. He downed its contents until sleep claimed him once more.

When he woke again, his leg stretched over the bed, and glass bottles clattered to the ground, pinging against the discarded ones on the floor. One eye opened and swept over the empty bottles piled against the side of the bed. Nudging the bottle's lip closer to his mouth, he was met with glass, not the mixture of sweet, salty, and bitter juices. It was empty.

"Curses," he mumbled. "Where'd it go?"

A high-pitch ring rattled to his right, and he glanced at the brass clock on the mantelpiece. A happy, golden cherub sat on the clock, and beneath his feet was the ticking minute hand landing on the eighth numeral.

The sands of sleep sealed his eyes, but another loud, sharp sound wrapped around his consciousness, forcing him to acknowledge it. Through the raw and irritable emotion, he identified the noise as a squawking bird outside his window.

Grumbling, he grabbed a pillow and forced it over his ears to block out the sound and go back to sleep. To his dismay, the sound persisted, growing louder and shrill, like...

Like a dog barking.

No longer able to ignore the sound, Henri threw the blanket from his body and approached the window. Amid the cobbled paths of the garden under the wooden, lattice arches, not far from where he stood, was a white dog. It was a small thing no bigger than a large cat with bat-like ears and chestnut markings. And it was looking directly at him.

What an annoying little thing. How did it get in his garden anyhow?

Although every muscle in his body screamed with fatigue, he stumbled, knocking into a reading chair on his way out the door. No one occupied the halls or down the east stairs, but he heard a commotion of voices coming from the foyer of his home.

Ignoring it, he shrugged it off as 'servant activity' and lumbered on. The east wing bore nothing on its walls except the stray hooks meant for hanging objects left by his ancestors. No light guided his way, he did not need it with his unnatural sight, but the dim morning spilled through the back doors around the corner. Pushing through them, a cool spring breeze swirled around him, but the wind could not penetrate through the thick layer of fur.

Even after the fall of rain, the garden was a graveyard of brown, twisted vines and branches. Wet, moldy leaves squelched under Henri's feet, leaving cloven hoof imprints in the mud. A wilted lilac crumbled to dust in his clawed fingers when he touched it. The flowers had all shriveled black and powdered upon contact.

The work of the curse.

He continued his search for the little dog and passed the labyrinth, which was nothing more than crumbling branches and wet stone. The fountain in the center was covered in algae and had not spouted water since the curse began. The hedges, designed in swirling, shell-like patterns, remained, but their lush leaves had fallen, and the remaining branches were white with death. Dried, withered bushes scratched his legs as he passed, and his ears twitched at the sound of barking.

Finally, he spotted it.

The dog scampered, sniffing the twisted hedges before running toward another path. Henri followed, careful not to startle it and force it toward the roses. Just as he came a little closer, the dog looked at him with a quirk on its head before trotting along again.

He sighed and clenched his teeth. This was getting ridiculous. With thinning patience, he increased his speed and followed the blasted thing around a corner of the hedge. The dog must have sensed his looming presence gaining on him as it began running. Around and around they went with unsuccessful attempts at scooping the dog until he was out of breath. After another failed swipe, the dog sprinted toward a different path, one he knew led to the rose bushes.

The last remnants of life within the garden.

"Oh, no, you don't," he seethed, running after the stupid rat-like dog.

Red blooms the size of oranges perked in the cloudy afternoon. Their branches were lush and green, contrasting the disease around them. Just as the row of untouched rose blooms came into view, panic burrowed under his skin like worms stretching beneath the earth.

The dog sniffed the lush, green leaves before circling and lifting a leg to urinate.

Rage ignited like a strike of hot lightning in his chest. No bush or branch stood a chance as he trampled over them like a stampeding bull charging toward its target. Before the dog could react, he swooped upon it in mid-stream. His claws dug into its scruff, lifting it high above him as it screamed and wriggled under his grasp.

"You'll pay for that, you little—"

A crack of a branch and a small gasp elicited from his right, and his head swiveled toward the offender.

His heart dropped.

9

Marguerite

T he monster looked at Marguerite with eyes blue and unyielding like the ocean. She opened her mouth, hovering over a silent scream. A trickle of sweat dribbled down her neck and seeped into her dress as she stood ever so still.

Its head towered over her own and could surpass the height of two men combined. Dark fur curtained it like a cloak over its broad shoulders and narrow waist, stringy and matted, but the creature's long hands were bare and curved into claws. Dark shadows hovered around its form like slithering snakes, twisting, and forming into various appendages—arms and legs—where none should have been.

Pale skin stretched over its elongated skull with tusks jutting from its mouth. Two horns lay on long, greasy black hair, but one had broken off with splintered fibers hanging from the stump. Only one descriptor came to mind:

Demon.

Her hands itched to form the sign of the Gods, but terror prevented her from doing so. She was trapped in an eternal stare-down with the monster who held Bonbon in its clutches. The dog whimpered for her help, but her feet were fused to the cobbled stone beneath her.

"Who are you?" the monster demanded.

Her heart jumped as she stepped back. Its voice was deep and unnatural, like rocks grating against stone.

"I said who are you?"

"I—I...I did not mean to—" she said but the words fumbled across her tongue.

"Answer me!"

Bonbon let out a high-pitched scream, and something beneath the layers of fear within her broke through the surface.

"Let him go!"

It was a shaky demand, one that fled from her mouth before she could rationalize the action. The erratic beating of her heart sent blood rushing in her ears like a roaring waterfall as she trembled before the creature. She did not expect him to comply, but he slowly lowered his arm with the dog in tow. He set the dog on the ground, and the shadows around his form dissipated into puffs of air until they all but disappeared.

As soon as his claws relinquished their grip, Bonbon flew to her and jumped, pawing at her cotton dress.

The sight of him so frightened shielded her fear, morphing it into rage. "Monster," she spat.

"Monster? Who are you to enter my estate?" the creature said, taking a step toward her.

"Get away from me," she sputtered.

"Answer me!"

"I said get *away*!" she shrieked when he took another step toward her.

Without another word, she bent down to pick Bonbon up and ran as fast as her legs could carry them.

"Miss? Miss are you out here?" someone called out. A panicked jolt rang through her limbs when she recognized the voice as Claude's. She could see his head bobbing above the labyrinth and through the pillars behind her.

"Ah, sir, you are awake. I have been looking for you," he said, and a mumbled conversation she could not distinguish ensued. Hopefully, it would give her enough time.

Charging through the brown hedges, branches crackled all around her. They snagged her dress and scraped her exposed skin. When she shuffled out of the hedge, onto uneven ground, the dog grunted within her grasp. She sucked in a breath but regained her balance. There was no time to waste. She ran across wet grass with Bonbon's head bobbing in her arms like a jackrabbit. By the time she approached the forest, she could hear clattering footsteps behind her.

"Miss? Mi-Wait—Wait—" Claude's voice cried, but she dared not even turn her head to face him. "No, please, don't go in there!"

Thump. Thump. Thump.

She was so close now. If she could reach beyond the trees, then perhaps it would transport her like it had that morning. She could only hope.

As she ran, she felt every single beat of her heart, every pound, the building pressure of it—she was certain it would burst before she could claim her freedom. It thundered in her ears, deafening her to the desperate shouts behind her. Her muscles quivered while anticipation for her capture loomed over her. She was not fast—Claude should reach her any second.

A shrill scream of terror ripped from her throat when a whisper of a touch grazed her back. With one jump, she launched herself behind the line of trees. Bonbon yelped when some of her weight came crashing down on him, but he squirmed out of her grip before she could roll over him again. She came to a stop on her back, staring at the treetops above her.

A small, wet nose came up and blew puffs of air into her eye. Bonbon began licking at her brow, and she slowly propped herself on her elbows to face her pursuer.

No footsteps crunched on leaves. Claude's voice did not call for her.

She twisted, her head whipping around in disbelief.

The gardens were nowhere to be seen behind her.

Henri

Henri's eyes burned like hot coals as he stared into the muddy cobblestone.

Who was the woman? Was she sent to him by the Enchanter? Was she the key to the curse?

Somewhere in the distance, Claude's soft voice had inclined higher and higher, reaching heights he had not thought the man was capable of. He took his sight off the ground and looked up to see the man's face puffing and sweating under the layer of fine, blond fur. Claude inhaled deeply from his round, black nose and he stopped directly in front of him.

"Sir, the-the woman, she—" Claude gasped, "she got away and—"

Henri cast him a hard glare. "Did you know she was here?"

Claude shrunk under his gaze. "Yes, sir."

"Why didn't you tell me?"

"I apologize, sir, but you were indisposed, and I meant to tell you as soon as you woke."

"You idiot," he hissed, "look at what happened because of *you*. Had you told me of her, none of this would have happened!"

The space around them darkened, sucking the light into shadows, and his form elongated into a series of silhouetted, ghostly limbs. The more his anger spread, the more he grew—longer, more crooked, and more wrong. Yet, Claude did not tremble before him.

"Had you kept your temper, she would not have run off."

Claude's words doused the explosion of rage, and the dark shadows wavered.

"Regardless, we cannot waste any more time. I don't care what should or should not have happened. We must find her, sir. I believe she is the one," Claude continued.

The darkness evaporated into cloudy puffs as he felt himself shrink into his usual, lumbering height, and he stared into the ground bitterly. "That is of no consequence to me," Henri snapped, and Claude's eyes widened.

"You do not mean that, do you?"

"Of course, I mean it. Why else would I have said it?"

"But...the curse—"

"Forget the curse and everyone in it! Let another unfortunate maiden come waltzing in then," Henri seethed, ignoring the image of the woman's frightened expression flashing through his mind. It reminded him of his ugliness—his nightmarish cage. And worse of all, it reminded him of his stepmother's disdain for him.

Claude straightened, a contrast to his frequent cowering. His large, hairy hands curled into fists, and Henri eyed them with vague interest. The tension matched the silence between them—heavy and unsettling before Henri snorted in amusement.

"What?" Henri spat, his arms folding in a challenge.

"You don't know if another will come," Claude said with quiet restraint. "This might be our only chance."

The emphasis on the word *our* was not lost on Henri. He knew the others counted on him to break the curse even in the haze of emotions. He was their only hope.

Yet bitterness washed through him at the memory of the woman's fear. How her eyes despised him. How quick she was to run from him. Why should *he* be responsible for someone who wanted nothing to do with him?

Shrugging, Henri turned and waved a dismissive hand. "If she is bound to the curse, she will return on the property soon enough. There is nowhere she can run to."

"Even so," Claude said, "you cannot be sure of that. What if she is free to leave? We don't know the Enchanter's rules. These are his woods. Regardless, I want to make sure she is well. She might be hurt."

Henri raised a hairless brow but refused to let concern rule over him. Yet, he could not help but ask: "What makes you believe that?"

"She took a tumble trying to run from me."

"Well, maybe we can rely on the Enchanter to care for her." He sniggered, but Claude did not join him in his mirth. The valet's face hardened, his lip turning upward to show off a gleaming canine fang. Was this a threat? His eyes narrowed.

"She deserves our help," Claude said slowly, enunciating each word with a firmness that reminded him of Daniel, Claude's father when he would lecture him as a child.

His chest gave a violent tug, but his mouth contorted into a scowl at the thought. What right did the older valet have to lecture *him*—his employer? "If it's so important to you, then go fetch her yourself," he said, pointing one claw toward the forest.

Standing in silence, neither moved nor made a sound. The air was so brittle it could snap, or Henri would if the fool wouldn't bend. Finally, Claude spoke.

"Very well. It will be done."

Without another word, the man spun on his heel and started toward where their guest had made her escape. Henri watched him with clenched teeth.

So, this is how it would go? What did the man think he was? A knight in shining armor? Claude was making a fool out of himself. If the forest brought everyone back, she would not be any different.

She would return as he had.

Huffing, Henri turned, pulling his fur cape to cover himself as he looked to his rose bushes.

A soft fluttering whistled until a bird with a shimmering blue and green belly sat on a decorative stone urn before the roses. Its burnt orange head was decorated with a yellow chin, and its eyes were masked with a thin black stripe. The bird stared at him, tilting its head unafraid until its eyes suddenly glowed green.

Ice surged so fast under his skin he thought he would faint. The saliva in his mouth thickened as bile rose in his throat. He recognized those unnatural green eyes. The memory of the Enchanter sent violent chills down his entire body and dissolved his pride and confidence into dust. The dead hedges behind him crunched under his weight as he stumbled into them, snapping their brittle branches like glass.

"As spoken, your garden has been dying. Nothing remains except your roses. Each rose bush now represents one month. Break the spell before they wilt. Fail, and you and your servants will be cursed until you die. May Kyros have pity on your soul."

The words were not heard aloud but were directly injected into his thoughts. It echoed repeatedly, and each time felt more mocking and sinister than the last. He cradled his head, shaking it furiously to cast the voice out of his mind.

"Get out of my head!" he roared, baring his sharp teeth, but the bird and voice had already disappeared.

"Sir?"

Henri whipped around, ready to strike. Isa stood outside of his reach, safe from his claws. She did not flinch or startle at his proximity.

It was difficult to read her face with those beady black eyes. There was a time when he had mastered interpreting her expressions when they were younger, but those days were long gone. Now she was a stranger ghosting through his halls.

"What happened? You look unwell," she said, her voice calm.

"I'm fine," he said, but his hands shook, and his heart pounded under his ribcage. He dug those hands into his thighs, clenching the fur there and willing them to stop trembling. The shivers persisted, running through his back as he avoided Isa's gaze. Seeing the Enchanter's eyes and hearing his voice was worse than any nightmare he had conjured.

"Time is running out," he said, quieter this time.

"What?"

"We have four months. The Enchanter spoke to me."

Silence crashed around them until she hooked a thumb behind her. "Then you better find her. For all our sakes, Henri."

Claude's voice called the woman's name, and the sound rang around the sighing wind. Henri's cloven feet shifted against stone while he clenched and unclenched his fists.

There would be no other choice then.

A growl leaped from his throat as he stormed away from the roses and the woman he did not wish to part from.

10

Marguerite

I t worked.

An incredulous giggle erupted from her mouth at the astonishing feat. She could not believe it worked.

The chateau, the gardens, and Claude were nowhere to be seen. Instead, she was surrounded by tall, thick trees clustered together in a tight circle where none had been before. Instead of grass, soft dirt cushioned her back as she stared upward. Whatever magic these woods held had transported her to a different part of the forest in the blink of an eye.

Relieved, her hands flew to her face and she exhaled deeply, attempting to soothe her blood buzzing like a swarm of wasps from her daring flight. "Thank you, Erus, Kyros, and Ghiana," she prayed sincerely, letting her fingers touch her lips before placing them above her heart.

Bonbon sat beside her head, and she peered up at him. His tongue peeked from his mouth, panting. "You poor thing," she murmured, but he did not acknowledge her sympathy.

Standing, she smiled down at the dog. "Let's go home, shall we?"

Another wave of relief washed over her when she spotted a dirt path carved between large, stretching trees. If there was a path, there was civilization.

Just as excitement took root, something flew past her face in a flurry. She squeaked and threw up her hands to protect herself, but the intruder had already escaped. Bonbon barked and pointed his nose toward the offender, and she strained to see what was in the treetops.

A bird. A colorful little thing with a teal stomach and a rustic orange head. Its yellow chin dipped up and down, bobbing from its perch. How strange.

"You scared me," she said breathlessly, and it eyed her with small, black eyes. She felt its peculiar stare on her while she approached the path and looked to her right and left, carefully considering both.

"Which way?"

The dog sat and looked up, and she imagined him saying, *you decide.*

"Well, the forest was south of the cottage, so if we go north," she said, turning to her left, "we should make it back. What do you say?"

Bonbon yawned, and she nodded.

"Just as I thought. Let's try left."

The path was not long. In fact, after a few minutes of stumbling around protruding rocks and branches, a clearing could be seen between the trees.

Could it be that easy? Would she be home so soon?

With renewed energy, she forced herself to run faster, with hope curling within her. The sound of fluttering wings buzzed by her head again, and she held back a startled yelp. The bird flew before her, racing her to the finish line. Laughing freely, she obliged the bird and began to run faster.

But as she reached the clearing, her lively steps froze into place. Hope disintegrated like ash in her mouth.

The chateau sat in the clearing with its wrought-iron gate erected in front. Its white walls stretched three stories high with a slate roof steeping into tall, conical slopes. The roof dipped into a parapet of stone and gabled dormers. Several half-crescent windows adorned by cream curtains lined the entirety of the building. Tall pillars with leaf motifs stood proudly beside the imposing, oak doors.

The same wilting trees lined the gravel path leading to the entrance. The same flower beds surrounding the gates were brown and brittle. Marguerite blinked once, twice, three times, and the color drained from her face when the image remained.

"Miss Dupont!"

The wind carried the voice to her, making her tremble like a leaf. Claude's call came from behind the chateau, most likely in the gardens where she had left him. If she turned around right now, she might have a chance to escape again.

But, from the corner of her eye, she saw the bird, the same strange creature that raced her here, hopping around in the grass. It chirped, bobbing its head before its black eyes glowed green.

The eyes.

A shriek rushed from her lungs, and she stumbled back into a tree trunk.

"No!" Her hands searched wildly behind her, only grasping air and bark, desperate to procure a different escape route. The bird bowed before flying up in a whirl of flapping wings and darted toward the gardens. Whatever it was, she had no intention of staying to find out.

Bonbon followed her obediently, and when she looked up, she blinked at the scenery around her. The dirt path she had been following moments before had vanished. She had been transported to a different area.

A new, wild grass swayed around her calves. Instead of the branches she had hopped over a minute before, a hoard of small, purple flowers dotted the detritus. Twisting around, she gaped. The clearing and the chateau had also disappeared.

This was not the path she had just taken; she was certain of that, but she needed to keep moving. Several minutes later, the trees thinned around her. "Maybe this time," she whispered, scarcely daring to hope.

She faced the chateau from the east but swallowed her despair with clenched fists. She refused to accept this. Whatever magic this was, it could not keep her here against her will.

She immediately turned back around from where she had come.

But, again, the scenery shifted. She followed a line of large, brown mushrooms until she faced the chateau from the west. Another voice called her name and joined Claude's frantic cries, but she marched back around.

As she jogged along, the trees began to blur together in a smear of greens and browns. Sometimes, it would take minutes, and sometimes, it would feel like an hour had passed, but she always found herself face-to-face with the monstrous chateau.

East, west, north, south, northeast, east again—she had lost count and begun to memorize every angle of the building and the grounds upon which it sat. And she turned back around with clenched teeth each time to face a new path.

After stumbling around, the cut on her foot flared, but the sound of rushing waters nearby drew her attention. Curiosity drove her toward the noise, and her slippers sagged against the softer ground. She wedged between large pine trees and felt their needles prickle her scalp as she passed.

A river sat beneath an embankment with churning water and white, turbulent waves. One step closer, she would tumble down the steep slope and be washed away by the current. The edge gradually ascended to her left, where a bridge had been constructed over the rapids beneath. It was not like the stone arches over the Sabine River in Avilon, but rather made of wooden slats supported by thin, wooden beams.

Bonbon wheezed beside her. Frowning, she sank against the lip, allowing her legs to dangle over the swirling waters. The rocks beneath her pressed painfully against her legs, but she did not have the strength to shift into a more comfortable position. Bonbon collapsed in a heap, resting his small chin on her thigh as he continued to gasp for air.

Frustrated tears pressed in her eyes, threatening to fall, but flapping wings sounded, and she spotted a familiar bird perched on a rock beside her. It had an orange head and a teal stomach. Its eyes blazed a frightening green, but she refused to cower this time.

"Who are you, and what do you want from me?" she hissed. She was cornered like a wild animal, and her teeth barred in a challenge.

"I am an Enchanter, and fate has chosen you. Time will now move naturally with your presence."

The words were not physically spoken but were embedded in her thoughts. She gasped at the rich, foreign voice echoing in her mind.

"What? Fate?" she spat. "What does that even mean? Why are you keeping me here?"

"Fate keeps you here. I am merely a facilitator and spectator of fate. I have no power to release you."

Marguerite raised her chin while balling her fists. Bonbon did not stir in her lap except to open his mouth in a wide yawn. She glared at the bird. "You can facilitate fate but cannot release me?"

"Break the curse, and you will be free."

"The injustice!" She gently urged Bonbon off her lap so she could stand. The bird—creature—hopped backward as she wobbled to her feet. "Who are you to curse innocent people and keep me against my will? How dare you!"

"I follow the will of fate—of the God who created me. It's by Erus' will, not mine."

Blood drained from her face, and she swayed in place. Erus? The God of the Heavens? If His will was fate…did that also mean—

"Is Erus responsible for my family's misfortune? Did he bring this upon us so that I—I could…"

"I do not know how you have come to be here, but the will of fate has spoken. You have been chosen to break the curse. The fate of everyone who is affected is in your hands."

Her back hit bark, and the ground rolled under her feet. "No, I don't want this. I cannot—I...I must go home. Do you hear me?" Her voice inclined higher, desperate. "I *must* go home now. I cannot stay and break curses! I don't even know what the curse is. How do I break it?"

"Follow your heart, and the curse will be broken."

She exhaled in disbelief. "What does that even mean? Why must you speak in riddles?"

"Follow your heart..."

The bird flew away, rustling the treetops in its ascent.

11

Marguerite

"*Follow your heart,*" the Enchanter had said.

But Marguerite wanted to escape. She wanted to go home. She wanted to forget the legends of Enchanters and old magic. Erus had called the angelic beings he created back into the Heavens long ago. They shouldn't be here. Not anymore.

"Fate or no fate," she seethed under her breath.

She braced the trees along the bank with renewed vigor and inched slowly across mud, rocks, and weeds. When she reached the bridge, she assessed the slick, green planks from moss and the gaping holes. There was no railing or rope to hold onto, and one cautious step told her it would require more than balance to cross. She would have to carefully choose where to step if she didn't want to fall through the dilapidated wood slabs.

"We can do this," she said, more to reassure herself than her silent companion.

Picking Bonbon up, she took a deep breath. She patted the first plank with the tip of her foot before putting the rest of her weight there. It creaked, but it did not crumble beneath her.

The next part would not be so easy.

Come on, come on, she thought, gathering her courage to move her next foot. It quivered in her hesitation, but she finally placed her foot next to her first on the bridge. Closing her eyes tightly, the plank did not crack or groan.

She exhaled noisily in relief.

She whispered a prayer and continued her steady path, one toe at a time. Before she knew it, she made it to the middle of the bridge, but her eyes widened at the white waters frothing beneath the cracks of the planks.

"Marguerite!"

She jolted. The wood collapsed inward without warning, trapping her ankle. Screaming, she lurched forward on her hands and knees, splinters biting and moss slickening her descent. Bonbon leaped away just as the hole opened like a dragon's maw. Her hands scrambled, searching for something to hold onto, but her fingers only met the empty air whooshing around her. She clawed the air until her fingers hooked around the edge of a supporting beam. The bridge swayed. She dangled, but a small splash drew her attention to the rushing current.

"Bonbon!" she screeched. "Bonbon, no!"

The dog, fighting to keep its head above water, was carried off by the turbulent waters. Tears pressed in her eyes, wailing when his body plunged beneath the waves. Those screams echoed as a sickening crack ripped through the beam she held onto.

"I got you."

Her eyes flew upward, and her heart floundered in relief. Never had she been so ecstatic to see Claude as she was in this moment.

"Take my hand!" He reached his arm to her, belly down on the remaining stable planks. Gasping and whimpering, she attempted to unlatch one hand, but her weight plunged her down before she gripped the beam once more.

"I can't," she cried, "I will fall!"

"I will not let that happen," he said, shimmying his arm as far as possible. "Just...reach. Take my hand. I promise I will catch you."

His hand, although a head above her own, felt leagues away. The beam whined in her ears, splintering under her weight, and her stomach leaped up in her throat. A shrill scream tore from her mouth as she kicked off the collapsing timber. Fingers brushing, her eyes widened as her body suspended in mid-air before descending.

Just when she accepted her doom, a strong grip caught her wrist. His claws dug into her skin, grunting with the new weight straining his arm. Wood bit into her stomach when he hauled her up while the opposite end of the bridge collapsed with a splash that burst over them like a tidal wave.

"We need to move now," he said, scrambling to his knees. "Come on!"

Before she could steady herself, warm arms dipped under her legs and back and pulled her toward his firm, lean body. He ascended easily, even with her added weight, and dashed toward the stable ground. Legs swinging, she braced herself by wrapping her arms around his neck and nestled her face in the layers of his cravat. His heartbeat drummed heavily against her ears, and she couldn't help but inhale the scent of dry cedar and resin clinging to his clothes.

After reaching safety on the other side, he craned his neck to inspect the bridge they escaped from. She followed his gaze and gasped as the rest of it bowed and slapped into the water.

"Well, that was rather close." He smiled down at her, chuckling. "Are you alright?"

"I...yes," she said, breathless. From this proximity, she could see every thick, blond hair covering his skin like velvety fur. The bridge of his nose was straight, like the statues she was fond of, but instead of ending in a point, a wet, black tip sat above his shapely, thin lips. His soft, brown eyes peered into hers, relief, and an emotion she could not name swirled in those coppery depths.

A mix of emotions also clashed within her, but the most concerning one was the warmth she felt fluttering in her chest.

Her eyes rounded at shrill barking, and she pointed toward the river. "Bonbon! We need to save him—"

But her words were cut short at the sight of a hulking beast clinging to a boulder against the current, holding a shivering Bonbon in his arm.

Henri

The water crashed around Henri like an icy bath. Its chill seeped into his fur and stole the heat from his body like a ruthless thief. Shivers erupted all over his skin. His teeth rattled in his skull while the weight of the water threatened to topple him over. The biting waves would have overpowered him in seconds if he were still human.

At least this monstrous form was good for something.

Large, splintered planks rushed toward him and struck his back like a battering ram. Hissing, he kicked the debris away and glared at the wood. Water doused his face, and he sputtered when another wave smashed over him and the dog. The little runt shrieked in his ears, and Henri growled.

Even now, he wondered why he did it—why his legs moved on their accord to save the blasted rat. Claude had scampered to save the woman, telling him to stay back since his weight would likely send the bridge tumbling down. It was true, though. He was too heavy to assist the woman, so he had to stand there while watching the mound of brown and white fur sink under the water.

Maybe it was how she grieved over the animal as it bobbed in the current, or maybe it was because a memory of himself surfaced like a swollen blemish. An awful memory—one when he was a little boy weeping over the stray cat he had named Enzo laying still in the gardens. Isa had kneeled next to him, her apron muddying, as she put her arm around his shaking shoulders...

The memory struck him like a lightning bolt, and he acted without further thought.

Shaking his head, he clenched his clattering teeth together. That was the issue: he did not think. Either way, this stupid dog had caused him trouble twice in one day, but this time it might end in both of their deaths. They would drown in these painful, freezing waters, their corpses bloated and washed up in tall reeds somewhere. Perhaps the curse wouldn't allow him to die, but all the same, he did not wish to test the theory.

Curse him. And the wretched woman he did it for.

"Sir," Claude called out above the white froth with the woman in his arms. At least she survived, and this rescue was not a complete failure. He could not say the same for himself as his sharp claws grated against the boulder.

"Hold on!"

"What does it look like I'm doing?" he hollered, but another wave drowned out his words. He gurgled and spat the water filling his mouth. He sank under, his legs tired from kicking to stay afloat, and his fingers screamed for release from his vice-like hold. Even as his strength failed him, he thrust the dog up above the water with one shaky arm. The runt could not die before he did.

Gasping, he surfaced again but yelped as pine needles stabbed his cheek. He looked at the offending thing with wide eyes. On the other side were Claude and the woman's faces, each holding on to the end of the branch from the embankment.

"Grab on, sir, we got you."

Henri obeyed and held on. One tug, and another, both woman and dog man, dragged him across the current. Closer and closer until he reached the slick underbelly of the embankment. He used the last of his strength to crawl up the steep, muddy shore. He grasped the edge, and two pairs of hands grabbed his arms and pulled him upward.

Weeds tickled his back as he rolled over them, and he panted like the dog lying next to him.

"Are you well, sir?"

Two faces hovered above him, blocking the sun. Their blinking, worried faces created discomfort in his chest, but he nodded wordlessly. "Yes...good work, Claude," he rasped, taking his offered hand.

Claude shook his head when he got to his feet. "It was Marguerite's quick thinking that saved you. You should thank her."

Henri looked at her through a half-lidded gaze and furrowed brows. "What do you mean?"

"She was the one to suggest we use the branch to help you. She saved you, sir," Claude said.

The woman said nothing but did not shy away from his open stare. He bowed his head and said, "Thank you, I owe you my life."

She opened her mouth but jumped as the dog shook, spraying them with water. She bent down and hugged it to her chest. "Thank *you*," she said, looking at him without fear or disgust. Was that a bit of a smile on her lips as well? "For saving us both."

"I am happy to do so," he murmured in return.

"Come, it's late," Claude said. "Let us rest, and then we can speak more tomorrow."

12

Marguerite

The tea Claude had given her had grown cold in her hands. She stared at it, hypnotized by how the amber liquid rippled by the slightest movement. The white porcelain felt smooth under her hands, a concrete reminder that everything was real—curse and all.

She had hoped everything was a terrible dream. But, her heart fell when she woke up the next mid-morning to a strange bed and an even stranger man by her side. Claude was kind enough to answer her questions and help tend to her needs, but this situation was absurd. Why was she trapped here? How could a forest belong to an evil Enchanter? And he cursed a Count and the staff into animalistic creatures, bound to a nameless spell?

That was one detail Claude omitted when she asked him earlier that day. He failed to mention what the parameters of the curse were, and she was sure there had to be a way to break it if the Enchanter had instructed her to do so.

And, as much as she wished she could help their cruel situation, she needed to go home. A knot settled in her stomach at the thought of her family, who were probably worried about where she was.

She looked to the door, where a knock sounded, diverting her worrisome thoughts, and she called for them to enter. The face of her temporary Lady's Maid entered, but the shock of her appearance still rendered her speechless.

The *woman's* eyes were like large, black orbs and placed nearer to her temples. Two, long wispy plumes sprouted from her white, fuzzy head topped with a linen maid's cap. A massive mound of white fur collared her neck and stopped at her sternum, while the rest of her body was slender under her cotton dress and apron. Behind her back were white, velvety wings whose tips hovered over the floor. An image of a white moth came to mind, but the woman's nose and mouth appeared untouched as she smiled at her in greeting.

"Are you done with your tea, dear?" she asked.

"Yes, yes I am, thank you," she said, steeling her voice from cracking with nerves. Jeanette crossed the space between them and held out her hands. The action confused her until she realized she was being cautious of touching her. It was evident that Jeanette did not want to frighten her more than she already had, and her eyes softened.

"Thank you," Marguerite said again, handing her the porcelain teacup apologetically.

"It's my pleasure, miss." Jeanette dipped into a small curtsey before taking a few steps backward to allow more space between them. "I have been given orders to help you dress for the dinner my master wishes to have with you."

This was unexpected. Her brows knitted together. "I thought...Claude had said that I could rest as long as I wanted. He did not mention dinner."

"Well, Mr. Alarie would like to discuss the curse with you in person. Do you accept his invitation?"

If it meant figuring out a way to go home, then... "Yes," she said, "I accept."

"Lovely. He is expecting you at half past seven."

That was in thirty minutes. "Oh." It appeared he had assumed her answer would be yes, regardless. How presumptuous.

Jeanette set the unfinished tea on the table and crossed the room toward the wardrobe. When it creaked open, she gasped at the sight.

Several dresses, shoes, undergarments, and jewelry lined the space and glittered in the light.

"Is it normal for your master to keep so many dresses for his guests?" Marguerite asked, squashing the temptation to race to the wardrobe and run her hands through the silky dresses.

"Oh, no, dear. It's all magic, see?" Jeanette waved her hand around the room with a soft, polite smile. The expression would have been more reassuring if it weren't for Jeanette's unblinking eyes. "The chateau provides for us well, at least."

"Do you simply open something, and it'll provide you with what you want?" she said, eyeing the ribbons her sister would most likely drool over.

"Well, not quite. The linens are always washed and clean in the cupboards, and our pantries are always lined with food. So on and so on. I don't think too hard about it and how it all works. I'm glad we don't starve since we cannot leave the premises."

And neither can I, she thought with a frown.

Jeanette turned to the line of dresses and picked one out. "I believe this dress will look lovely on you." She pulled out an amethyst silk dress for her to inspect.

The style and colors were dated, yet she did not have the heart or spirit to protest the option.

"Very good, miss. The color will look splendid against your complexion." Jeanette approached the bed at her side. "If I may..." she gestured to her.

"Of course," she said, squashing her uneasiness and climbing out of bed. Despite her efforts, she still flinched at the woman's velvety touch.

"I'm so sorry, dear!" Jeanette said, but Marguerite corrected herself and sought her hand again.

At first, the process did not stray from her familiar routine. They replaced her dirty shift, and the stockings, garters, and shoes followed, but the stays were peculiar. They fastened in the front rather than the back, and it came down slightly longer than she was used to. There were no pockets or kerchief, but a red, silk petticoat sat underneath a deep plum skirt. A matching, tight mantua draped over the skirt with a golden stomacher.

Her mother would have had a fit if she had come out of her room looking like this. A lady was meant to wear light, pastel colors with delicate lace and ribbons. It was supposed to be loose-fitting, effortless, innocent, and graceful. Everything about this dress felt mature and sensual—words that should never be uttered together. A flush crept up her neck as she looked down at the narrow, curve-hugging material.

However, the dress was not entirely foreign. She recalled portraits of her grandmother that used to hang in their estate. She wore a gown like the one she was wearing. Granted, it was painted thirty years ago.

After she was ready, Marguerite followed Jeanette with nervous emotions swarming around her heart. They came around a corner where candelabras lined the walls.

There was something strange about the place, she decided. A peculiar power hummed inside the walls, mimicking the forest's unusual aura. She could not hear or see it but felt it thrumming around her.

A few paintings adorned the hallways, and one of Erus on his throne, surrounded by his Enchanters, caught her eye. She had prayed to the God of the Heavens all her life and believed him to be a merciful creator of her soul. Erus' wife, Goddess, and maker of the world, Gallia, was in another painting with her fae and other magical beings she created. In the next painting, Kyros of Judgement stood with his whip in the Inbetween, a land of spirits and luminescent blue light.

These were the Gods she believed in. But were they as compassionate as she was taught to believe if they forced her here?

After reaching the bottom of the staircase, the very ones she had tripped down yesterday, they continued until they reached a set of open doors into the dining room.

She could not brace herself enough when she found the beast's blue eyes glowing toward the end of the room. Flickering light from a candle toward the opposite end of the table reflected in those eyes, fire clashing with ice.

Claude stood and gestured, pulling out a chair for her. Despite his friendly demeanor, she hesitated to comply but sat despite the urge to flee.

"Miss," an unfamiliar male voice said from beside her. She jumped, placing a hand over her racing heart. She looked to her right to see a stout, plump man with two black, vertical stripes up his eyes staring at her. How she did not sense him, she did not know. Maybe he moved quietly for his stature and quickly at that.

In his hairy, clawed hands was a bowl of scented water for her to dip her hands in. By the look of his white and black hair all over his body and his round, black nose, she guessed that he was a badger, perhaps a butler.

Steeling herself, she dipped her hands in the water and looked toward the sound of the door being pushed open near her left side. The brief light from the kitchen highlighted the woman's features before the door shut. Despite seeing three creatures already, the fourth one was no less jarring.

The maid had a crow's beak as a nose, round, beady eyes, and black, gleaming feathers under her maid's cap and down her throat. She pushed a trolley with platters of food and placed one before her.

"Enjoy," the beast said in a low, rumbling growl.

13

Henri

Henri observed his guest from the comfort of shadows. Entertaining guests had never been his strong suit, and women even less so. Perhaps his stepmother was to blame, but his hands sweat, his heart raced, and his mind scrambled for a plan of escape.

Most boys outgrew this awkward phase, but fear still clung to him even through manhood. Up until the Enchanter came pissing on his life, he had avoided most women and dreamed of becoming a comfortable recluse.

The only woman who ever made him feel at ease was the woman who set down his dinner and refused to look at him.

Isa...

An ache filled his chest, but he shook off the unwanted emotion and returned his attention to his important guest. But what to say now? How was he supposed to start this conversation? Claude had helped him think of various conversation starters, but each one eluded him.

When the main course arrived, he realized he had sat there too long without eating his appetizer or saying anything. Marguerite sat stiffly and cut into her chicken with delicate knife strokes.

"Dinner was wonderful, thank you," Marguerite said after dinner.

"We do have dessert," he said, attempting to keep his voice light. "Are you fond of custard tarts?"

Her face brightened. "Oh yes, I am. That sounds delightful."

"I am glad." Another lengthy pause followed, and he feared it would prolong until she retired to bed. He had to speak now.

"Are you—"

"May I ask a question?" she asked simultaneously, their voices colliding.

"Oh," he said sheepishly, "you first."

"No, you."

"I insist," he said.

"Very well..." she folded her hands in her lap and nodded thanks to Isa, who replaced her dinner with a small plate of custard tart. "Thank you for taking this time to speak with you," she said when the silence became uncomfortable again.

"Of course."

"I wanted to address our current circumstances with you. Both of us are trapped here. And if I am to stay," she paused, her frown turning wistful. "I want to spend all my energy helping you break this curse. I want to go home, and I assume you no longer want to be trapped in your current bodies?"

He nodded, jarred by her bluntness but grateful for it all the same. "You would assume correctly."

"Good. Let us help each other then. Do you have any leads on how to break the spell? Any idea at all?"

"I am unsure," he lied easily. Claude and Jeanette had suggested he keep the curse-breaking a secret. *Love must come naturally*, they had said, and he agreed.

"The Enchanter did not tell us how to break the curse, and we have yet to find a solution. But I have been told that we are restricted to time," he explained.

"How long?" she pressed.

"Four months."

"Four months?" she repeated in disbelief. One hand came up to her mouth, and she shook her head, "I cannot wait that long!"

"If given a choice, neither would I."

Her face fell, and her fingers tightened over her silverware. The fork clattered as she took a sip from her wine and looked down at the glass in despair. "I have obligations to fulfill myself. I am eager to help you, but all the Enchanter told me was to follow my heart. I don't know what that could mean."

He shared a look with Claude, who offered his silence in return. Keeping his face neutral, he said, "He spoke to you?"

"Yes, he came as a bird and spoke in riddles. It was difficult to understand."

"What else did he tell you?" he asked and ignored the way his blood began to rush up his neck in panic.

"Something about being unable to free me because of 'fate'. Does that mean anything to you?"

So, Claude was right. There would be no second or third choice—she was the one he was destined to fall in love with. The words of the curse came back with full force:

A woman fate shall send
She is the key to the curse's
end
Only by learning to love and
be loved in return
May you break this curse
and find what your heart
truly yearns

He inhaled deeply, grateful he did not have to lie through this one, "I suppose it must mean you are the key—the only person—who can break our curse."

"I do not see how or why," she murmured.

"Maybe the answer will come in time," he said, looking away from her wary gaze.

"How long have you been cursed?" she asked.

Leaning back, the chair groaned, and he clicked his claws against the glass. Where was she going with this? "About six months, perhaps."

"I ask because I have been thinking about what the Enchanter said about time. I almost forgot, but he said something about time moving naturally now because I'm here. And I cannot help but notice the way your servants dress." She gestured to Claude, who wore a dark blue overcoat. "And the dress you provided me. I also do not want to appear ungrateful—"

"I'm not sure what he could mean. But is the dress not to your liking?" he asked, wondering if the wardrobe the Enchanter had left them had failed them.

"No, I think it's beautiful, but..."

Oh no. Nothing good came after the word "but." Too many remarks from his half-sisters and stepmother had taught him that.

"But I have not seen such fashions in Avilon," she said.

Tilting his head, his fingers ceased their drumming. "Truly? I have been to Avilon, and I can assure you that you wear the finest fashions led by Madame Beauchamp herself."

The crackling fire popped in his ear like small, bursting cannons as her lips parted and closed. "Madame Beauchamp? The late king's mistress?"

"Yes, surely you have heard of—"

Words caught in his throat like a bear trap, snapping and tearing them in two. Had she said what he thought she said? But, no, she must have misspoken, or maybe he misheard her.

Swallowing, he cleared his throat. "*Late* king? No, miss, the Star King might be in his prime, but he is only fifty-two years of age and not ill from last I heard."

She leaned forward. "Sir...Do you know what year it is?"

Chuckling to suppress the flip of his stomach, sweat collected in his large, naked hands. "O-of course I do! It's the year fifty-four fifty-one."

Every tick of the clock on the mantle sharpened into distinct beats. Her eyes widened, and shock washed over her face. She shook her head slowly. "I am afraid it's not, sir. It's the year fifty-four eighty-one. The Star King died five years ago."

"What? No," he said and stood from his seat. The calculation blurred in his mind, and his heart stammered at the answer.

Thirty. Thirty years. Three Gods above.

"No," he insisted, "you lie."

"I am so sorry," she said with her hand to her heart. "I swear to you. I speak the truth."

He could not detect deceit.

An invisible hand clamped down on his chest. There was not enough air in the room. His eyes scanned the walls, his thoughts blurring into incoherent words and images. His ribs threatened to collapse inward. A clatter sounded behind him. It was the chair, he realized vaguely. The floor was swaying. "No, that cannot be possible. How...how is that..."

Suddenly the face of Claude was right there, smoothing, placating Claude with his mouth opening and shutting, but the words were a distant garble, spurring his panic.

His feet were wobbling, and the weight of his own body would bow them in half if he didn't move. A gentle hand rested on his shoulder, but he shrugged it off. Isa, but he found her touch burned, singing the last piece of his rationale. More voices called to him, saying words that didn't make sense.

Get out. Get out. Get out. It was a demand, the instinct to run.

Lurching forward, he pushed against the pacifying hands and barreled through the double doors. Faces blurred past him, surprised, shocked, worried faces of the doorman, the butler, the scullery maid, all of them blended and melted into each other as he scrambled around the corner. Claws scraped against the herringbone floor, and he barreled into familiar doors.

Slamming them closed, he stood in the darkness of his study. The silence soothed his beating heart and twisted lungs. There were no more hands, voices, or faces to distract him from the mantra repeating over and over.

Thirty years. Thirty years. Thirty years.

A roar, long and strained like a wounded animal, burst from his chest. Claws found chairs and shredded the cushions with one swipe. Feathers burst up in a cloud as he swung them into the wall. The accent table was next, and it flew, smacking against a bookshelf. Books rattled and fell until the shelf groaned over and thudded to the ground. Nothing was safe—the rug, a globe, the paintings torn, battered, and ripped to shreds. And soon, his hands were searching for his desk, plunging through the piles of papers and envelopes until he found the one. The last letter from his father before his passing. It shook in his hands, crumpling as he read.

My dearest son,

I wish I could have spent the Yulefest with you. I know you are angry with me since you chose to spend it alone...

"Curse you," he hissed, scanning the rest of the contents with burning eyes. It was not his choice to spend it alone. His stepmother had made sure of it.

I love you.

Tearing it in half, the pieces fluttered slowly to the ground.

The doors creaked open behind him. "Sir," Claude said.

"What am I to do?" he whispered, feeling tears stream down his snout. Swiping them away, he turned to him.

Claude closed the door behind him, stepping over the books and broken pieces of furniture. He did not speak but stopped a few paces away.

"I did not think *thirty years* had passed, did you?" Henri continued, breathless, while rubbing his hands over his face. "I mean, I've heard the old legends about the fae realm and their twisted sense of time, but...I didn't think he—He's not fae! He's an Enchanter and...Everyone I know is likely..." Closing his eyes, he swallowed down the word he dared not utter. "And those who live will think I have met my end. Not that they would care," he sneered. Those within his circle wouldn't care if an illegitimate lived or not.

He turned to the scattered papers over the desk and shook his head. "Am I fifty years old? I don't feel like I have aged, but..."

He clenched his fists. "Even if she falls in love with me and I fall in love with her...wh-what am I supposed to be? My title, my estate...everything. Who will I be? How will we fit into this new world?"

"I don't know," Claude answered quietly. His valet usually had the answers, but now he was as lost as Henri. What was the point of this curse if he had to restart his whole life after?

"We might as well spend the rest of our days as monsters," he said, looking up at Claude. But his valet's eyes were no longer filled with uncertainty but a blazing ferocity.

"I don't wish to die like this," Claude whispered, "and I doubt the others would either."

His lip curled into a scowl. "Of course."

"What is that supposed to mean?"

"It means...While you can find a new master, I will be floundering in the waste of my title. What life is that? Tell me, Claude, what kind of life is that?"

"Are you giving up then?" Claude asked, raising his chin and balling his fists. "After we saved Marguerite—after everything that has happened?"

"Do not patronize me," he snarled back. Claude didn't understand—none of them did. How could they, when they always knew who they were and where their place stood within society? Meanwhile, he wrestled with his existence and fought to find meaning.

The only thing that gave him worth was this title he didn't even want.

But he couldn't say this to Claude. Too many emotions weighed him down to near exhaustion. Too much hurt and confusion clamped down on his lungs, making it difficult to breathe.

"Do you think me stupid?" Henri settled on saying instead. "I leave her in your hands for now."

Claude moved the overturned table and stepped around it to draw closer to him. "What does that mean?"

"It means exactly as I said. Take care of her. Do whatever you can to make her happy for me. I don't care." Henri waved a hand and turned his back on the valet.

"What will you do then?" Claude asked.

There were too many questions and too many thoughts. Henri wanted to shout and break all at once. "I want to be left alone."

"So, you're giving up?"

The stinging accusation hit its mark. "I said don't patronize me! I am your master."

"And I thought I was your friend."

Henri whirled around. Why wouldn't Claude leave already? He made it clear he wanted to be alone.

Always alone.

"You thought wrong," Henri started with a growl. "Your pathetic excuse of a father always pushed me to play with you as children, but you were always insufferable. Always a stupid, cheerful little *dog*. Know your place and leave me."

Claude's mouth tightened into a grim line, his face a rigid slab of stone as he turned, strode away, and shut the doors behind him.

14

Marguerite

The book snapped shut with a cloud of dust stinging Marguerite's eyes. She blinked away the irritant, sighed, and set the book on top of one of the five tall stacks she had made. Glancing up at the ceiling, medieval crests of a rose with two swords intersecting the flower were painted around the perimeter—a symbol of a family rich with history and nobility.

And her heart ached for their living kin hiding behind these walls.

Three weeks had passed since Mr. Alarie, and herself had spoken in the dining room, and she had not seen him since. Even when she inquired after him, she was told that he was unavailable. Servants floated through the halls with empty stares and worried frowns as they continued their duties as normal. Even friendly Jeanette spoke little to her but continued to provide and tend to her when needed.

If thirty years passed while she was trapped in the chateau, she shuddered to think of what she would do, how she would feel in their place. Her parents would most likely be dead, and her siblings would undoubtedly be well in their prime: ages fifty-two and forty-eight, respectively. And what would they think seeing her as youthful as she did when she left them?

At least time would move normally now, and she would not have to worry about the years passing without her knowing. Or so the

Enchanter promised. Still, she must find a way to break the curse as soon as possible.

A deep sigh exhaled from her lungs, and she gazed toward her pile. Only one book mentioned the magical creatures that once inhabited Gallia before they disappeared. It spoke of the fae, their curious realm, and how time had moved differently for them there. Perhaps the same logic could be said for the Enchanter and his magic, despite being a different creature, which caused the misfortunate time-skip to occur.

Otherwise, there was little information about curses and how to break them, for that matter. A few books of religion and poetry were also littered in her stacks, but those had proven as fruitless as the rest. There were still hundreds of books she had yet to investigate, but the first ten bookshelves had been scanned or read within the weeks. Only thirty more shelves to go.

"Any luck today?"

She whisked around and put a hand to her heart. Claude stood in the front of the white archway, his canine teeth sharp in his wide grin. Although he was always full of smiles, they had not reached his eyes since the day in the dining room. Today was no exception.

"Oh, Claude," she said after her heart settled down. "I did not expect you." The statement was not quite a lie, considering he usually came in to check on her at noon, in twenty minutes, according to the clock on the mantle.

"I apologize for startling you," he said while bowing his head. "I had some extra time to spare and thought to see how you were faring."

It was an innocent statement, but his words nonetheless warmed her heart. Throughout the weeks, he had been so thoughtful of her, talking to her when she was lonely and ensuring she never skipped a meal. Although his visits were brief, they made her day as she scoured through the library.

It should have worried her—this comfortability around him, especially when her heart skipped when she thought of the day he saved her at the bridge. That day he held her in his strong, sturdy arms. The comfort she felt.

Heat rushed to her face, and she opened a book on top of one of her piles to keep her hands busy. They were alone, and even though he was a servant, her mother would have certainly scolded her for not having another female attendant by her side. Like Sophie...

By the Gods, she missed her. If Sophie were here, she'd help her find the answers to break the curse. She'd cheer her up.

"How is your master?" Marguerite asked abruptly to shake the thoughts away.

"The same," he replied with his mouth dipping. "He is still unwell."

"Is there anything I can do? I still haven't heard from him."

"He'll be fine, don't worry. Time will help, I am sure."

"It seems like that is what has caused his grief in the first place," she mused out loud. "I wish I could help him and all of you. I know you said you are well yourself, but thirty years is a lot to take in. How are you managing?"

"It's a lot," he murmured, and his eyes darkened like a bleak, gaping hole, but it vanished quickly with another practiced smile. "But no matter. I am managing fine. It's of no consequence now."

"It seems like a huge consequence to me," she countered. "I cannot fathom what you and everyone must feel."

His eyes widened, no doubt surprised by her candid remark. She cursed her loose tongue but could not ignore the sadness hovering over him like an oppressive storm.

An emotion wrestled over his face before he straightened. "I appreciate your sympathies," he said quietly, almost too soft for her to hear. "But I suppose there is no use grieving over what I cannot change."

"Even so," she said, disliking how easily he could brush the pain away.

"You have been slaving away in this library for quite some time," he said, gesturing to her stacks. "It's quite impressive."

A twinge tugged at her heart, but she found she could relate to wanting to avoid such topics. She would humor the subject change and close the book in her hands. "Well, I don't read all of these boring books without good reason."

"Not a fan of reading?" he asked, picking up a hefty tome and squinting at the calligraphy painted on the cover.

"I know, it's a crime to confess. But I would rather paint than read if I had a choice. The print is too hard on my eyes."

"Ah, a painter?" His eyes glinted with curiosity as he put the book down. "And what does the lady like to paint?"

"Oh, well," she said, twisting a curl around her finger and thinking of the landscape her mother had sneered at and claimed was an *uninspiring and a cheap imitation of nature*. "Nothing of importance, really."

"I cannot believe that to be true. I think painting is a noble pursuit," he said. "It shows creativity and passion, certainly things worth praising."

She certainly had not received the praise he spoke of. Another mocking face came to mind, and her lips pursed at the thought of Gustave and his friends who spurned the portrait she made of her brother when they were but fifteen. It was then she had decided she would never humor the thought of marrying him.

Ironic, she thought. Desperation had its way of swaying even the most stubborn of hearts.

"Hm, I can see why your master hired you," she said, walking to another pile and brushing dust from one of the covers.

"What do you mean?"

"You are skilled in flattery and would put many gentlemen I know to shame," she said lightly.

"Is it flattery if it's genuine?"

She blinked at him owlishly, and a blush combed through her cheeks. A fan would have come in handy to hide the evidence, but she turned to the bookshelf behind her. "Sincerity is rare."

"Perhaps, but would you believe it more if I asked again?" he teased.

It was difficult to repress the smile threatening to curve on her lips. One finger trailed over book spines as she said, "If you must know, I paint landscapes and portraits. I have always wanted to start a trade in painting portraits on snuff boxes, but my mother discouraged it. She believed women and business are bad luck." She shrugged and glanced over her shoulder at him.

"And do you believe that?" he asked, and when she turned to look at him fully, he continued, "Do you believe such superstitions?"

"Do you?"

"Absolutely not," he said those two words with such conviction she was tempted to believe him. But the sincerity of his eyes, the closeness of his face made her heart flutter and her doubts melt away.

"And neither should you," he insisted earnestly, disrupting her thoughts. "I would be happy to see your work, and if I had the means, I would be honored to be a customer."

She giggled at the image of him owning a dainty, decorated box meant for women. "That's very flattering, but I don't know what you would do with such an item."

"I would find a use for it," he said with all seriousness. "Maybe even use it as coin storage. But any painting would do. I could hang it in the servants' quarters. Perhaps liven up the place."

"Well, if you have any oil paints, an easel, and a blank canvas, I could attempt to paint something."

"Just for me?" he asked. She averted her gaze just as his grin disappeared. "But, of course, I don't mean to speak to you with such complacency. Forgive me. I forget myself."

Her mother would have pitched a fit by now and might have demanded he be thrown out of the room. She might have turned her rage on her for how they had been speaking so comfortably all this time—as if they were pleasant acquaintances.

Even the implications of such a relationship between lady and servant would have been frowned upon by her mother, her peers, and the society she once belonged to.

Belonged to. Past tense. That's right.

Being paraded around in fine, lovely gowns had made her forget, but she was not above him in status at all. In fact, she realized his duty as a valet outclassed *her* now temporarily. She shook her head at the irony of the situation.

"There is nothing to forgive," she found herself saying instead of the rebuke her mother would have encouraged. "Please speak freely to me. I enjoy your conversation."

His eyes darted to her hesitantly. "Are you sure that's wise?"

"I do because..." she paused, wondering if he would treat her like she was inferior rather than an equal after her confession. But honesty and the secret desire to hear more from him—all of him—won over. "I don't bear any title of lady, at least, not anymore. My father was a wealthy merchant until we lost everything. We are now in very humble circumstances that don't warrant all these rules of propriety."

His eyes lit with understanding, and instead of a sneer or any indication of disappointment, he said, "I am sorry for your circumstances. That must have been terribly difficult for you and your family."

The sympathy in his voice unearthed despair she had painstakingly shoveled under her heart, but she waved it away with one delicate hand. "It's of no consequence now." She shrugged, echoing his own words back at him. A small smile lifted at his lips. "It simply means you don't have to worry about making a friend out of me."

"Is that what you wish? For us to be friends?" His eyes shone with something akin to awe that made her smile.

"Of course. Especially in these strange circumstances. It's always best to have a friend by your side, is it not?"

"Indeed," he murmured as he folded his arms and leaned against the desk.

"Besides, it also means that as your friend, I would be happy to paint you something. Free of charge. You most likely do not have such items, but it would be a nice way to pass the time." They did have a little over three months left, after all.

"Alas, the master is not a painter," Claude said and frowned. "Perhaps when the curse is broken, then?"

"Yes," she smiled. "When the curse is broken."

"It's a deal," he said with confidence slowly warming his voice. "I look forward to your grand magnum opus."

"Oh, please don't set your expectations so high," she laughed. "I don't want to disappoint you."

The playful tone shifted as his gaze softened, "I don't think that's even possible."

Her mouth opened and shut within the same breath. Looking away, she cursed the heat rushing to her neck and cheeks. Realization of what he said must have struck him because his hands began to fidget at his sides.

"Would you like something to eat?" he asked suddenly. "Bonbon has had his lunch already, so I suppose you would like some as well. Not his, of course." He grinned.

She chuckled. "I would like that very much," she agreed much too quickly while tucking a curl behind her ear.

"I will inform the cook then," he said with a slight bow to indicate his leave.

Just as he reached the archway, her heart leaped as she called out, "Wait, Claude?"

"Yes?" he asked, turning.

Slender fingers clenched the navy-blue satin at her sides as a wheel of emotions spun inside her stomach. "Thank you."

His expression grew puzzled. "What for?"

"Well," she clasped her hands behind her back. "I'm happy to have a new friend."

For once, his smile stretched across his mouth and pulled at his eyes. "So am I."

15

Henri

E mbers in the fireplace wavered like drunken fireflies over the remaining logs. Carvings of leaves and crawling vines decorated the marble, and mischievous pixies danced across the mantle. One eye lazily studied how the wood glimmered and breathed heat under the small flame. The fire would be extinguished soon, and a servant would replace it. Henri lost count of how often he watched the flames ignite in greedy waves until it withered into a pathetic spark—an all too familiar sentiment.

His title lived a short lifespan as well.

Voices beyond the door flitted around Henri's ears. But, the concerned tones, the hushed whispers did not phase his mind, drifting in and out like a restless tide. Time didn't exist. It hadn't, for however many weeks, drained around him. None of it mattered.

Reaching for a bottle nestled by his side, he licked the sticky wine remnants until a light hit his eyes. Grunting, he shifted away and pulled the comforter over his head, exposing his cloven feet to the cool air.

"Close the door," he barked.

"Sir," a feminine voice said. "I've brought something for you to eat." The door clicked shut, and darkness washed over the room once more.

Henri shifted, swiping the duvet, which caught on his one good horn. "I don't want it. Just tend to the fireplace and leave me be."

Wheels turned over the wooden floor, and the rustle of skirts fluttered by his bed. "Eating will help, sir," the blunt voice said.

When he did not answer, glass clinked on a metal surface, and he pulled the golden comforter to peek at the shape of a woman bending over and placing the bottles on her trolley.

"Leave them."

Her ebony eyes met his before she continued to place three more on her cart.

"I said leave them," he slurred.

"They are empty."

Oh, he knew that voice. It sounded clearer when it was right next to his ear. "Isa."

She did not respond but rather continued to scoop the piles of glass from his bedside. When they disappeared, she grabbed a bowl of water with a rag floating on its surface and bent on her hands and knees to scrub the remnants of scarlet liquid staining his floor. As she hunched over, the grooves of her spine stretched across her cotton dress.

"Why'd you do that?"

Isa dipped the rag back into the water. Twisting it, pink-stained water dribbled over the bowl and down her hands. "Why do I do what?" she asked but no emotion laced her words. Her indifference slapped him across the face.

"Clean when I am nothing," he moaned.

"I don't follow."

"I am nothing. Nothing!" The bed creaked as he flopped on his belly, the pillows muffling his voice. "I am no Count...no master of anything anymore."

"You are still the master of yourself," she said, avoiding his gaze when he rolled on his side to face her. Even in the darkness and blurry gaze, he admired how she washed the stain with deft fingers. Calloused fingers he had threaded with his own, fingers that once curled into his dark hair when they were teens. The memory of her lips, dry but soft, searching his own and stealing his breath when no one was watching danced in his mind. Happier times.

"You are so nice," he said, extending a clawed finger to the cascade of black feathers down her neck. They were soft under his bony touch. "So beautiful. You used to sing so pretty too. Why don't you sing anymore?"

The rag clenched in her hand. "What are you doing?" she asked, her tone low in warning.

"We were friends, you know?" His claw smoothed the silky fringe down. "Do you remember?"

"Of course, I do," she whispered, wrenching her head away. Sitting up on her knees, she stared into his bleary vision. Unyielding and soul-searching. Her small, gleaming eyes pierced through him, threatening him to silence.

But his half-intoxicated tongue wouldn't listen.

"You were my only-only..." Curses, the words were slipping around his mouth like a bar of soap. "Friend."

"And Claude," she countered. "He was your friend too. You seem to forget that a lot."

"He, well, yes." He leaned down so his elongated, hairless muzzle was inches from her beak nose. "But Claude's different, see? I...I lov—"

"Don't say it," she said, teeth clenched. "You swore to never speak of it."

He did? Memories swam together in a mixture of swirling images and sounds, but his mind somehow made sense of the one she was referring to.

"You said it, Henri—you told me that you—"

"Sir," he had said when they were eighteen. "You will address me appropriately from now on. Never speak my name informally again. And to your claim? It never happened, it was never true, and you will never hear me utter it again."

That memory. Those words. Ah, yes, she was right. He had been the one to break the relationship...to break her heart. Even so—

"I lied."

The words had dislodged out of his mouth, from deep within the caverns of his heart, but he found the confession felt good on his tongue and soothed his hazy conscience. Her hands balled into fists in her lap, and she bowed her head.

Silence blanketed them in a suffocating embrace. A log broke and crackled in the fireplace.

"You are drunk," she said at last. A tremor laced her quiet voice, but his muddled brain raced over the detail.

"Not drunk enough," he exclaimed loudly, rolling back. "You see...it goes—" He reached for the bottle by his head and made a thrusting movement across his chest and up in the air, "—right through me. Can never stay drunk for long."

"It's no surprise considering your size," she said frankly and bent to finish scrubbing.

"Wha'd you doing?"

"Cleaning."

"But I-I was talking."

"Yes, you were," she said, wringing the rag over the bowl and slapping it back on the floor with furious swipes.

"And you did not listen," he said, waving the bottle around. Why wouldn't she see what he was trying to say? "I said I *lied*, Isa. I lied, lied, lied," he sang loudly while closing his eyes. Talking was taking an extraordinary amount of energy.

"I know."

His eyes flew open. "What?"

The bed creaked when he sat up. One of his horns scraped the canopy above as he bent over to reach her. She'd known all this time? What did she feel? What else lay beneath her icy exterior?

"I think I am finished here, sir." She got up and evaded his reaching claws. Brushing her apron off, she turned, put the bowl away, and set a tray by his side.

"Are you leaving me?" he asked, suddenly afraid to be in the dark like he'd often been as a child. Alone.

"Not before I say my piece."

Somewhere in the back of his foggy mind, he knew he should mentally brace himself by her sharp tone, but there was nothing to hold onto. "What do you want to say?"

"You are being selfish."

"Selfish?" he echoed back like a dumb buffoon.

"Do you believe you are the only one who has lost something precious?" she demanded, sweeping her arm out. "You're only thinking of yourself, wallowing away as you are. Have you ever considered the rest of us who've lost family or friends?"

"I..." Her words did strange things to his head, clearing it of its fog. A sliver of soberness pushed through the drunkenness. She'd never spoken to him like this before. "What do you mean?"

"My parents are likely dead. I know it. And even if they are alive, who would be there to take care of them? No one."

Shame, an emotion he went out of his way to avoid, crawled up his spine. "I did not think—"

"Of course, you didn't," she reprimanded. Something in his chest recoiled at her tone, and he couldn't look at her. Instead, his eyes retreated to the duvet in his lap but it refused to give him the comfort he sought. "You haven't thought of anyone but yourself for these past two years. Ever since your father became unwell, you became obsessed with nothing but obtaining his title and getting your revenge."

The space between his brows pinched together. An ache formed beneath. "I did it...I did it for you too..."

"You did it for you," she responded coolly, storming toward his side. The feathers down her hair were a testament to the curse wreaking havoc on her body. They quivered across her skin when she pointed a finger toward him. "You ended things with me for your sake. And you dragged me here because of your inability to let go."

Henri reached for the nightstand, steadying himself despite sitting down. He hadn't seen this coming but felt he should've prepared for her ire all the same. His thoughts swam like dizzy leaves in the wind, but it didn't stop the self-loathing from taking over. "Isa—"

"No. Don't 'Isa' me. Just tell me if I'm right. Tell me that's why you forced me here with you."

She hadn't raised her voice this time, but the eerie calmness in her words, the truth of them, could gouge his core out. Shame rose into flames in his throat. Mouth dry, he nodded.

"That's what I thought."

The statement hammered another blow to his conscience. She stood before him, her face a stone slab, but her eyes betrayed tumultuous emotions. After a beat of silence, the tightness around her jaw slackened, and the rest of her face folded, softening.

She continued, "I understand your title meant everything to you. I know you wanted to be seen as more than your father's illegitimate son...trust me, I understand. You did not deserve the horrible treatment you received from your stepmother either. I hope that woman lives in misery for the rest of her life. But you cannot undo what has been done, and you cannot abandon the others who want to be free."

Chin trembling, he bowed his head. "Others like you?" He glanced up just as her expression solidified to stone again.

"Especially me. Henri, I will say this once and only once. If you have a shred of a heart or any decency left, you will get up, you will stop drinking, and you will go out and break this curse for us. It's the very least you could do."

The steam from a salty vegetable soup wafted to his nose when she set it carelessly by his bedside. It sloshed and dribbled down the side as she rolled the trolley away.

"Isa?"

"What, Henri?"

"I'm sorry."

Turning, she expelled a weary sigh. "Tell me when you're sober enough to be sorry. In the meantime, get up. You have another woman to fall in love with."

The door shut behind her, and for once, he did not reach or summon another bottle to appear in his bed. Instead, he allowed her words to take their fiery course around his sobering mind as he stared into the darkness.

16

Isa

When Henri's door clicked behind her, Isa's hands flew to her face. A silent scream tempted her lips, begging to be let out, but she swallowed it down. Her body yielded, but it forced the emotion to burn her eyes instead. Blinking away the urge, she steadied herself with a deep breath.

She couldn't recall when she'd last been angry with Henri like that. When she'd last been honest with him. Two years, perhaps—much too long. She hoped he would finally listen to reason and break this curse once and for all.

Her fingers found solace against the trolley's handle, whitening beneath the small feathers growing across her skin. Feathers, which wouldn't be there if it weren't for Henri. For his foolishness. His selfishness.

It was his fault she was here at all. It was his fault for dragging her to this place when he could have let her go to Avilon and live out her dreams as an opera singer. He knew she dreamed of joining the troupe and singing on stage. He could have sent her on her way, but he kept her instead. Like a caged bird.

Yet, after all he did, she could not hate him. The soreness around her heart, the reminder of their shared past, crushed any ill will she had for her childhood friend.

How could she despise him when memories of his sad, boyish face came to mind? The loneliness in his eyes, the longing for a family...the neglect. There was only so much she could do to fill the ache inside him—a responsibility she learned was never hers to fill.

The proof was in their curse.

With a sigh she felt deep in her bones, she rolled the trolley forward, away from the man she once thought she'd share her life with. Although haughty, his love had run deep and fierce like the winds sweeping over the hillsides to beat upon the windowpanes. Starved for affection, he greedily drank every gesture of affection she gave him. A subtle glance, fingers brushing, a whisper in the dark. It was so easy to please him.

Perhaps his desperation for company was the only reason why he'd fallen in love with her. If she hadn't been there as his only female companion of his age, would he have ever noticed her at all?

Her stomach clenched in waves at the thought. It hadn't been the first time the idea crept into her mind, whispering doubt to the legitimacy of their love. But then, a happier memory rose above the skepticism, soothing all her doubts.

A smile tempted her lips at the image of them sitting beneath the oak tree on the east side of his father's manor—the area he was confined to by his stepmother's orders. She would fill his time, distracting him by singing songs her mother taught her, and he would bring out books to read to her, to teach her to read, until she would be called away to her duties.

There were no secrets between them. He told her of his dreams to travel far away from his stepmother, and she told him her secret desire to sing on stage. With interlaced pinkies, they promised each other as children that they would help each other fulfill their dreams.

One afternoon, years after their settled routine by the oak tree, a stray leaf fell on her hair, and he reached out to remove it. His hand strayed for a second too long, their eyes meeting in a moment of desire before he leaned in. Soft lips slanted over hers, dampening them, searching, and exploring softly.

They were sixteen. Young and hopeful. Lonely but found.

Blinking, she found herself pushing through the open dining room doors, but she could not remember the journey there. She would have to be careful about allowing herself to reminisce on happier times, of a happier Henri. No, she couldn't allow those old feelings to creep back in.

Schooling herself, she took in her surroundings and found two others occupying the space. Their laughter filled the room, unaware of her presence.

"And Rosalie snored so loud, she woke herself up!" Marguerite said at the table while holding her arms across her stomach as if to contain her giggles. Claude sat next to her, an inappropriate gesture for his status, with a large smile on his face. Warmth filled his eyes while he leaned forward to be closer like a moth drawn to a flame.

To the woman fated for Henri.

"What did she do then?" he asked with a laugh.

"She blamed *me* for snoring!" Marguerite rolled her eyes, but her grin pulled at her cheeks.

"She sounds like a handful."

Marguerite nodded, but her eyes softened with fondness. "She might be a handful sometimes, but she's young. My mother, on the other hand..." she said, frowning. "Well, let's say she is harder to please than my sister. No matter how hard I try, it seems I can never get her approval."

Claude stretched out his hand, aiming for Marguerite's shoulder. Isa cleared her throat, and when they saw her, Claude launched himself from his seat, and Marguerite's mouth fell open with surprise.

"Was your meal to your satisfaction?" Isa asked, nodding to the empty plates in front of the woman.

"Yes, thank you. I finished up just now, and Claude was keeping me company," Marguerite said in a rush. Pink dusted her cheeks, and her chair scraped backward.

"Is there anything you need, miss?" Isa asked.

Marguerite shook her head. "No, but I should go back to my research, though." She stood, gave Claude a small, bashful smile, and whispered 'thank you' before rushing past Isa.

Claude stared at their guest's retreating form and scratched behind his ears before saying: "It wasn't what it looked like."

"I trust you wouldn't be stupid enough," Isa said, pushing the trolley forward. "Especially after what you saw between Henri and me."

His face fell in understanding. "No. Nothing like that will happen."

"Good. It would be wise to back off."

"I'll be more careful," he said and pushed in the chair Marguerite previously occupied. "But someone has to keep her company."

Isa inclined her head, scrutinizing the valet with pursed lips. "Just don't forget who you are."

"And what does that mean?" he chuckled and gathered the plates from the table.

"You're not her friend. You're a valet. You should remember that."

His hand hovered over a fork before he turned to her. "I know what I am. You don't need to remind me."

"Clearly, you need reminding," she said, motioning her chin to where he had sat close to their guest. Shaking his head, he seemed to understand what she meant but continued to clear the table.

"Did you talk to Henri?" he asked with his arms full of glassware. The subject change didn't go unnoticed, but she would not press the matter after sharing her piece.

"I did."

"And?"

She shrugged and pushed the trolley toward the kitchens. "We'll see."

17

Claude

The kitchen was filled with bustling servants and scattered ingredients. The heat from the brick oven warmed Claude's face as he entered through the back door. Kitchen maids went back and forth to the walk-in pantry, which was filled with spices, vegetables, and hanging meats that magically replenished each day.

Paul, a bald, stout man with an extended pig-snout, looked up from basting a chicken and nodded to him. He returned the gesture to the head chef and Anna, the cat-like cook kneading dough. Another cook placed an omelet from her pan onto a plate, and he glanced over her shoulder to check for mushrooms in the dish.

Marguerite always picked out the mushrooms.

"Very good," he said after confirming it was safe. The cook turned toward him and glanced down at what he was carrying. He cleared his throat. No one commented on the freshly plucked wildflowers in his hand, but he felt their eyes follow him as he pushed his way through the swinging double doors.

He froze in mid-step, and he whipped the bundle around his back. Two occupants were at the table—not one as he had expected.

Henri sat across Marguerite like an imposing mountain, stooping over his first course.

Isa deserved a raise in her wages. Whatever she had said to him worked when others, including himself, had failed for three and a half weeks. Only ninety-five days remained for his master to fall in love with Marguerite, not that he was counting.

Visions of their last encounter in his master's office flashed in his mind. Hurt from his *friend's* words still seeped like tree sap, but he swallowed it and let it disappear under the smile stretching over his face.

"Good morning, sir." He bowed his head. "And miss." Bonbon perked from his spot beside Marguerite and wagged his tail at the sight of him.

"Oh, Claude, look who came to join me for breakfast," Marguerite said with a smile. "Isn't this so exciting?"

"It is," he agreed despite the nerves rippling around his stomach. "It's a pleasure to see you well again, sir."

Henri took a bite out of a buttered croissant and narrowed his eyes. "Our guest was telling me that she has been doing a lot of research in my absence. We were just talking about you."

Claude swallowed, attempting to patch where the sap of emotions oozed from his chest.

"Yes, he's kept me company while you were gravely ill," she said before placing a pear slice in her mouth.

Henri's eyes grew sharper on him. "Is that so?"

Before he could explain it was all a misunderstanding and that he had nothing to worry about, Marguerite continued, "Yes! I don't know what I would have done in his absence. I would have probably forgotten to eat without his reminders since I was so focused on those books," she chuckled. "You have a fine man in your service, Mr. Alarie."

"Do you hear that?" Henri asked, raising his glass and tipping it toward him. "That's high praise from the lady."

"I was simply doing my duties," he said. *Getting to know her and keeping her comfortable as you asked me to,* he thought grudgingly. While Henri appeared satisfied, Marguerite's face fell, and his gut followed. "But I'm happy to have been in her service as well. She is a remarkable guest."

"Very much so," Henri agreed quietly. The dangerous tone told him he had misspoken, but it was worth it to see the delight dance in her eyes once more.

Silence blanketed the room until Marguerite tilted her head with furrowed brows. "What is behind your back?"

His heart leaped, and his grip tightened over the stems.

"Yes, show us what you have, Claude," Henri insisted, his long claws steepling together.

Finally, he revealed the flowers. Many of the small purple and yellow flowers had wilted, depleted of their life as soon as their roots were exposed to air, but the daisies stood proud as if they had not been plucked by clumsy hands. Every white petal glowed with a kiss of pink at their tips in the morning light. His traitorous heart fluttered when Marguerite's eyes softened. "I thought the table could use a little decor," he said lamely.

"Oh!" Marguerite sighed and placed a hand on her heart. "They're—"

"Hideous," Henri finished for her with a scoff. "You expect us to stare at weeds while we eat?"

He stared at the sad bouquet and nodded in agreement. It was a stupid idea. He shouldn't have wasted his time.

"I think they're lovely," she said, and his head perked up.

"My dear, if these gardens were what they used to be, I would give you a *proper* bouquet. Not this sorry excuse," Henri said and sipped his tea.

"Daisies are my favorite," she said, and both he and his master stared at her, stunned. A flair of thrill ran down his spine. "I would like them on the table. If you wouldn't mind."

"Yes, of course," he said quickly and ignored the piercing glare burning through his back.

Within a few moments, he returned with a round glass vase that cinched upward into a scalloped edge. He placed the flowers in without much grace or skill and set them on the table closer to her side.

"Thank you, Claude. They're so beautiful," she said, leaning over to touch one of the pearly petals.

"If you wish to see beautiful flowers," Henri began and glanced at Claude while he retreated to the wall, "then we should take a stroll together today and view the roses. They are particularly beautiful at this time of year."

Claude could not help but wince at the staked claim Henri made on Marguerite. By all accounts, it was fair for his master to do so, but a small part of him, one he should not entertain, whispered that he hoped she would not fall for such tactics.

"Perhaps later when the weather is cooler," she said. "I would like to let Bonbon out to relieve himself and then do some research first, if you don't mind."

"Of course," Henri said, directing another malicious glare at his head. Despite the intimidation tactic, Claude resisted a grin from pulling his cheeks.

When they finished, servants swooped in to clear their dishes. Marguerite excused herself, and they watched her exit the door near the tall, vertical windows with Bonbon at her heels.

Her shadow crossed the linen curtains, and his eyes followed her figure as she passed within their sight.

Marguerite paused in her steps and turned to his watchful gaze. The sun poured over her as she lifted one hand to wave at him before twisting one of her brunette curls around her finger. A light spray of freckles dotted her nose and cheeks. She was a blooming flower amongst the decay surrounding her in the gardens.

Even as he waved back, he quashed the emotions tightening in his chest as his eyes followed her. *We are friends*, he reminded himself as she sat on the edge of a fountain. Bonbon trotted about as her hair glimmered in the sunshine, and he inhaled deeply.

Nothing more.

"Are you enjoying the view?"

Claude jerked from the window before turning to the voice growling from the table. Every servant in the room stilled.

When Henri stood, his horns jostled the crystals dangling from the chandelier above. Those cerulean blue eyes sliced right through him.

"You did not answer my question. Are you enjoying the view?"

"Y-ye—I mean no. No sir, I am not," he said in one breath.

"Come now." Henri angled his chin toward the window. He was calm as a sea before a vicious storm. "Your words would wound her. She is not so hard on the eyes, look." He pointed toward her. "Some might say she is adequate. What do you say?"

It was a trap.

But he had no choice but to follow the command and look back at the woman basking in the sun. "Yes. Adequate," he said quietly and turned back around.

Henri kept his piercing stare on him as he said, "Leave us. I have a few words to say to my valet." Within moments, servants scurried off with the dirty dishes, and his heart hammered as they filed into the kitchen one by one.

They were alone.

Words suddenly flew from his mouth, "I meant no disrespect—"

"What nonsense are you pulling?" Henri demanded, cutting him off as he rounded the table to face him. Claude clenched his teeth together to remain calm under his towering presence. It was the same dance they had performed since Henri was eighteen. He just had to say the right words to avoid Henri's wrath.

"I am unsure of what exactly you mean—"

"You know well what I mean."

Of course, he knew, but he hoped he could have eased into the topic better. "Allow me to explain, sir."

"By all means." Henri swept his arms out in a mocking gesture. "Explain why my trusted valet has become so enamored with our guest while I was unwell? Pray tell, why would you threaten our very lives with this foolishness?"

Anger flared at his master's hypocrisy. Claude could say the same to him while he wasted time, drinking himself into nothing. It took two deep breaths to steel himself and ignore the jab stinging like a barb between his ribs. "Marguerite was lonely. I talked to her on occasion. I agreed to be a friend and nothing more."

"Do you bring flowers to all of your *friends*, Claude?"

"She had mentioned it in passing. I wanted to help her feel more at home here. Believe me, I am on your side, sir."

"Do you think I'm stupid?" Henri snarled, baring those awful, sharp teeth at him. He could see his nervous reflection in those large, white tusks. "I saw you with my own eyes. You cannot fool me. I saw the way you looked at her."

"I feel nothing for her," he said firmly, even as his own words struck and twisted into his heart like a knife. The sensation startled him, but he refused to let it surface on the expressionless mask he had created. Besides, it was a cruel trick of his imagination. She had served as a friend and a distraction from the sadness creeping into his thoughts. Thoughts of his father most likely dead. It was preposterous for him to feel anything for the woman who was fated to be with his master. To break this curse.

To save them all.

"Nothing?"

Her hazel eyes came to mind. The way they sparkled when she laughed, and the rosy blush that painted her cheeks commandeered his thoughts and pummeled the justifications away.

I feel...

"Nothing," he said rigidly.

Henri eyed him with suspicion just as he questioned the emotions seeping from his heart.

"And what about you?" Claude dared to ask.

"What about me?" Henri challenged in return, straightening his back.

"What do *you* feel for her?"

Those icy eyes widened in surprise before sharpening like daggers. "I care for her enough," he snapped. "I need more time to get to know her better."

You could have had three weeks to do that already, he wanted to retort but smiled instead. "Well, while you were away, I was able to gather more information for you. I can help you woo her."

"And I will have no need to worry about you?"

"No," he said, even though he doubted his word already. "You will not need to worry about me."

18

Marguerite

Marguerite sat up with a yawn. Amidst the span between awareness and disorientation, she expected to hear her mother's voice scolding her father from downstairs. Rosalie would be heard from the next room and whine about a dress that no longer fit her while Phillipe would pass her door and wave. But the voices of her family did not come. Her maid, Sophie, did not come in to greet her, pat her cheek, and smooth down the fly-away hairs from her face. Instead, there was only darkness and the cascade of crimson drapes and golden sheets to dwarf her body.

The faces of her family had been so vivid in her dreams, but they, too, began to slip away as she wiped the sleep sand from her eyes.

Her family was not perfect. She could be the first to admit that. But, despite the tension between her and her mother, she found herself missing her fiercely. Sure, her mother was shrewd and perhaps overbearing, but she also knew how to make others feel welcome in their home. Mother carried a grace she only wished she could measure up to. As much as Marguerite wished she could dislike her, a part of her still wanted the sweet mother she dreamed of. Maybe it was fruitless to wish for such things, but could she blame her inner child for yearning?

Marguerite clenched the sheets by her side as her eyes landed on the furry mound at the end of the bed. Bonbon. The dog snored softly, reminding her of how her sister snored in her sleep. Her sister might blame her for their misfortunes, but Marguerite couldn't help but miss her too.

Light gradually illuminated her room into a dull, gray color, and she reached for the journal and quill by her bed. It had been empty when she discovered it, and Henri provided the writing tools for her use. Fat drops of black ink spilled on the page as she made a swift line by two others. She placed the soft plumes of the quill to her mouth while she counted each mark.

Thirty-three days. *Normal days,* she sighed with relief. And all that time in the library had yet to pay off.

She sighed deeply, filling her lungs before she exhaled noisily. If Henri had not vied for her time so often, she might have been able to spend more time researching. Between meals, he often insisted they take a stroll around the gardens or sit in the parlor while he read his favorite story: The Knight's Betrayal. It would not have been inconvenient if he were not so stiff and awkward around her or if Claude could accompany them.

She missed his conversation.

The cold, herringbone floor chilled her feet when she finally removed the covers and stood. It was much too early for Jeanette or any servant to enter the room, but she made her way to the large wardrobe with her white shift floating around her like a translucent spirit. Every morning, Jeanette would open the large armoire, and dresses of varying colors and textures would appear, and they would fit as though she had spent hours standing with pins at her side at the tailor. She would have her pick of the thirty-year-old styles and never wore the same dress twice.

Curiosity drew her closer as she grasped the brass handles, and the walnut doors easily swung out. An array of dresses, jewelry, hair accessories, and shoes lined the space in organized sections. She reached out to touch a lavender dress and admired its softness. The pastel purple was her favorite despite it being quite expensive to produce. Father could never afford to buy her one, but it hung in the wardrobe with an air ease despite its cost. She stared in awe as the fabric stretched out effortlessly when she pulled on the skirt to inspect it closer. The cream lace at the sleeves and velvet bows were the exact likeness of the one she admired in the shop of a window in Avilon.

The skirt rippled like a ribbon caught by the wind as it slid out of her hand. This was the very dress. It was here, in this wardrobe.

Blinking, her hand found its way over her heart and collarbone. Magic, indeed! Not only had it procured the dress of her dreams, but it had also provided other dresses she had fawned over—dresses of *her* time. But how? It never gave anything other than the outdated styles when Jeanette assisted her.

Perhaps it answered to the one who opened it?

"Oh, you're up already," Jeanette said.

Bonbon perked from the bed but did not bark at the intruders. Marguerite turned to Jeanette, who stared at her with those large, unblinking eyes from the doorway. The sight of them used to send shivers down her spine, but now they were a welcome sight. She came in with the maid, Isa, rolling her cart behind her. A bouquet of daisies sat in a crystal vase alongside an ornate, white, and gold teapot with matching cups and saucers.

She could not help but grimace.

"We come bearing gifts from the master." Jeanette gestured to the flowers and did not acknowledge the look of distaste on her face. "He is very insistent you wake up to them, but no matter. They are lovely regardless."

"Yes, they are lovely," she said, even though she was given the same vase of daisies every morning since Mr. Alarie became well again. The gesture was kind, even if the sentiment bordered on romantic. Only suitors gave their lady of choice flowers as often as Mr. Alarie did, but perhaps traditions were different thirty years ago?

"And what do you have there?" Jeanette gasped while Isa quietly put the vase on the small table.

Marguerite returned to the open wardrobe and pulled the lavender dress off its hook. It was heavy as she attempted to bring it flush against her body with a slight twirl. "Isn't it gorgeous? I have only dreamed of something this beautiful."

"It certainly is," Jeanette said with furrowed brows. "Is it supposed to billow out like a house gown?"

She chuckled. "They are designed to look effortless and comfortable."

"Hmph, comfortable indeed. Do you still wear a stay under all of that fabric?"

"Of course!"

Jeanette approached and held out her ghostly white hands toward her. Handing her the dress, the maid's wispy plumes from her head twitched as she caressed the silky fabric. "Come, look at this, Isa. Isn't this fascinating?"

"Yes," Isa said quietly after glancing up from pouring the steaming tea into a cup.

"Come, don't be rude, come look and see," Jeanette insisted.

The other maid hesitated with the teapot hovering over the full cup. Under that black, sharp beak, her mouth dipped downward. If Marguerite's mother were here, she would have put the maid in her place, but Marguerite waved a hand in a placating manner. "It's fine. I'm sure she can see it from where she is."

"Very well," Jeanette said, and Isa looked up at her with a curious glint in her eyes. It was the most emotion she had seen in her stony expression since she had arrived. She wondered what it could mean.

"Oh, I almost forgot," Jeanette said, placing the gown over the bed. "The note. The master had a note."

"A note?"

"Yes, here it is," Jeanette said and plucked it from the cart and handed it to her.

It was a folded piece of cream parchment with a wax seal of the same crest she saw decorating the library walls—a rose with intersecting swords. She peeled it open with furrowed brows and read:

My dearest Marguerite,

She paused over how he chose to address her in such an intimate fashion.

I have a surprise waiting for you before breakfast.
Meet me downstairs in the parlor.

Your Gracious Host,

Henri

Her stomach coiled tightly like a spring in a clock over the few seconds it took to read the note. The daily strolls, the flowers, and now a surprise gift? Was this more than genial kindness? No, it couldn't be. He had said he wanted to make up for his absence. He was simply being a good host to her.

"Your tea, miss," Isa said, interrupting her thoughts while handing out the cup and saucer.

"Thank you," she said, but her throat clamped down, and the words felt strained in her mouth. The thought of her host taking an interest in her as more than a guest made her insides churn with nausea. And, not because he was a lumbering beast, but she could not fathom being with a man so awkward and foul-tempered as he.

"Shall we get you dressed in this? I am sure the master would approve," Jeanette said, bringing the lavender dress up with a cheeky grin.

Her heart stuttered at the thought. She pointed at one of the dresses hanging in the wardrobe. "That one."

"Oh? I thought you were very fond of this one," Jeanette said with a frown.

"I think I will save it for a different day. Thank you."

"Very well." Jeanette carefully stored the lavender one away. "This one it is."

Henri

"Are you certain this is what she wants?" Henri asked, wringing his large, clawed hands together while pacing before the cold fireplace. He eyed the covered item with uncertainty before looking up at his valet, who stood by the wall closest to him.

"Yes, I am," Claude said calmly.

"Is everything accounted for? Am I missing anything?"

"No, everything is accounted for, sir. She will love it," Claude said with a taut smile.

"It's just so...unusual. I have never given anything like this."

If it weren't for Claude, he would never have thought to give it to her. Nor would he have sent her the flowers or walked with her every day. Those were Claude's suggestions above other things, but he could only manage a few gestures at a time. He wouldn't know where to start if it weren't for Claude.

All this wooing felt so complicated, unlike being with Isa. With her, everything was as easy as breathing.

"Trust me," Claude said with the same unwavering patience. "She will love it."

"And if she doesn't?" he snapped, his heart racing at the thought of the repulsion on her face. Once was enough after the incident in the gardens, and he never wished to experience it again.

"I know, I know," Claude said, raising his arms. "It will be on my head."

The sound of footsteps echoed beyond the door, and Henri's heart quickened and tightened all at once. He looked to Claude, who smiled in reassurance.

"Just act naturally, sir."

"What does that even mean? 'Natural' is subjective," he hissed.

"Relax, then. Do not look so stiff and intimidating."

"What? How do I even—"

Three knocks sounded before the door opened to reveal Jeanette leading Marguerite. He frowned. A silver dress wrapped around her and did not match the warm undertones of her skin. As she walked, it belled around her hips, almost swallowing her willowy figure. It was quite plain, and her hair was pinned closer to her head rather than cascading in a fountain of curls as per the fashion. It was not his favorite.

"Good morning, sir." She curtsied, and her eyes softened when they met his valet. "Good morning, Claude."

In return, Claude gave a polite nod, and Henri loudly cleared his throat. "Good morning, I-uh-I see you have received my note?"

"Yes," she said, folding her hands in front of her. She avoided his gaze as he stared at her, waiting for any other response. None came.

"Good, very good," he said when he realized he should speak again. "I have something for you." He groaned internally, *stating the obvious: why don't you?* She did not say a word but followed his gesture toward the tall mound covered by a sheet. "I hope you like it."

He pulled it off in one sweeping motion before she gasped. The easel stood as tall as she, with a large, blank canvas on its shelf. A tray sat on the floor at her feet filled with glass jars of oil paints, charcoal, waxes, resin, and brushes. The pressure around his chest squeezed when she slowly placed her hand on her chest. Was that a good sign? When she looked at him, her eyes were glossy. Did he do something wrong? Why was she crying?

"Is it not to your liking?" he asked.

"It's more than I could have hoped for," she said and bent down to touch one of the brushes. "Ox-hair," she murmured. "But how...Claude said you did not have anything like this—"

"The chateau bends to my will the most. I can imagine what I want, within reason, of course, and it appears in my room. Probably to cure boredom, perhaps. I see it has done the same for you, in a way." He gestured to the odd dress she chose to wear.

"Incredible," she said and glanced down at herself. "Yes, it appears it has. It only needed my touch, it seems." She lifted the tray from the ground with a large smile. "I cannot thank you enough. This is the most thoughtful gift anyone has given me. How did you know?"

"I—uh," his first impulse was to look to Claude, but he did not want to give himself away. A lie. He needed a lie and quick.

"You mentioned it before," Claude said. "Isn't that right, Mr. Alarie?"

"Yes—yes," his head bobbed up and down, catching onto his valet's quick thinking. "I remember you speaking about being an artist."

"How thoughtful and...insightful," she said, clutching the tray tighter to her chest. By her tone, it did not seem they fooled her well enough.

"Of course," he grunted, "anything for you."

She shifted her gaze to the gift in her hands. "These are expensive and time-consuming to make," she said quickly. She turned away and set the tray on the small table between the red velvet chairs. Her face brightened like a child receiving gifts on Yulefest, and she picked up two jars filled with red and gold paint. "Like these. These pigments are only found in the East and are quite expensive."

"I assume they are adequate then?"

"They are more than adequate. I can tell this mixture is better than anything I have mixed myself. See how smooth the texture is and how bright the colors are?" She beamed, and she continued to show him each bottle and explained its use to him.

Her happiness was contagious as she talked, and warmth slowly spread through his limbs. Was this normal to feel? This emotion of...whatever this was? It did not feel like pride, but it had the same tingling effect in his chest, like when he gave flowers to Isa for the first time. If he gave Marguerite more gifts like this, would she open to him as she was now? Would she smile in a way that could melt any bitter heart?

Maybe this curse was possible to break after all.

"I don't know how to thank you," she said, breathless from her chatter.

"There is no need to," he said. "As long as you are happy, that is enough for me."

A look of alarm painted her features before she chuckled nervously. "Well, thank you again. I appreciate your thoughtfulness." But her eyes darted from his and landed on Claude beside him. "I will not forget your kindness."

19

Claude

A hiss sounded before light erupted on a wooden splint; the flame wavered as Claude lit the wick of a candle. Its light produced nothing more than a small glow when he brought it up by its handle, but his altered eyes could make out the shapes of his small room with a clarity not possible when their guest had first arrived.

A small bed with a simple, brown, wool blanket sat to his right. Hay poked through the old mattress, but he hadn't the time nor care to mend it. The nightstand held a small basin for face washing and a clock to mark the time, and a dresser crowded the left side of the room. Shrouded by darkness, those shapes had become sharper in his vision over the past few weeks, and knots formed in his stomach at the change.

Whispers of conversations he could not hear as a man became clearer over time. A mixture of sweat, dust, and grease from each servant beyond his bedroom carried under his door, and he scrunched his nose in disgust. The smell was the most unfavorable sense to be heightened and worsened each day.

Pushing the thoughts to the back of his mind, Claude undressed for the night. When he stripped down to his white shirt tucked into breeches, he caught a glimpse of himself in the distorted mirror.

Mirrors were banished from the premises, but Henri had not bothered to check or enforce the rule for his room. While the other servants threw their mirrors out, he kept his to remind himself of what was happening to him and to provide proof that he was continuing to change.

He reached for it and held it close to his face while turning his head from side to side. He opened his mouth and checked his incisors, which appeared sharper—longer, and his ears, which were flat against his head, had also grown outward and hairier than a month and a half ago. Even his light brown irises had grown to the point where it was difficult to see the whites of his eyes.

What was happening to him?

By the end of the curse, he imagined he might transform into a full-fledged dog. Maybe that was their fate.

Suddenly, he stiffened, clenching the mirror at the sound of hurried footsteps against a cobbled path. A small yip followed, and from his window, he caught a glimpse of brunette hair and sapphire silk trailing around a hedge. Placing the mirror aside, concern lit his chest, and he stuffed his feet into his shoes before exiting his private room.

He followed the familiar scent of daisies and lavender perfume and found her sitting on a fountain's edge. Bright moonlight cast a halo around her features as she sat with pursed lips. Moss grew where water should have been, but Marguerite stared at the green pool, her eyes distant. Her dog trailed around the fountain and lifted its leg to do its business before he approached.

Marguerite whipped around, and her hands came up like knives, ready to carve him in half. He bit back a chuckle when recognition lit her eyes, and those sharp hands came down to smooth her blue robe.

"Claude," she said with a shaky breath. Her hands gripped her robe tighter. "What brings you out here?"

By her flushed cheeks, he stopped and averted his gaze. He, too, became very aware of what she was wearing, and heat rushed up his neck. "I was startled to see our guest wandering alone at night and thought to check on her. You are not thinking of trying the woods again, are you?"

"Oh, no, not at all."

"Then what brings *you* here?"

"I could not sleep," she admitted and frowned. "Neither could Bonbon."

He mirrored her frown. "Is there something keeping you from sleeping?"

Her brows pinched together while she fiddled with the leash in her lap. The white dog came around and sat at her feet, breathing loudly through its mouth. Its dark brown eyes stared at him while its curled tail wagged excitedly. "It's just..." she glanced up, then averted her gaze. "I'm rather homesick."

Her voice had a faint crack, and her throat bobbed up and down. His eyes softened as faces of his own family, particularly his father's, were conjured in his mind, and for a moment, he wished he could sit near her, but remained rooted to the spot. It was not his place to comfort her in that manner, but his conscience, or what he believed the nagging warmth in his chest was, would not allow him to remain silent.

"It must be difficult to be away from them," he said, his thoughts straying to his aging father. "To not know how they are faring without you or if they are healthy and safe."

She nodded, and her loose, wavy hair fell around her shoulders. "Yes. Some days it hurts so much to think about them that I try not to think of them. But then I feel shame for abandoning them altogether."

"You are not abandoning them," he said, daring to step closer.

Her frown curved into a strained smile as her glossy eyes looked down in her lap. "I am, though." Her chin quivered. "They will need me, and I am not there to save them."

She dabbed the corners of her eyes and straightened her posture as if to will the tears away. The distance between them closed with one cautious step at a time. It was a dangerous action, one stirring his heart into a warm soup of emotions. It would only lead to heartache because Henri was right after all: a valet had no business having an informal relationship, friendship, or otherwise, with the woman who was fated to break their spell. Even so, he sat beside her on the fountain's ledge, leaving a suitable amount of space between them.

From this close, he noted every freckle dotting her forearms as she raised a hand to push her hair around her ears. Since she had been out without a parasol every day, her sun-kissed face glowed under the contrasting moonlight shining down on her.

"Save them?" he asked gently. "Save them from what?"

She inhaled and exhaled a steadying breath, "I have mentioned my family has faced financial ruin recently..."

"Yes, I remember."

"What I haven't mentioned is that I struck a deal with someone. I promised to marry him in exchange for a partnership with my father's business. He is on leave with the navy, but when he returns...I must be there."

His face remained neutral, but panic was set aflame in a rush of heat. Why would fate send a lady already spoken for? Their circumstances were difficult enough, as it was, with teaching a beast to love. Why make it impossible, then?

However, another emotion wriggled under his skin, one making his teeth clench together: disappointment. It was foolish. It was unthinkable.

Breathe. He needed to calm himself.

"I see. That is worrisome indeed," he said with an attempt to keep his voice even. He failed.

"Yes, and even though his character is...distasteful, it's necessary."

Hope flared like a burst of fireworks despite himself. He tried to convince himself that it was hope for Henri and herself to break the curse, but something in the back of his mind whispered it was for a far more selfish reason. "You are not fond of your intended?"

"I suppose 'intended' is a strong word. He said he would consider my proposal after he returned, and I don't know when he shall, but no. I have no feelings for him."

"When did he say he would return then?"

She shrugged. "He said four months. He was unsure. I have wasted almost two already, so I must find a way to break this curse as soon as possible. Not just for all your sakes, but mine as well."

"That is a considerable burden you bear," he said.

"Burden, duty, are they not one and the same?" she scoffed. "Mother reminds me of it all the time."

"Duty can feel like a burden," he agreed.

"You speak as though you have experienced the matter yourself."

"I suppose I know a thing or two about feeling indebted to family," he admitted, even though reason told him it was foolish to reveal anything about himself. This one-sided vulnerability had worked for them so far. If he added his own, it would only create more confusion.

"You do?" She peered up through those short, thick eyelashes, and his resolve was undone.

"Yes," he said. "I may not have to worry about loveless marriages, but I come from a line of servants. My father, and his father, and so on. They all prided themselves in their work and expected the same from me. When your option is to serve or risk the streets, the answer is obvious."

"Do you miss him too?"

He blinked, surprised by the question. "Who do you mean?"

"Your father," she said quietly, almost shy to ask. "Do you miss him?"

"Um," he began and cleared his throat. Her genuine concern, for him, a valet, unlocked the tumultuous emotions he locked away these past few weeks. Since learning of the time passing, he had worked tirelessly not to think of his father passing on without him. The man would be eighty years old if he were still alive, but deep down, Claude knew a life of servitude was too harsh for anyone to live that long.

A soft hand touched his own, and he snapped up in surprise.

"I'm sorry." She removed her hand. "I figured it might be difficult for you to talk about this considering..."

"Considering how much enchanted time has passed," he finished for her. "Yes, I admit it's difficult."

"What is he like?"

"My father?"

"Yes," she said. "If you don't mind sharing."

Hope and anticipation filled her face, and he succumbed to those sparkling eyes. "He is a good man. Loyal and kind. He took care of Mr. Alarie in his youth, so perhaps that speaks for itself."

She giggled, and something loosened his tongue and opened his heart as he shared stories of himself with Henri and his father. He and Henri would play make-believe games, fighting werewolves in the east garden. They would pick up sticks and pretend to be knights until Claude's father lectured them about weapon safety.

He even told her of when Henri tried disposing of a wasp's nest that had settled underneath one of the garden arches with a slingshot. He laughed at the memory of Henri's face when the wasps chased them into the house. Claude's father pulled them by the ears for that stunt. Despite Henri's status, his father treated him like his own son. With every story he shared, her face lit up.

She giggled. "Your father sounds like he has a heart of gold."

"He does. I want to be like him."

"From what you described, you would make him proud."

Warmth spread through his chest as he stared at her. The sincerity of her statement filled him with the comfort he didn't realize he needed. "I try my best."

"You are succeeding," she said with earnest. "I hope you know I mean it. I know it's your duty to tend to me, but I have also felt your kindness to be genuine. It has made my time here less daunting with you as my friend."

A small grin stretched over his quivering mouth. "I am happy to hear that," he said and knew, deep down, his father would be proud. "I hope to continue to be someone you can depend on even after the curse."

"Which, I was thinking," she said. "What will you do after the curse?"

"What do you mean?"

"Mr. Alarie may not have his title and may be unable to keep you in his service. What will you do then?"

"I suppose I will have to look for work elsewhere," he shrugged. "Unless my master finds a way to retain his nobility."

"Perhaps," she said, and for a moment, there was nothing but silence between them as she fidgeted with the folds of her robe by her side. He wondered if her skin would feel like the silk she pinched between her knuckles, but he quickly dispelled the thought when she looked up at him. "Perhaps when I find a way to break the curse, and I marry Mr. Bellanger...I could employ you. Perhaps even employ all of you here. Then you would not have to worry about searching for employment. Of course, I could also help Mr. Alarie too."

The offer was so genuine and sweet. He was tempted to press his large hands around her own and thank her. But his hands remained on both sides of his legs. "That is a most gracious offer and one I thank you for, but..."

Why was he hesitating? It would be ludicrous to refuse, so what was it that was keeping him from saying yes?

"But?" she pressed.

His eyes scanned over her oval face, down her neck where two dark birthmarks lay at the hollow of her throat, and he found he could not bear the thought of another man grazing his hands over her freckled skin. It did not matter with Henri or this Mr. Bellanger because in the end...

It would be too painful.

"We shall see when the time comes," he settled for with a tense smile to reassure her. He stood suddenly. The urge to remove himself from her was overwhelming as he placed his hands behind his back. "It's getting late, though, and I hear my master has a special plan for you tomorrow. Would you like to retire, or should I leave you with your privacy?"

She grimaced, whether from his formal tone or his sudden urge to leave, he did not know, but he waited for an answer, nonetheless. "Is it another gift?" she frowned.

He did not expect that answer. "I cannot reveal that, but you do not seem pleased."

Huffing, she smoothed down her robe again. "It's not that I am ungrateful, but Mr. Alarie has been acting familiar toward me, and I'm unsure of what to think of it."

That was not promising. He needed to tread carefully. She would suspect something if he hesitated too long, but if he answered too quickly, it would produce the same result. And so, he counted to two before saying, "Familiar? In what way?"

"Well," she said, standing and pacing before the fountain with Bonbon in tow. "The flowers, for one. He has sent me daisies every morning since he discovered they were my favorite. The walks in the gardens, reading his favorite book to me in the evenings...the gifts. I cannot seem to find any time for myself since he vies for it so often." She settled her animated hands back by her side. "That is partially why I am out here so late. I feel like I need some fresh air without him near me."

"Are you sure I am not disturbing your fresh air?" he teased.

"Not at all. In fact, I welcome your presence. You are much easier to converse with than your master but don't tell him I said so. I don't want to offend him. It's just..."

"Just what?"

"I feel, despite our time together, I know little to nothing about him. And it concerns me that he would rather spend our time walking the same path here in the gardens rather than finding answers in the library. I don't understand his reluctance. Does he not wish to break this curse?"

"Have you spoken to him about your concerns?"

"No." She sighed and ceased her pacing. "I have not. Well, I have tried but never directly. But to be honest, I am afraid of his reaction."

"You do not need to be afraid of him," he lied. "He cares too much about your opinion to disregard it."

"That's what I am afraid of," she said quietly, but his ears picked them up easily. Even with his newfound feelings aside, breaking this curse would be more difficult than he thought.

"But," her voice inclined higher. "You might be right after all. He might listen if I confront him on the matter, and I have just been acting foolish this whole time. I wish I were not so intimidated by him."

"That is no fault of your own," he said. "His appearance is quite frightening."

"It's more than that. I have seen him when he was angry, and it frightens me. That day in the gardens haunts me. I had never seen such a transformation before."

"It's true. He is most horrifying in that state."

"It's like a nightmare," she whispered.

"Indeed, but, beneath the anger, I know there is a good man. Be patient with him, and you might see it for yourself."

"Perhaps." She sighed. "I am glad you are here, though. Thank you for being my friend."

"It's my pleasure," he said.

After silence settled over them, she stood and wrapped her arms around herself. "Would you be so kind as to walk me back to my room?"

It was a simple request, one he should agree to, but he hesitated at the racing of his heart upon the request. If he were to decline, perhaps the bursting emotions would not bother him, but he found he could not deny her.

"Of course. I would be happy to."

She beamed, and it was then, he realized he would do anything to see her smile like that more often.

20

Marguerite

Marguerite plucked a white clover and twisted it between her fingers. Its petals whirled in a blur while Mr. Alarie's voice droned in her ear. He sat beside her with his cloven feet tucked under his legs in a crisscross position, reading from a book in his lap. She placed more clovers over the wool, tartan blanket laid over the unkempt grass; a large charcuterie board sat in front of them decorated with piles of grapes, figs, peaches, cheese, and cured meat that had been slowly picked at as she fiddled with the clovers at her side.

A breakfast picnic—Mr. Alarie's surprise Claude warned her about.

Thirty minutes prior, Jeanette had led her outside the chateau gates, where the grass was greener, and found Mr. Alarie standing in front of the display with wringing hands. The vase of daisies and a bottle of wine nestled next to the loaves of bread did not go unnoticed, but his nervousness swayed her. She could not bear to confront him when he had gone out of his way to have a pleasant breakfast with her. The weather was perfect, and the food looked delicious.

The confrontation could wait.

Thus, she found herself quietly tying a long stem over the neck of another clover as he read.

"The king threw the woman into the tower for her father's lies. 'If you cannot turn this straw into gold, you will perish,' he said. The miller's daughter then wept at the impossible task before her until a strange, impish man appeared in the tower..."

The puckered skin between her brows relaxed when she succeeded in tying a third clover to the chain.

"'I can turn your straw into gold,' the imp man declared. 'How?' she asked. 'By magic, of course,' the man said with a wicked grin."

Her hands stilled over the clover link as one word struck her in surprise. *Magic.* "Wait, wait," she said, sitting up on her knees. "What are you reading again?"

Mr. Alarie paused and looked up from the thick, black book. The oval reading glasses perched above his elongated snout slid down when he acknowledged her with pursed, thin lips. "*Tales of Old*," he said, raising the cover for her to read. The bold, golden calligraphy stared back at her. "It's merely a collection of folk tales. Fantasy, really. Do you want me to continue?"

"Yes, yes," she said quickly, scooting closer to his side as excitement bubbled within her. He stiffened, but she could not help but peer at the words imprinted on the pages. This could be it, the type of book she had been scouring his library for. "I would like to, but I couldn't help but wonder if there were similar tales like this?"

"There are, and we can read through them if you are interested."

"I would like that, actually. And other books like this as well."

The translucent skin over his brow bones stretched upward, a gesture that would not have made her as uneasy if there were hair there. "Well...yes, if that is what you so desire, Ms. Dupont."

She clasped her hands together. "Thank you, thank you so much."

"You're welcome," he said gruffly, rolling his shoulders back. "Now, shall we continue?"

"Of course." She settled back into a more comfortable position with her legs folded to the side under the layers of her pale pink skirt.

He continued reading, and she smiled when he added more inflection to his voice as though bolstered by her interest. It was a welcome addition to the flat tone threatening to lull her to sleep, and she listened intently while popping another fig in her mouth. In this version, Rumpelstiltskin helped the miller's daughter for three nights, and on the third evening, she vowed to give her firstborn to the strange man. After the king married her, Rumpelstiltskin came to claim his prize when she had her first child. However, she bested him by guessing his true name...

"...and Rumpelstiltskin was never heard from again. The end."

She clapped, an action usually done out of politeness, but today she felt it was more earned. A rosiness spread over his gaunt cheeks.

"What did you think of the story?" he asked, averting his gaze.

Although it was a routine question, she usually opted for a polite, *I enjoyed it,* or, *it was quite interesting* considering her lack of interest in the tale. The conversation would end there, and he would plow through the awkwardness with another reading. However, *this* story wove emotions within her, whether due to his better reading skills or the story itself, she did not know, but for once, she had a more substantial answer. "To be honest, I found it sort of tragic."

"Oh? For whom? The villain?" he asked.

"I was thinking of the miller's daughter."

"Interesting, explain."

"Well," she began, as her nerves took flight in her stomach at his expectant stare. "The miller's daughter was only desirable to the King when she could satiate his greed. He married her after she proved useful to him. All that emotional turmoil for a man who did not love her..." her thought trailed to a halt in her mouth as the weight and irony of her situation clamped over her heart.

My circumstances are different, though, she told herself. *I am not forced into this. I am choosing Mr. Bellanger for the sake of my family. That is the difference.*

Mr. Alarie interrupted her quiet resolve. "Love is not a matter of importance in marriage, but perhaps she learned to love him."

"Perhaps," she agreed and searched for differences between the fictional and real characters of her life. "But it would be difficult to love him when he treated her so poorly." *As if Gustave has never treated you poorly?* she thought but forged on. "She was from modest means, and he threatened to take her and her father's life for an impossible task."

There. Mr. Bellanger never threatened our lives. He is better than the King, surely, she thought.

As if leaving us to live as paupers doesn't count? another part of her whispered.

Those icy eyes softened in acknowledgment, and he bowed his head. "Is he irredeemable then? Is that what you are saying?"

The defeat in his voice was unmistakable, and she bit back a sigh. How did the conversation twist in this way? "I didn't say that."

"You did, though. You said you wouldn't find anything re-deemable about a man who did such things."

"I said it would be *difficult* to," she said, careful to keep her voice neutral and controlled. "Especially if he is not remorseful about it. That's the difference."

"So, it *would* be possible to love him?"

Her spine went rigid as heat swept through her veins. There was an implication that went far beyond their conversation, and she swallowed thickly. "I suppose there could be a possibility, yes. But one that would require more than forgiveness or remorse."

"What would you require then?"

"To love him? Or anyone?"

"Anyone."

"I suppose if we are speaking hypothetically." She needed to clarify for both their sakes. "I could not see myself loving any man who was not kind or respectful, but that is a bare minimum of requirements. I suppose I would want..."

What did she want?

As a child, she wrote down a list of attributes she found admirable in a partner, but when her mother found it, she sat her down and told her that these "expectations" were simply unreasonable. *"You are not to expect anything except his salary and children he will provide you,"* her mother had said, *"To wish for anything else would be a path of disappointment."*

Unearthing those secret desires might lead to heartache, as her mother had warned, but she was not planning to marry Mr. Alarie, so it was no concern of hers whether he approved of them or not. At least, that is what she convinced herself of before clearing her throat.

"I would want someone interested in me, not just as a wife but as a person." Claude's face appeared in her mind, startling her. She shook the image away and ignored the sudden intrusion. "So-Someone I can have easy conversation with. Someone who supports my pursuits and dreams and one who I could proudly do the same for."

Silence enveloped them as though she declared she wanted to frolic naked through the trees. She reached for another fig and popped it in her mouth, keeping one part of herself busy while he stared at her. Swallowing, his eyes did not relent, and her hands found solace in smoothing her skirts.

"Of course, this is all hypothetical," she said, the words spilling out her mouth like drool.

"I see," he murmured in acknowledgment. Those unyielding eyes finally found a different target, and she sighed in relief. "Those are..."

Laughable? Foolish?

"Commendable desires," he said in all seriousness.

Her lips parted, flustered and unsure of how to answer before saying, "Well-well, thank you. But what I want does not matter, hypothetical or not."

"Why is that?"

"Because I am to be married to a Baron regardless of what I want." A weight lifted from her chest, freeing her of the pressure.

She finally started the confrontation she had been meaning to have with him.

"I know," he said nonchalantly like they were discussing the color of the sky.

"You know?" Then why did it feel like he was still trying to woo her?

"Yes, Claude told me," he said, reaching for the meat and cheese. "He tells me everything."

An unknown force clamped down on her ribs as though Jeanette had laced her into an ill-fitting stay. All she could exhale was a soft "oh" in response. Was it all a charade? Memories raced through her mind, attempting to find where his smiles and kind words were disingenuous, and she could not find any. But was he simply obligated to speak with her because of his master?

"You look surprised."

"It's nothing, really," she said, forcing a smile. "He is your valet, after all."

"Precisely. He keeps nothing from me."

The pressure tightened. The sting of his words had not lessened a second time and only created more doubt where fondness had bloomed.

"Anyhow," Mr. Alarie said to break the silence, "shall I continue? Perhaps the next story will be more uplifting?"

By his tone, she realized it was an attempted jest, but she could only nod in response. Even as his eyes burned through her, she found solace in the clover chain in her lap.

"Are you..."

There was hesitancy, a touch of concern in his voice, but she refused to tear her attention away from the wilted flowers. He sighed and abandoned whatever thought he wished to say and read:

"Once upon a time..."

21

Marguerite

The prince approached the princess lying still as death, Marguerite read. The book Henri lent her propped in her lap as she sat up against the golden headboard of her bed. She was already familiar with most of these stories—Phillipe would tell them to her at night when she was a child—but there were many versions of the same tale. Some argued if they were fiction or accounts of real people, but she wanted to believe they were real when she was younger. Bonbon snored softly beside her, and she reached over to pat him on the head.

A few candles glowed in the darkness, allowing her to read the print, which often blurred together when close to her face. Although she was not fond of reading, keeping Claude out of her thoughts was a welcome distraction.

She knew it was an overreaction—this pain. After knowing her for only two months, Claude did not owe his loyalty—his friendship—to her. He served Mr. Alarie as he should, just as her servants had served her. Yet, knowing this did not stop the hurt in her heart.

Was it because she trusted him and believed he sought her company because he enjoyed it? Maybe. Was it because he may or may not have been using her for information? Information for what she dreaded to know. Or was it something more?

Curse it all. She was thinking of him again.

Shaking her head, she sat taller and gathered her attention on the print once more. She had lost her place and had to go back three paragraphs since she had glossed over them when her thoughts wandered. But as she readjusted her focus, her forehead ached with tension.

'She is dead,' the dwarves cried, and the prince was moved to tears at his loss and the loss of those who loved her. 'I must seal my goodbye with a kiss,' the prince declared, and kissed the fair princess. Life filled her cheeks, and she opened her eyes. The dwarves shouted with joy, 'True love has broken the spell!'

True love?

She placed the book down. This was not the only tale to mention such things, and if she remembered correctly, the tale of *Sleeping Beauty* had a curse lifted by a kiss of true love.

Could that mean...?

No, she grimaced. It was a reach at best. Besides, the story of *Cinderella* had no *'love'* to save her. Even if there was no curse to break.

Perhaps *she* needed a break.

She placed the bookmark in the pages before shutting it and placing it on the nightstand. Removing the covers, she slipped out of bed, and Bonbon perked up as she moved. She crossed the room and pulled the tarp off her new easel.

It was a wonderful gift, more than anything she could have hoped for. Yet, knowing Mr. Alarie would not have given her such a gift without Claude's assistance. She knew she had not mentioned her beloved hobby to Mr. Alarie. There wasn't room for conversation when he kept her busy with his reading.

Still, it was not a gift she would spurn.

After being forced to sell the one she had been gifted as a girl, a part of her felt silenced and caged. Painting was her only escape and safe harbor from the storms of contention her mother often swept into their conversations. Countless hours were spent at her easel, but only three were spent on the new one.

Those three hours of work stared back at her, and her throat clenched. There must have been magic in the air because the paint had dried as soon as she deemed it finished. There were no smudges or lingering fumes when she packed her easel from the gardens and hid it in her room.

It was a portrait of Claude—or how she imagined he would look if he were not touched by the curse.

Dark golden locks curled at his nape and swept over his forehead—wavy and effortless. Instead of a wet, black nose, its bridge ended in a thin, round tip over his shapely lips. Without the fur, she imagined him clean-shaven with large ears covered by his locks. Even though he wore many smiles, she opted for a more neutral expression like the portraits of nobility.

He was handsome in her eyes. Her sister might have sneered at the size of his ears and oblong face, but the kindness radiating from him that won her over.

But what had she been thinking, painting something like this? Even though she had promised Claude a portrait of something, she dared not share this with him now. It would not only be humiliating if her interpretation was inaccurate, but she dreaded knowing he had only told her what she wanted to hear.

Her hands hovered over the canvas as her heart pulled in different directions. Was it worth keeping? Should it be discarded?

A knock on the door startled her into action, and she grabbed the tarp from the ground.

"Marguerite?"

Oh, good Gallia.

"Don't come in," she squeaked, throwing the tarp over the canvas.

"I brought something for you," Claude's muffled voice said.

Curses. Of all the timing. "One moment," she called back, straightening the material so every corner was covered. She then strode to the door while tightening the ties of her robe together. It was nearing ten in the evening, so why was he here this late? What did he want?

She had no battle plan, no idea of how she should feel or what to say to the man burning a hole in her chest. Finally, she settled for a smile, opened the door, and came face to face with a cup and saucer.

"Tea?" she asked, puzzled as she made eye contact with him. His soft brown eyes glinted green against the darkness, a sight she witnessed with cats and dogs—animals. They had not shined so brightly before.

"I uh, saw your light from your window," he explained. "Even though it's late, I saw you were still awake and thought to bring you this." He lifted the saucer in emphasis.

The servants' quarters were on the first floor to the right of her window, so it was possible he saw the light shining from the third story. She eyed the amber liquid in the cup and back up into his hairy face. Was this another act?

"Thank you. What is it?"

"Something my father used to make when I had trouble sleeping," he said and handed it to her.

Steam wafted from the cup, warming her hands as she held it. It smelled sweet of chamomile and other herbs she did not recognize. "*You* made this?" she asked, not liking how her emotions muddied with both delight and suspicion.

"Indeed, I did. Father's secret recipe," he said with a soft smile. "I know it has been difficult for you to be away from your family. I know it keeps you up at night, so I thought this might help remedy that."

If she had not suspected him of insincerity, she might have sipped from the cup and complimented him for the drink. However, the cup sat still in her hands as a frown worked its way on her lips.

"Is there something amiss?" he asked gently.

She did not want to look into his face and see those eyes that might deceive her. "Did Mr. Alarie send his regards?"

"What?"

"Did he put you up to this?" she clarified, her voice quiet but on edge.

"I am unsure of what you mean?" His face contorted with confusion and concern, but it was possible he was skilled in acting with his years of servitude.

"Mr. Alarie has informed me you tell him everything I say. Is that correct?"

His brows shot upward, but he schooled his features with ease. "Well, yes," he said, "I do. Mostly. He is my master, and I tell him what he wishes to know when he demands it of me. He wants to know more about you and your welfare."

It didn't sound like a lie. He didn't deny it, which was a good start, she supposed.

When she opened her mouth to speak, he said, "However, I came here of my own volition. My master had no say in making you tea past bedtime."

Despite his gentle teasing and the smile threatening to stretch on her lips, he was not absolved from suspicion quite yet.

"Did he tell you to spy on me?"

His expression turned grave, but his eyes did not narrow in outrage at the accusation. "No," he said after a moment. "I was not ordered to spy on you. I was only asked to look after your welfare."

"Even if Jeanette could do the same?" she countered.

"He trusts me the most and feels the most comfortable speaking with me. But that is not the only reason why I seek your company."

The way he looked at her, with a tenderness softening his gaze, flitted over her face and created a pleasant warmth in her chest. She looked down at the tea in her hands, unable to hide the heat crawling up her cheeks. How could she deny the sincerity in that look? She knew her fears were not unfounded, but she knew men whose eyes were hollow when they lied to her, and he showed nothing but unfeigned emotion.

She could not help but smile in relief. "I am glad."

With the tension evaporating, he mirrored her smile. "Were you worried that our friendship was a farce?"

She avoided his eyes. "The thought might have crossed my mind."

"It's alright. I understand. Though, I am curious as to what you think Mr. Alarie might need a spy for?"

"Oh," she said, chuckling at her insecurity. "I don't know, exactly. Maybe he needed information to woo me or something? Why would he do that? I do not know." She took a sip of tea to dispel the awkwardness and was tempted to sigh at the sweetness filling her mouth. "This is delicious. What is your secret?"

She looked up as a strange look disappeared from his face. It flashed so quickly she thought she might have imagined it before a toothy grin spread on his lips.

"Ah, ah," he tsked, "it would not be a secret if I revealed it."

"Curses," she drew in a noisy breath for a dramatic effect and made a show of batting her eyelashes. "Surely you could make an exception for me?"

"Well," he put a finger to his chin as though contemplating her request. "Father was stingy about his recipes and made me promise not to tell. But..." He noted her best impression of a doe-eyed look and smirked. "How about this? If you can guess the ingredients, I will simply say yes or no. That way, I will not be breaking my promise, and you can know the secret. Does that sound acceptable?"

Delight spun within her. She loved a good game. "Yes, yes, it does. But first, tell me how many ingredients you used. Excluding water, of course."

"Of course," he smiled cheekily, and his eyes shined gold-green in the flickering candlelight. "There are seven others."

"Seven," she murmured, leaning against the doorframe. "I know one is chamomile."

"Very good. Correct."

She took another sip and recognized a distinct tanginess. "I taste...lemon?"

"Correct again. You are too good at this."

"I am simply fond of my teas," she said before taking another sip and allowing the liquid to sit in her mouth a little longer before swallowing. A part of it made her breath feel fresh and wintery.

"Mint?"

His slender arms folded over his chest as he assessed her with squinted eyes. "Are you sure you didn't know my father?"

She laughed. "Am I correct, then?"

The skin around his eyes puckered under his fur. "Yes, four more."

Again, she sipped the tea, but the other flavors felt familiar yet muddy. "Jasmine?"

He tsked and shook his head. "Here I was thinking you were a tea expert."

Huffing, she tilted her chin up. "For your information, I was simply testing you."

"Oh? Testing me? And how would that work in our little game?"

"By throwing you off. If I didn't get at least one ingredient incorrect, you would have suspected me of witchcraft. And we both know what happens to witches," she said in a light, matter-of-fact tone.

"Fair enough," he said. "But you still have three more to go."

"Well, if it's not jasmine...It must be lavender, then."

"Ah, we finally have a winner," he winked.

One by one, she guessed the other ingredients with a few hints thrown in by Claude. She accepted the hints begrudgingly but did not miss how his eyes sparkled with amusement when she grumbled at being incorrect.

"Catnip? I would have never guessed."

"You could not, without *my* help," he said with another charming smirk.

She reached out and swatted his arm. "I did well, admit it. I got three on my own, thank you very much."

He shrugged. "Not nearly fifty percent. What a shame."

Lifting her chin, she sniffed delicately. "I still got your secret recipe."

"Shall I write it down for you, so you won't forget?"

There was a mischievous glint in his eye when her tongue poked out. She laughed at her childishness, but the heaviness weighing her heart felt lighter than it had in months. Speaking to him in this way reminded her of her brother, Phillipe. He knew how to rile her competitive spirits and then tease her into submission when she lost. He was the only man in her life who was privy to that side of her—a side not ladylike in nature and scorned by her mother.

"Your ambition is unbecoming," her mother once said to her. *"No man will find it attractive."* Yet, here Claude stood, smiling through their banter. More worrisome, though, was the way he kept looking at her like he was now.

It made her want to swallow down the foreign emotions bubbling from her chest.

"Fine," she said, waving a hand. "Write it down if you must but mark my words. I will remember it. I'm already feeling its effects."

"I am glad it's working for you. If you need more, let me know. I hope you sleep better tonight."

She realized he was ending their conversation, but she found she yearned for more. However, she folded her arms and was suddenly aware that the candles behind her had dimmed. How long had they been standing there at the doorway? A wave of self-consciousness took root as she nodded and handed him the cold, empty cup.

"Thank you. It was very kind of you to think of me."

"Of course. Please do not hesitate to ask me for anything."

Even for your company? she thought but dared not say it aloud. She knew it was a foolish request, even if it would make her stay more pleasant. Time would pass more quickly with him by her side.

They bid their farewells, and she closed the door behind her. The easel in the corner called to her, and she took the tarp from the canvas once more.

"One day," she said to herself. "Maybe one day I will show you."

22

Henri

"A nd they lived happily ever after." Henri closed the book with a snap, and his reading glasses slid down his snout when he spotted Marguerite across from him. The orange hues from the setting sun flitted through the parlor curtains and danced across her closed eyes and open mouth. He sighed.

This was not the first time his reading put her to sleep, but her recent enthusiasm for fairytales had given him hope that she would remain alert.

Setting aside the book, his eyes slid shut as he inhaled deeply. Two months had passed since her arrival, and there was little progress to show for his work, let alone his own affection for the woman. He opened his eyes just as she let out a loud, unattractive snore from her nose.

What was he doing wrong?

Reading to Isa strengthened his relationship with her growing up. When he was forced to spend his days away from the rest of his half-siblings, Isa would sneak into his room, and they would tell each other stories of made-up far-off places. More importantly, he taught her to read and write. She taught him how to throw a punch and catch frogs. They were sweet memories. A smile crept on his lips at the thought of one of her fanciful tales of a magic broomstick that would sweep them far, far away from the home they both grew up in.

Marguerite, on the other hand, had not warmed up to his favorite pastime. Although she politely accepted every offer, he could see in her eyes that she was not fully present with him. It was...

Disappointing.

He did everything Claude told him to do. He gave her daisies—her favorite flower. He gave her the easel and paints. He avoided asking for mushroom dishes for their meals. He read the fairytales. He attempted to spark conversation with her. He kept his temper in check. What else was he missing? What more did he need to do?

His eyes narrowed on the sleeping woman.

The Enchanter could have sent him an impossible woman as a slap to the face. Her personality was stiff as a board, and she didn't appreciate his time or beloved hobby. How was she supposed to love him if she was so callous as to fall asleep in his presence? The audacity. How dare she? Isa would never—

Suddenly, her head began to nod forward, and she jolted awake.

Bleary eyes found his own, and she straightened in her seat. "Oh..." she said, realization dawning in her eyes as she spotted the closed book on the circular end table. "Oh, curse it all. I did it again, didn't I? I am so terribly sorry about that. I suppose our walk in the afternoon tired me out."

I doubt that, he wanted to say. Claude or Isa would remind him to be kind, and so he said, "It was rather warm today."

"Yes, yes, it was." Her head bobbed up and down. "I'm simply exhausted."

Silence followed as it usually did in their conversations. It was always up to him, wasn't it? He always had to break the silence. Why couldn't she be better at conversation then? She could say something, but she never did. Why was it *always him?*

If she does not wish to be here anyway, then I will do her the favor.

"Well, since you are exhausted," he said, but it came out like blunt nails scraping dirt. "You may be dismissed then."

She fidgeted in her seat. "Is...are you sure that's alright?"

"Of course," he clipped. "I would not have suggested it if I wasn't sure."

"It's just," a pause followed as her hands clasped together on her floral, cream skirts, "I cannot help but feel as though I offended you."

She was seeing right through him. He chuckled, alleviating the nerves and frustration swimming to his throat like rancid vomit. "Offend me?" He took the reading spectacles off and set them on the book. "Pray tell, why would you think I would be offended?"

The air of nonchalance in his voice felt too cheery and false in his mouth, like a sweet that had gone stale on his tongue. The act was unbelievable, even to himself, but he could not stop how his lips curled upward in a smile. It was the fake, reassuring expression he had learned to plaster on his face in front of his stepmother, but his guest did not take the bait. She grimaced and looked away. It must have been the fangs.

Or perhaps he was not as good at pretending anymore.

"Well, you seem upset. And I can only assume it was because I fell asleep," she said.

When she put it like that, it made him feel foolish. Soft, black tendrils of smoke ghosted over his hairy arms. "Nonsense. It's only the fourth time it has happened."

"I apologize, Mr. Alarie—"

"There is nothing to apologize for," he gritted as the heat grew hotter in his veins, egging on a more monstrous transformation.

"But—"

"It's *nothing*."

"I cannot believe it's nothing when you sound—and look," she gestured to the obvious darkness surrounding him, "so angry," she said, leaning forward in her seat.

"If I say it's nothing, then it's nothing," he insisted, but the dark tendrils danced around his arms like a fervent waltz.

"We can discuss this, though—"

"I said there is nothing to discuss," he shouted suddenly. "If you're really that tired, then go!"

The words reverberated through the parlor, leaving her stiff and white in her seat. His face fell, and words of apology swarmed in his mouth, but his lips refused to sound them out. Without a word, she stood, avoiding his gaze, and brushed past him in a whirl of skirts.

"Ms. Dupont—" he called while shooting from his seat, but she had already closed the door behind her.

"Curses," he hissed, "curse it all." The cushions wheezed under his weight when he plopped back down. Cradling his face, he was tempted to run his claws through his skin at his idiocy.

Why was this so difficult?

If this went on any longer—this tentative, rocky thing called their acquaintance—he feared the curse would never be broken. Maybe the Gods and that blasted Enchanter were laughing at him and their little experiment. To put two different souls in the same room and force them to love. What a good show. He hoped they got their money's worth.

Growling under his breath, he enjoyed how it rumbled under his chest and rippled through his limbs. None of it was fair.

The door creaked open again, and he spun out of the chair so fast that it toppled over. But the face of Claude stopped his beating heart in its tracks.

"Oh," he said, "it's you."

Claude eyed the fallen chair and stooped to pick it up. "What happened, sir?"

"A misfortunate match happened, that is what," he sighed, reaching for the cold tea on the small, end table. "That insufferable Enchanter is mocking me, I swear it." Taking a sip, the herbs did not soothe his nerves like a good Haut-Brion would. Curse his promise of sobriety. He needed a drink. Badly.

"I assume your time with her did not go as planned?" Claude asked, standing by his side.

"You could say that," he took another sip but grimaced when the soggy, cold herbs hit his tongue.

"She appeared angry," Claude said. "Did something happen?"

Yes. Something did happen—his anger got the best of him despite himself. Admitting it would only make him feel more ashamed than he already felt. "She fell asleep. Again." It was a lame explanation, he knew, but it was the truth nonetheless.

"I see."

Even without his confession, Claude appeared to know exactly what happened. The way the man eyed him and then looked straight ahead inspired nerves of humiliation to dig under his skin, heating his neck and face. Henri knew his valet was judging him—or worse, disappointed in him. Like Henri's own dead father. But what right did either of them have to judge?

"I am trying, Claude," he blurted out. "I don't understand what I'm doing wrong. By the way, she acts, one would think I am the dullest and most uninspiring man in the world. Is that what she has said of me? That I am intolerable to be around?"

For a moment, Claude looked as though he were to say something but shook his head instead. "She has not said anything of the sort."

"Then what has she said?" Henri edged forward on his seat, eager to know what Claude knew, and if the man would have the gall to confess his actions with Marguerite.

The hesitation was more obvious in the man's eyes before he clasped his hands behind his back and pursed his lips. "She has said little about you."

So, Claude wouldn't be honest, then. Pity. He thought better of him. "Then what were you talking about last night?" With smug satisfaction, he watched Claude's back stiffen and his jaw clench.

Yes, he had seen them together. Alone. Although their figures were shadowed in darkness, the light from their guest's room illuminated their backs. He had watched her smile at Claude and even intimately touch his arm from outside when he took a much-needed stroll. He saw the way Claude lingered in the hall and turned his head toward her closed door when they bid their goodbyes.

Henri's bony, clawed hands clenched over the armrests. "After everything we discussed, you still went to see her without notifying me?"

"She had reported she had trouble sleeping recently. I had given her something to remedy that."

The man wasn't telling him the whole truth. Henri could sense it by the way Claude's hands were wrung together. It didn't make any sense. Did he really have feelings for Marguerite, or was he deliberately sabotaging the curse for all of them? He expressed a heated breath and asked, "Did it need to take more than thirty minutes to do so?"

"I could not be rude to our guest by not engaging in the conversation she wanted. She asked me questions, and I answered."

"What did she ask you about?"

"Nothing important, really."

The teacup clacked loudly when he set it beside himself. "Why do *you* seem reluctant to talk about it?"

"Because..." Claude began before turning to him. "Because she trusts me. I don't want to compromise that when she already distrusts *you*. I am working to ensure that changes, but if she feels I am your informant, you will lose her too."

Henri spread his arms to gesture around the parlor. "Is she here now? Do you see her anywhere?"

"No—"

"Exactly. So, tell me how withholding information from me gains her trust? Is she supposed to feel comforted by your silent acts of chivalry?" he demanded. "What she doesn't know won't hurt or help her."

"You don't understand, sir."

His hand twitched at his side, tempted to slap it over his face in frustration. Instead, he stood and glared down at the man. "What...do I not understand? Because what *I* understand is that you are willfully keeping things from me that could hurt our chances at breaking this spell."

Claude shook his head. Stubborn git. "No, you are already doing that yourself."

"What?"

"If you want her to fall in love with you, you must do the work yourself. I don't want to be your middle-man—your *dog* anymore. I don't think it helps anyone, including your chances with her."

"You think I've been sitting around doing nothing?" His arms flapped out with a snarl. "That I have not spent countless hours being in her company and trying to please her? I have done everything you have told me to do, and nothing makes her happy. I have asked her about her day and the books we're reading—"

"*You're* reading," Claude said coolly, and Henri gaped at him. "I think you mean the books *you're* reading."

One clawed finger pointed behind him where she had exited. "*She* has asked that I read these stories in the first place. Do you know how difficult it has been to find anything she was remotely interested in?"

"You don't know a single thing she is interested in." His valet's rounded eyes narrowed in a glare despite having to crane his neck to look up at him. The accusation—the audacity—stung like sharp nettle and fanned the flames of his anger—of his incompetence.

"I know—"

"No." Claude took a step forward. "You don't. You have relied on *me* for that, and yet you remain oblivious. You don't know her passions, her dreams, or why she tolerates your presence at all. I have done that work, not *you*."

Anger came like a rushing current sweeping his veins in roaring waves. But, denying it was futile, he would only look like a stuttering fool, so the truth erupted.

"I couldn't care about what she wants. I don't care to know—curses. I don't *want* to know. Do you know why?" Darkness shrouded him like a heavy, sulking cloud. Shadows formed hazy appendages around his figure, and they waved around him, limp and boneless. "I don't want to fall in love with her. I didn't choose her! Why should I be forced to love her?"

Claude glared at him. "We've had this conversation before. You know why you must try."

"I am trying!" he roared. "So blast the curse. She has no care for me, and I have no love for her—happy?"

"Are you?" Claude spat and took another step, so they were mere centimeters apart. Henri bared his hideous mouth full of fangs and tusks, willing for the man to back down, but he refused. "Are you happy knowing we will all die as animals then? Because that *will* happen if you do not fall in love with her, and by some miracle, she falls in love with *you*."

"What?"

Both Henri and Claude whipped around simultaneously. When they saw the figure, they froze, afraid to move lest they spook the woman at the open doorway. He had been so occupied with Claude. He had not heard her enter. How long had she been listening?

Long enough, he thought as her fingers clenched over the golden doorknob with large, shining eyes.

"Ms. Dupont—" Henri said.

"Marguerite—" Claude started.

She swiftly held up a hand to silence them. The shock melted from her face and was replaced by a hardened expression that dared them to defy her. Releasing the door handle, she marched forward, her heels clicking against the polished floor. For a moment, he thought she would storm up to him and slap him, but she pushed past them and picked up something small and glittering from the chair she had previously occupied. Clamping it to her ear, Henri realized it was an earring that must have fallen while she slept.

Despite her ferocious glare, Claude stepped toward her with one hand stretched out, but she shoved it away.

"Don't touch me."

"Marguerite, wait—"

She spun back around on Claude, "You *knew* how to break the curse." She pointed a finger at him and then to Henri. "Both of you knew." Shaking her head, her accusing finger turned back to Claude and trembled in time with her voice. "It all makes sense now. And I was a fool to believe anything that came out of your mouth."

Although the statement was not directed at him, Henri felt the prick of it all the same. And he watched Claude—the man who always kept his composure, the man who did not waver, and the man who saw reason when he could not—stumble back in despair as she twisted around and walked out the door.

A stupefied silence possessed him as her footsteps echoed down the hallway until she disappeared around a corner. His gaze turned to Claude, who stared at the empty hall.

"This is all your fault," Claude said with clenched fists. The skin around his mouth and brows puckered upward like a snarling dog about to strike.

"My fault?" he retorted, swooping down so their noses were a hair's breadth away. "*You* exposed us."

"None of this would have happened if you had an ounce of care for her."

Henri looked down at the man's fists trembling at his side, itching to be raised. "Go ahead. Try it. See what happens," he said, and Claude's hands flexed outward, defeated. "That's what I thought." Retreating, Henri headed for the door, hoping he could sleep off his newly formed headache.

"You did this to us," Claude said, low and barely controlled to his back. Henri turned and saw the man's face still smoldering underneath his stony expression. "This is all your fault. *You're* the reason why we were cursed. *You're* the reason why any of this happened."

Fists were unnecessary when his words came like a blow to the gut. It left a stinging, empty hole where his stomach should have been. Curse Claude's boldness. He expected a swell of anger to come to his rescue and negate the truth eating him alive, but it did not come. Words wanted to leave his lips, but he could not form any. All he could do was stand there as Claude advanced on him.

"Do you understand, *Count*?" The title spat out like bitter bile. "No one has had the gall to say it, but we all think it—we all know it. You were the reason why that-that *thing* cursed us. If you had treated him with more decency, we wouldn't be here. We could have lived without this curse—without looking like *beasts*.

"And now we are all afraid. Afraid of your stupidity—of-of your anger and most of all...we are afraid of dying like animals. All because you are too selfish to look past yourself and fix the mess *you* made. Do you hear me?" Claude jabbed a finger into his large chest, his voice cracking. "You always said your stepmother was a monster, but you never stopped to consider how much you turned out to be just like her. I wish I had never been in your service and left you when you relocated us here. You're a selfish byblow, and I wish your father had the nerve to disown you from the start!"

Monster. Byblow.

The hole in his stomach was now a giant chasm he could not mend together. The word had been used against him his whole life but never had the man—his friend—uttered it until now.

He stared at him, his mind numb as the older, dog-like Claude melted into a younger, freckled one in his memories. That toothy grin and the dirt on his chin came to mind. Claude's cheerful disposition had annoyed him, but it was because he was jealous the older boy could live as free as he did. Despite his servitude, Henri was also chained to his title—an unstable promise of power lest his stepmother gave birth to a baby boy. Claude was there to comfort him when every pregnancy was announced. Those days were spent with gleeful card tricks and harmless pranks on the other servants to distract him from his crushing anxieties.

Fortunately, she bore nothing but girls. Or perhaps it was not a fortune at all.

Because now that same child, his friend, had grown into a man and bore nothing but resentment toward him. Both he and Isa.

Both their words crashed down on him, and for the first time, he felt...

Like he deserved it.

Silence enveloped them while purple hues bathed the room as the sun began to disappear behind the trees. Claude stood with his eyes gleaming against the light, his fists still clenched by his side.

"Why didn't you leave then? Why did you stay by my side?" Henri asked, afraid of his answer.

"Because," Claude's eyes softened, his fists unclenching. "My father asked me to. He saw the way your stepmother and half-sisters neglected you. He felt powerless to help you and thought I could help fill the void they created."

"Oh." Disappointment should not have whipped him in the face, but it stung all the same. He was not a pity case, especially not to those whom he was supposed to command. "I don't need you to fill any void."

"I know."

"Then why?"

"I know that *now*," Claude clarified. "I should have realized it a long time ago. I cannot change you. Not Marguerite and not even Isa. You are the master of your person, and so I wash my hands of you."

He sucked in a breath and attempted to neutralize the biting truth. "Even as my friend?"

Claude tilted his head, his frown twitching upward. "I thought I wasn't your friend?"

"You know I didn't mean what I said. You've always been my friend."

"Your words always mean something, Henri. You must understand that."

Flashes of conversations between himself, Isa, and Ms. Dupont came to mind, and he begrudgingly nodded. It was difficult to squash his pride. "I know...I'm working on that."

"Good, you *should* work on it," Claude said, and Henri bit down the burst of irritation at the man's confirmation. "But I hope you know I also saw the same thing my father saw in you."

"A monster?" Henri chuckled wistfully.

"No." Claude's expression grew earnest, "I saw a man with potential—a good man and a true friend."

Despite the words warming his heart, he shook his head. "I am neither of those things."

"You can be."

"I don't know how. I don't think I have ever been those things before."

A hand touched his arm, and he saw Claude's reassuring smile. "You have been. A long time ago, but it's in you, somewhere." He winked.

Henri rolled his eyes but could not help but smile. "That's *very* reassuring."

"Ha, there's that old spunk," Claude laughed and patted his back. "See? It's not so hard."

"Sure. Not difficult at all," he sighed.

"I'm sorry for calling you a byblow," Claude said suddenly. "And for what I said about you being disowned. That wasn't fair. Here I was telling you that words mean something. I went and said such hurtful things."

"Well, I literally am a byblow, so it's not like it isn't true."

The hand on his back slid to Claude's side. "It doesn't make it right, though. I realize I said things in anger, so I want you to know that you are more than just your father's 'mistake.' Because you are not one. You never were, and I know you have had difficult feelings toward your mother, but I hope you know that my aunt loved you more than anything in this world."

So many emotions had already lashed through him, but a new one surged through his heart. It was a strange feeling thawing his chest, making his eyes prick. It was also the first time Claude had mentioned his mother in this way. Although everyone knew he was a product of an affair, Father wanted to keep her anonymous.

He said something about protecting Claude and his family. They would be kicked out if others knew they were related to Henri by being associated with a woman who was a part of the affair.

Cheeks burning and eyes watering, he cleared the phlegm coating his throat. "I...umm..." What was there to say? How could he sum up the feelings he was experiencing? "Thank you," he murmured and cringed inwardly. It had been a long time since he uttered those words, and even then, they did not encompass what he felt he should say.

"I know she is watching over you. So...please...don't let her down."

Taking a deep breath, he willed the quivering of his chin to cease. "I will not. I promise."

23

Marguerite

She should have known. She shouldn't have ignored her gut feeling—the answers staring back at her in the fairytales: *Love. True Love.*

That had been the answer to breaking the curse all along. It made sense now. The flowers. The gifts. The reading.

The *spy.*

She ran, and the halls closed in on her, narrowing until she felt her breath flatten from her lungs. All those conversations, the tea, and the blasted portrait she painted of Claude flew through her mind. She cringed when she recalled each of his stinging words behind the door:

"I could not be rude to our guest by not engaging in the conversation that she wanted. She asked me questions, and I answered."

"I don't want to be your middle-man."

"...because she trusts me. I don't want to compromise that..."

"I have done that work, not you."

It was just *work* to him.

All those sweet words were empty, meaningless. The pain of it burned. But why? Why did it hurt this much? Why was it spreading like fire in her chest?

An image of him came to mind, one she treasured from last night. It was the look in his eyes—how he gazed into her own and made her feel she could sprout wings and fly. He was just delivering a cup of tea, she reasoned, but there was more to it than that: he had listened to her, saw her for her "unladylike" nature, and still looked at her as though she could do no wrong. No man had looked at her that way after seeing those parts of her. And she...she...

No.

She refused to admit what those emotions could imply. She would not say them—she would not think them. But how could she have been so stupid?

Stupid.

Stupid.

Stupid!

Suddenly, she crashed into someone's back, forcing them both to careen to the left. After catching herself and steadying the person in front of her, a pair of black eyes and a beak greeted her, and she recognized the woman.

"S-sorry, Isa," she stammered, and without another word, she ducked her head before picking up her skirts and dashing out the nearest door.

Distance was all that mattered, and the warm, summer night filled her lungs. Wispy clouds speckled dusty mauve skies as she ran past the hedges. Fire swirled in her throat, but her eyes remained focused on the line of trees behind the gardens. She needed answers.

She needed them *now*.

Finally, she crossed the line between the gardens and the forest and skidded across the dirt and crunching leaves. Golden red beams of light from the setting sun shimmered above her, casting her in a fiery glow amongst the thin tree trunks. The twittering of nightingales filled the silence in time with her labored breathing. Heart racing, she cupped her hands to her mouth.

"Enchanter? Mr. Enchanter, sir?"

Nothing. No rustle of leaves, no bird appearances, or green, glowing eyes in the shadows.

"Please," she said, "I must speak with you."

A breeze pushed through the trees, and a twig cracked when she slowly spun around, but no one appeared before her.

"Enchanter?"

"I am here, child."

Her head shot up as a chestnut squirrel darted down a tree to her right. It scampered to her and perched itself on a rotting tree stump. Its dark eyes flashed green, and she took a step back.

"Is that you? Are you the Enchanter?"

"Yes, you called for me, did you not?" He tilted his head while his voice echoed in her mind, deep and resounding. Chills ran down her spine; she would never get used to his voice injecting into her thoughts.

"You were a bird last time," she said, suspiciously eyeing the creature.

"I take many forms. Ones that are less intimidating to the human eye." His bushy tail twitched back and forth. "Would my true form be more fitting for you?"

Blanching, she did not want to see his 'true form' again if it were the same image she saw when she first came into the forest. Her palms grew sticky with sweat at the thought.

"No, thank you. But I...I want answers." She planted her hands on her hips but then realized how her stance must look, so she placed them behind her back. "Please," she gritted out.

"You understand the nature of the curse, now."

"Yes." Her eyes narrowed on the squirrel, who looked far too innocent and cute for her taste. Even though he looked small and vulnerable, she had to remember he was a powerful and magical being capable of curses. Who knew what spell he could cast on her?

"I know the questions you are afraid to ask me. You wonder why I could not tell you the nature of the curse, but I could not tell you. I placed the curse under the direction of the Gods, and it's up to those affected by it to handle it how they deem fit."

"But." The logic was strange and frustrating all at once. "But sir. I don't understand."

"What do you not understand?"

"Well, I am just as affected by this curse as they are. But I did not choose this. I did not ask to be a part of this. I am held here against my will for months on end, and I want to go home. So, it makes little sense as to why!" She needed to stop. It was difficult, though—her words were rushing out in an angry torrent, but she could not risk upsetting this creature. After a moment, she lifted her arms up and down in defeat. "Why me?"

The squirrel's nose wiggled back and forth, and a paw gestured to her. "I have already addressed this question before. You know the answer to this already."

Exasperation claimed every nerve, but she suppressed the urge to scoff. "I know. Something about fate and the Gods."

"Correct. They chose you."

"But, please understand. I already have a life. I am promised to be married to someone else. My family is counting on that marriage, so I cannot fall in love with this man. It's impossible."

"Why not?"

"Why not?" she echoed in disbelief. "Have I not just explained myself?"

"It still does not answer my question. Why is it impossible to fall in love with him?"

Pursing her lips, the pent-up frustration burst like trapped steam from a kettle. "Fine! Mr. Alarie and I are very incompatible. We have nothing in common, and I do not see myself finding anything endearing about him. He-he's awkward and boring, so I am confused as to why I am forced to love him?"

"You are not forced to love him. You have a choice, Marguerite."

She huffed, folding her arms. "It does not seem like I have one."

"There is always a choice," he insisted.

"So, am I supposed to wait out another two months? Am I to just sit and watch as they become beasts forever? I will be set free after, correct?"

"That is also a choice you are free to make. But, yes, after time has run out, you will be set free."

"But what if I choose to leave and have another take my place?"

"That is not possible. Fate has already—"

"Chosen me," she sighed, pinching the bridge of her nose. "I know. I know...But...How is that fair? I do not love him, and I do not want to love him. And I am positive he feels the same about *me*. So, what is the purpose of all this? It feels cruel."

The Enchanter did not say anything for several moments and allowed a thick silence to wash over them. Finally, the words slithered in her thoughts, creating echoes of his voice. "Then heed my word: *Love is a choice, precious and free, treasure the one who is suitable to thee. Know that all is possible but choose well. Only then can you break the spell.*"

An unflattering groan escaped her lips. She hadn't meant to sound so petulant in front of the magical being, but her frustration was reaching a boiling point.

"But..." She raised a hand to her aching forehead. "What is it supposed to mean?"

"You will know in time. All things will be revealed." Before she could register what was happening, the Enchanter-squirrel nodded to her and dashed in the opposite direction.

"Wait, don't go—!"

But he was gone—disappearing in the trees until she could no longer hear the skittering of his paws. For several moments, she stared at the treetops blanketed by indigo shadows.

None of her questions were answered, or at least, not how she had wanted them answered, and she stood there more confused and angrier than before she had confronted him. The sun set, hidden behind the distant hills, and the stars twinkled back at her grimace. Tears pricked her eyes, but she swallowed the slimy texture running down her nose with trembling lips.

There was nowhere else to go. She had to return. Every footstep felt heavy as she returned to the line of trees behind her and felt relief when she saw the scenery had not shifted as it did the day she attempted to flee. Perhaps the magic only happened when she wanted to escape. How delightful.

Suddenly, she jumped at the sound of crunching footsteps. Her heart stammered, believing the Enchanter had transformed and was coming for her, but a feminine face with a beak approached her instead.

"I-Isa?" she stuttered, her eyes widening. She wiped the tears from her eyes and straightened herself. "What are you doing here?"

"I wanted to make sure you were not running off again." The woman's blunt voice was not cold, but it surprised her, nonetheless.

"Oh." She patted her skirts down. "I-I was not. I know I cannot," she chuckled. *Even though I wish I could,* she thought. The maid stopped a considerable distance and stared at her with those beady eyes of hers.

"That is good. It would not be wise, especially at night," Isa said at last, regarding her from head to toe. "Are you alright? I heard what happened between you and the sir."

It should not have surprised her to know Isa knew because servants had ears, and they talked, but she was taken aback all the same. "I suppose I'll be fine."

"But you're not. Right now, that is."

Marguerite's eyes widened as the truth hit its mark. "You speak rather plainly," she said lightly with a sad smile.

"I've watched you interact with the others and know you wouldn't mind."

"Oh?" She was curious now.

"Isn't it true? You are different than most who come from your station. You listen and are kind."

The sadness in her smile melted. "Thank you. I suppose you are right. I don't mind if you speak plainly to me."

"Good. Because I've also noticed you are a little too kind to some."

Heat rushed to her cheeks. Was she speaking of Claude? Granted, she knew she had spoken to him the most and had become fond of him, but it was nothing more than that. "Are you insinuating that there is an inappropriate relationship between me and another?"

"Yes. With Claude," Isa said. "I've seen the way you look at him."

"Wh-what?" she cried, the back of her neck growing rigid with heat. "There is nothing between us, and I could not possibly be with him because of his status, and he doesn't have a decent salary—"

"It's alright," the woman said calmly, and Marguerite could not detect a single ounce of judgment from her. "I have seen it time and again. Besides, isn't it normal for those of your station to take up lovers of any status? Married or not? Salaries don't matter when it's an affair. People even turn a blind eye to them as long as you're married to the *right* person." Isa's lips tugged upward ever so slightly, a hint of venom tinged her voice, but it did not feel like it was directed at her.

"We-well, I certainly do not plan to take on any lovers," she said stiffly. "Besides, there is nothing between us." *Not anymore*, a voice in the back of her mind betrayed her. Shaking her head, her brows pinched together. Where was this conversation going? "I don't understand why you would bring this up. Why would you follow me here to tell me all this?"

"Because." Isa took a few steps to cinch the distance between them. From this close, Marguerite could see how her hair without her cap was formed of long black feathers. They glimmered green and purple in the moonlight. Matching feathers trailed down her neck like a cowl and disappeared under her servant frock. However, she looked down to see some of the skin around her exposed hands that appeared puckered and red, like a plucked chicken. "I heard you speak to *him*. The Enchanter. I heard what you said about Henri and your situation."

"So, you did overhear? Could you hear what he was saying?"

"No." Isa shook her head. "I couldn't. But I heard what *you* said. I know you're angry, and rightfully so. I know you don't want to fall in love with Henri and don't want to try."

Marguerite squinted at her. "Did your master send you out to me? To speak with me or convince me to be with him now that I've discovered his spy?"

"He didn't send me. I followed you here on my own."

Half of her wanted to believe what she was saying. The woman was straightforward, but it was difficult to tell if she was lying. How could she trust *anyone* here now? They could be telling her anything to get her to break their curse. "How can I believe what you say?"

"You don't have to," Isa said, but the edge of bluntness had softened from her voice. "You don't need to believe me. But know I'm not trying to trick you with fancy words." Marguerite winced inwardly, thinking of Claude. Perhaps Isa had been watching more closely than she let on.

"But you are here to still convince me to do it, aren't you? You came out here to try and tell me I should still fall in love with your master even though he has lied to me." Her fists balled together as anger swam up her throat. "Everyone has kept it from me. Even you. So why should I listen to what you say?"

"We kept it from you, hoping love would happen naturally—like it's supposed to."

Marguerite scoffed and pointed toward the chateau. "There is nothing natural happening between us."

"I know," Isa said smoothly. "Which is why I have personally come to you now. I ask that you consider how this arrangement could benefit *you*."

"Benefit me?" she exclaimed in disbelief. "How?"

"You said you were engaged to someone else, correct? And that it was important for your family? Why is that?"

"Because..." Was it wise to tell her? Maybe not, but she was curious to see where her logic was going. "It's because my family is financially ruined. We are living like paupers in the countryside. We are not equipped to live like that. We don't know how to till the ground, and I fear we may starve by the end of winter if I don't marry this man."

"So, it's money that's the issue, correct? It's not because you love someone else?"

No—Yes. She dispelled the image of Claude that surfaced and nodded. "Correct."

"Well, you realize that Henri is a Count, right?"

The fact that a servant woman had addressed her master by his first name a few times struck oddly informal, but Marguerite decided she would not address that. "I thought Mr. Alarie's title would be moot now."

"Maybe, but maybe not. We don't know what will happen. Regardless, he has kept all his wealth with him in this chateau. He has been stingy with it, and so whatever debt your family had, he could pay threefold."

Marguerite's face slackened with understanding. She had not realized that perhaps there could be enough wealth *here*, right under her nose. "And the faster I fall in love with him—"

"The faster you could leave and help your family. Maybe even have the time to take on another lover." Marguerite blushed again at the statement and was glad it was dark, so the woman could not see the pink invading her cheeks. She was implying she could have both men—Claude and Henri in the end. However, despite knowing many among her circle in Avilon who took up lovers, she had never thought she would take one herself.

But Isa must have sensed her inner turmoil because she said, "Or not if you really do love Henri. And who knows? If his title is restored, you could live richer than you'd ever been."

It was so simple. And yet, it felt so perverse. "How is that love if I am just motivated by money? I thought love was inspired by more pure motivations?"

"Isn't that how some love starts? An attraction? Whether it be for looks or money, it's the same. And now we don't have much of a choice. It doesn't matter *how* it starts now. What matters is that it does. And then you'll not only be helping yourself but helping everyone here. Everyone wins."

"But how?" she asked, swinging her arms out. "Where am I supposed to begin?"

"Be honest with him. Talk to him. *Listen* to him, and maybe you will be surprised at what you find." Isa said, but Marguerite wondered why her voice had thawed into tenderness. "He might be a monster now...but he was not always that way. You might like the man that's underneath if he ever comes back. If he doesn't, you have every right to run. You are not responsible for changing him. And we will *all* understand."

There was a graveness in Isa's eyes that gave Marguerite comfort. It was relieving to know there was a clear, spoken permission between them that if Mr. Alarie's behavior continued to sour, it would not be her fault—she could walk away from him guilt-free without feeling responsible for his lack of change. They would not blame her even if it meant the rest of them would be punished.

"I appreciate that, Isa."

"So, you will do it? You will try?"

Would she? It was a hefty task that could leave her emotionally raw and heartbroken with little to show for her work. She could leave empty-handed and still miss the opportunity to marry Mr. Bellanger. But what other choices did she have? Even though the Enchanter had insisted she had many, her other choice was to sit here twiddling her thumbs for two months until time was up. Like Isa said, if it worked out, she could be married and still help her family. The logic made sense even if she had been begrudged to agree to anything Isa had proposed.

But who knew? Maybe he was handsome, too? And even if he was not, it did not matter with his salary and their...*love*.

Love.

What a strange thing. Even the word felt foreign in her mind. Despite not factoring in that detail with her future husband, having a sweet bond between them before they married would be a nice addition.

Like how Claude made you feel? a voice in her mind whispered.

No, she reasoned acidly. *None of that was real. But maybe it will be with Mr. Alarie instead.*

Finally, she looked up and nodded once more. "Yes, I will try."

"Good." Relief visibly seeped from the woman, and her features relaxed for the first time that evening. "I know this is a lot to ask of you. If there were any other way, I would not have gone out of my way to seek you out. But it means a lot to me—to all of us here." Isa hooked a thumb behind her toward the chateau.

Although an actual 'thank you' was not spoken, it was there, warming her heart and giving her confidence in her decision. After a moment of crickets singing in their silence, Isa turned away.

But, before she could, Marguerite called after her, "Why do *you* care about this, Isa?" When the woman gave her a pointed look along with a gesture to the feathers on her body, she continued, "I mean, is there more to it than becoming human again?

"I just want something similar to what you want," Isa said.

Marguerite's face scrunched in confusion. "Similar how? Do you have an obligation to fulfill?"

"No," Isa said softly, but her lips dipped into a frown under her beak. "I want to leave this place. Go far away from here and never look back. I don't think I could stand it here once the curse is broken..."

"Where would you go?" She was surprised that the woman was honest with her in this way.

"Avilon. I would try and work with the Opera troupe if I could. Maybe see if I could eventually become a singer."

"You sing?"

"I did. And I will."

"Maybe I could convince Mr. Alarie to help you get there—"

"No," Isa blurted loudly, and Marguerite jumped in surprise. "I mean...no," she said more gently. "I don't want him to know that I plan on leaving or where I'm going. So, please don't tell him."

The request was strange, but she nodded anyway. Whatever reasons she had, she would respect them. "I promise I will not...but...Isa?"

"Yes?"

"I hope you get to sing on stage. I would love to see that."

"Thank you. I appreciate that, and I hope you'll continue to succeed with your art." She smiled a close-lipped smile under her beak, and Marguerite felt her wish to be genuine. "Just promise me another thing."

"Of course. What is it?"

"If the opera accepts me, and you come to see me...Don't bring Henri with you."

Marguerite's mouth opened in surprise. "I'll keep that in mind," she said. Perhaps Henri had been a cruel master to Isa and the woman didn't wish to see him more than she had to.

Another wave of relief washed over Isa's strange face, and she beckoned them to return to the chateau. With a sigh, Marguerite obeyed.

24

Henri

The envelope had never been open. Edges of the wax seal crumbled, and the crisp paper mottled yellow. Henri had kept it pressed in an old, religious text given to him when he was a boy.

Now he held it for the first time in fifteen years. Forty-five, to be accurate, considering the nature of the curse.

It was a letter from his birth mother, given to him by his father when he was ten years old. The seal had not been broken because he had refused to open it even when his father had said, *"This is from your mother. She wanted me to wait until you were older to give it to you."*

A huge smile had spread over his face as he hugged his father for the first time in months. Before he could speak, his father held him at arm's length, put the letter in his hand, patted him on his head, gave him a sad, pitying smile, and then walked out of his bedroom—leaving him alone once more.

Always alone.

At the time, his emotions circled and changed like sails under a turbulent storm when the letter was placed in his hand. Anger was the first to course through him since his father had rarely come to visit him, and he all but spent a few seconds with him before leaving. Fear was the second to grip him by the neck as he stared at the envelope—wondering if the whispers had been true.

"Whoever that boy's mother is, she's a whore," he had heard a guest say as he watched them from between the gaps of the banister above. Their fan opened as they whispered to the other.

"I heard she seduced the Count!"

"Horrible, really. It's probably for the best that the boy never met her."

"My thoughts exactly. She might have poisoned his mind."

Poisoned him with what he hadn't understood. But whatever they meant, if they had been right, it would destroy him.

So, he never opened it.

And now he stood as a monster—a grown man—alone in his study, holding a piece of his mother he dared not open. Claude had been right when he had mentioned he had difficult feelings toward the woman he had never met. As a child, in his darkest moments, he blamed her for his misfortunes and the life she even gave him. If he had not been born of an illicit relationship before his father was married, perhaps his life might have been very different.

At the same time, hope nestled in the back of his mind, hope that the woman he never met had loved him and would have cherished him if she were still alive. When he thought of her in that way—as a gentle mother who would have comforted him in his need rather than a wicked temptress—his heart would swell until he thought it would burst.

Those feelings swung back and forth his whole life until a false indifference settled into his adulthood.

The paper crinkled in his clawed grasp as he recalled what Claude said, *"My aunt loved you more than anything in this world."* Was this proof of that? He wanted to believe it. With his valet's encouragement, he sought the envelope out for the first time. *"Read it. Read all of it, and you may be surprised,"* Claude said before leaving him alone in the parlor.

Raw emotions battled within him, but a gnawing *need* ate at him to seek the truth despite the emotional blow-up between Ms. Dupont, his valet, and himself. Even though their guest had been seen running through the gardens, Claude had reassured him that

Isa had gone after her. She would be safe and would need time and space from him anyway.

There were no excuses then. Nothing stopping him from opening the letter.

Finally, he slid one sharp claw beneath the seal and popped it open. The letter felt delicate in his hands as he opened the folds and found crude handwriting rather than elegant and flowing as he had been taught. It was incredible to him that his servant mother could write at all.

My dearest son, my love...

Already his eyes were burning, but he kept reading.

Oh, how I wish I could see your face now and see how you've grown. I wish and regret many things, but most of all, I regret I have not been there for you. My heart aches knowing you will never know who I am or how different your life could have been if I had been at your side. I wish I could have seen your first steps, heard your first words, and have seen you grow up into the man you will become.

But I am sad to admit the sickness in my lungs is stronger than my wishes. Even so, I am afraid even if I were not ill, I would still not have been able to see you or raise you as my own. These circumstances are complicated, and for that, I am so very sorry. However, your father has promised to take care of you.

I also write to you to explain the truth of our relationship. I know your father has most likely kept it from you because he is too pained to speak of it.

Henri paused with a thick swallow. *His* father? Pained? Granted, she was right. His father never spoke of how he had met his mother or why he had the affair with her. He read on:

You may have already been told by others, but I wish for you to hear it from me. I served under your father's household all my life. I worked for his family as a housemaid. We never spoke or had reason to interact until he had rescued me from a lecherous guest of his. Even though he was engaged to be married, I had caught his eye, and he pursued conversation with me. I was reluctant—I knew it was forbidden, but your father was so charming and handsome. We fell in love so fast. Before we knew it, I was pregnant. It caused grief for both of our families. Your father was married soon after despite my pregnancy, and he claimed you when you were born.

My son, I wish so much for you. I wish for your health and happiness. I hope you grow into a kind and loving man. One who is strong and compassionate to all *those around him—even to those you may think are beneath you. Be free to give, and when life is difficult, lean on those you love, even when you feel the most broken. Love can mend even the most broken of spirits. I would know. When*

*despair had taken me, your little kicks inside my
belly had given me the peace and comfort I needed
to bring you into this world.*

*Even when the world is cruel, please do not give
up. Know that you have always been loved, and
I will always love and cherish you from above. I
wish I could write more and more, but I am growing
weaker even as I write. Forgive me, my son. I love
you. Always and forever.*

—Mama

Adaline

It was difficult to breathe. Nose runny, he sniffed loudly and
lifted his face toward the ceiling to prevent tears from rolling down
his cheeks.

A kind man? Compassionate? For shame. Claude was right. He
was not a good man. She would be so disappointed in how he had
treated Isa, Claude, and all his servants—the people who raised
him.

But love radiated from her words like the sun's bright rays,
blanketing him from the top of his head all the way down to his
cloven feet. All the pain and blame he had poured on her in his
childhood slowly seeped away as he clenched the paper at his
side.

Now he understood.

When others had spoken so poorly of his mother, he believed them. It was because she was a servant girl—some idiotic, anonymous, lowly girl who must have seduced a wealthy man with her charms. But it was the opposite. It was his father who had essentially pursued *her*. His father knew. They both knew the consequences, yet *he* should have known better. Father had more power, wealth, and status over her, yet...

The tension building in his forehead relaxed as revelation struck him. Maybe there was some good in him. After all, if he had the decency to end things with Isa, regardless of the pain it put them through, he mustn't have been too despicable.

Even though his title hadn't been secure until his stepmother had finished having children to attempt to have a male heir, it hadn't been fair for them both. Their statuses clashed, and there was no way he would repeat history.

No child should be treated like he had. All for being an illegitimate child.

A knock sounded, and he quickly stuffed the letter back in its envelope and shut it in the book's pages.

"Yes?" he asked.

"It's Marguerite. May I come in? I think we should talk."

Ms. Dupont? He had not expected to speak to her so soon. He wiped at his eyes and felt foolish for the action, considering how monstrous he had already appeared. Removing any trace of tears would not change that, but he cleared his throat and said, "Of course. Come in."

A face appeared behind the door, and he first noticed how swollen and red her eyes were. Pins had come undone from her simple updo, popular in her time, leaving tendrils of wavy hair dragging down her neck. A stab of guilt shot through him, but she held her head high like she was the Queen of Varis herself.

"May I sit?" she asked, gesturing to the velvet red chair opposite his desk. He nodded, and she fanned out her pink skirts before sitting.

"If I may—"

"Ms. Dupont, I—"

They blinked owlishly at each other before he held out a hand in gesture. "Apologies. You may speak."

"Thank you," she began and adopted a serious expression. "I would like to address three things with you if I may, and I would like for you to answer my questions truthfully. Can I trust you to speak the truth this time?"

It was an honest query, but it felt patronizing all the same. Even so, he...he deserved it, curse it, he did. He had not been truthful with her. *Speak kindly*, he reminded himself, thinking of his mother's words, before saying, "Yes. I swear to speak honestly. What is on your mind?"

"Good." She sniffed delicately. "The first matter I would like to discuss with you is the nature of the curse and how it began. Please tell me what happened that day and what the Enchanter said. I know the nature of the curse, but I still want to hear it from you. I doubt the story you told me before was accurate."

Her words stung worse this time. This would be difficult. But finally, he sighed and related the tale to her. This time, however, he did not embellish the story or leave out unflattering details. He shamefully told her the truth—all of it—how he had been angry with the man at his door, how he had lost his temper and threatened to harm him. And lastly, he spoke of the words the Enchanter had ingrained in his memory. When he finished, she sat, perplexed.

"Only by learning to love and be loved in return...May you break this curse and find what your heart truly yearns..." she repeated with her eyes wandering on her skirts. She frowned. "I was hoping there would be more clues, some other way."

"I wish there were," he said, and her eyes went wide, and he recognized his mistake. "No offense. I think you are lovely, but it's not how I imagined I would find a...a..." heat pricked his neck, "a wife."

"None taken," she said lightly. "I have been feeling the same as you. And I cannot, for the life of me, understand how that fits with what the Enchanter spoke to me about."

He shot up in his chair. "He *spoke* to you? *Again?*"

"Yes," she admitted as her hands fidgeted in her lap. "I sought him out. I...I was unsure if he *would* come, but I wanted to understand. I figured he might be in the forest where I last saw him and...I know it sounds foolish, but I called for him, not knowing if he would answer. But he was there, and he came to me. And he told me something which is puzzling me now."

"What did he say to you?"

She then told him all the Enchanter said about fate and the riddle, and his confusion sank deeper into his mind when she finished.

"Suitable to thee?" he echoed. "Choose well?"

"That is my thought too. He said I had a choice in the matter, but I do not understand what it could mean."

"Well, from my understanding and what I have told you already, all I know is that someone would come to me...and that is who I was supposed to learn to love."

"Exactly," her frown deepened.

"And if the Enchanter himself said you are fated to be here, then there is no other, just as I suspected. You are chosen for me."

"That is what I was afraid of..." she said. "I thought...I thought maybe it *might* mean something else, but the choice seems clear to me. *You* are the suitable choice if this curse is to be broken."

"Right," he said as they avoided each other's gaze.

"Well, no matter," she said, perking up. "This brings me to the next subject I wish to discuss." The candelabra at their left did little to brighten the room but illuminated the determination shining in her gaze.

He braced himself for the worst. "Very well. What is the next matter?"

"I will do it."

Had he not been sitting, he might have tripped where he stood. "Wait, you mean—"

"Yes. I will comply and do my best to fall in love with you. I cannot assure you that it *will* happen, but I promise to put all my energy into trying." Those eyes stared at him with unflinching resolve. "Will you do the same?"

Shock and relief wrestled through him until he said, "Yes, I will do the same. I swear. But...I do not understand. What has convinced you of this?"

"Let's just say that I've been given a reason as to how this may benefit us both. Which brings me to my last inquiry."

He steepled his claws together. "I am listening."

"I will agree to attempt to fall in love with you upon certain conditions."

He nodded. That was fair.

"One," she continued, holding a finger up in emphasis. "When we are married, I wish you to help me save my father from his debts and help restore his business. Two, I will not tolerate abuse. And three, you are to allow me to continue my art as I see fit. In return, I will be your loving wife and support you equally in all your endeavors. I will bear your children and raise them to be good heirs of your title. Does that seem fitting and fair?"

Despite what she thought, Henri had already planned on taking whatever financial burden her family was in the moment Claude mentioned it. If they were to be married, it would be his husbandly duty to do so. He knew that much, at the very least—he was not *that* uneducated on marital matters.

Overall, the decision was easy. "It's fair. I promise to uphold these requests. But are you sure that is all you ask? I am unsure if I will have my title, but if I did, I could provide you with a new summer home in the south if it pleases you. Or provide you new dresses of your choosing or—"

"Those are all very kind gestures," she said, raising a hand to stop him. "But I only ask what I have already listed. Anything else is up to you to provide, and I will be grateful to receive them."

"Very well. I will do my best to see that I am worthy of you," he said with a wistful smile, hoping against hope this curse could finally be broken.

The statement must have surprised her because she looked away from him while twisting her hands together. "And I of you..." she whispered. "However..."

"Yes?"

"I also request one last thing if you don't mind."

"Of course, anything."

"I wish for us to be honest with each other from now on. I believe that may be the best for both our sakes. I cannot fall in love with someone if I feel we cannot be truthful with each other."

Nodding, he realized this may be the most difficult request yet. However, he would try for everyone's sake. "Yes. I agree. I promise to be honest with you, Ms. Dupont."

"Marguerite," she said, peering up at him shyly. He blanched as the weight and implications of their agreement sank to the bottom of his stomach. "You may call me Marguerite."

"Very well. And you may call me Henri, of course," he said, shifting his gaze away from her as awkwardness crept up his spine.

"Well...thank you...Henri." His name on her lips sounded just as awkward as he felt, but it held promise for a better beginning for them both.

"No," he shook his head and reached his hand out as a peace offering. For a moment, she looked at it, confused before she slipped her hand against his massive one. He gently curled his claws around her small fingers in a light handshake. "Thank *you*."

25

Claude

Claude should have been happy for Henri—for himself, really.

He should have felt an overwhelming sense of relief when he had been informed of the deal between his master and Marguerite. There would be no more back-and-forth messenger duties. The curse could be broken—there were no more questions of "how" but "if," and he should have been celebrating with the other servants. There was more hope to believe he would not die as his cousin's *dog*.

It should have been comforting.

But none of those feelings came. Instead, he clenched his teeth until his sharpened molars protested when he fluffed Henri's napkin in his lap for lunch. Marguerite sat across from him, speaking casually about the weather at a garden table they set up between two white pillars outside. Large cotton clouds covered the sun, and the shade relieved them from its warmth.

Despite everything that had happened last night, they were sitting pleasantly as if the lies that had been exposed curled into smoke above their heads. The tension was visible but slowly disappearing.

The only difference was that Marguerite refused to look at him even as he came to her side. This was the first time he had seen her since he had watched her come out of Henri's study last night.

He had not approached her then, but each step he took toward her now inspired sweat to bloom under his arms.

An apology sat on his tongue, begging to be released. If Henri had not been there, he would have spilled his heart into her lap, but he reached for her napkin instead. Her lips twitched as he laid the cream fabric over her lavender dress, but never once did she extract her focus off Henri as she took a sip of wine.

It was a beautiful gown—one he appreciated with a heavy heart as he skillfully glanced at the details of her bodice and arms. Golden lace skimmed down from her elbows, and the sheen of the lavender material tapered from her bust down to her waist in a flattering 'V' shape.

By the Heavens, she was too beautiful.

Flushing, he quickly situated her napkin, but from the corner of his eye, he watched as she attempted to place her glass down. With all her focus on Henri, she miscalculated.

The base overlapped with her silverware and tipped it forward. A loud squeak rose from her throat as he jerked forward to catch it. No wine spilled, but his side brushed against her, and she stiffened at his touch.

"Great catch," Henri chuckled, raising his cup of tea. "That could have been a disaster."

She did not offer a similar remark but retracted herself from his touch like he was a viper. He quickly did the same, ignoring the ache he felt stewing in his chest as other servants swooped in to give them their meals. Retreating, he stood with his back to the chateau and laced his hands at his back. His eyes were weighted with lead as he stared into the dead gardens. It was not much of a view, but it was better than staring at the woman whose clutch over his heart had turned cold.

"You look beautiful today," Henri said, albeit awkwardly, echoing his thoughts. "I am worse for wear, I am afraid. Perhaps I should have gotten a trim to match the special occasion?"

She chuckled. "Thank you, but I suppose today *is* a special occasion."

"Oh?"

"Yes, today marks the first day of the rest of our lives together, does it not?"

A strangled choking sound ensued, one he wanted to match, but then he glanced over to see Henri pounding on his chest and clearing his throat. "Well, um, I-I suppose...but, uh—"

"We are not married, I know. But I would like to propose a toast...to us."

Something deep and fragile within him twisted painfully. She raised her glass, and Henri, looking taken aback momentarily, raised his teacup with hers.

"To us and to breaking the curse," she said.

"To us," Henri said before sipping his tea.

His brows raised. Perhaps Henri was serious about breaking the curse after all. So, why was his stomach clenching in nauseating waves? He looked at Marguerite and saw her smile—a curve of teeth, but something was amiss. Her cheeks had not lifted into rosy apples, and the crease under her eyes was absent. Claude remembered those smiles, the ones where her eyes crinkled into almond slits as she beamed up at him, warming him with her happiness.

But, as he looked at her now, all the memories of sparkling smiles sank to his stomach.

Marguerite

Marguerite raised the mallet high, grunting at its weight, and swung. The ball rolled directly through the hoop and veered right toward the next stake. Clapping sounded behind her, and she turned around with a modest curtsey.

"Well done," Henri said from beneath the large canopy they set up in front of the gates. Servants, including the person she wished would disappear, ceased their clapping and resumed their proper stance with their hands behind their backs. She eyed Claude with a frown, her gut twisting before Isa came forward and offered her another glass of wine.

"It appears my skills haven't abandoned me yet." She took a sip and handed the glass back, enjoying the richness that filled her mouth. It was her second glass of the day, and she appreciated how it made her feel warm and flush. Confidence for conversation came easier in waves of crimson in her belly. It was an addicting sensation. She looked to a happy, panting Bonbon and crouched to pet him.

"Indeed," Henri said as she approached his side underneath the red canopy. "You are quite skilled at this. Round three, and you remain undefeated."

"Well, I played this for many afternoons with my brother, Phillipe. I think of him when I play," she said and stood.

"Do you miss him? Your brother? I know we have briefly spoken about your family, but..." he trailed off.

"I do miss him," she said, realizing they hadn't spoken of such things in detail before. She motioned for Isa, who held her fan, and the woman gave it to her. Their eyes met, and she tilted her head in secret acknowledgment. "I have him to thank for the many skills I have today."

"Including your art?" He bit into an apple a servant offered him. The way his teeth smashed over the meat of the fruit, with pieces sticking to his tusks like an animal, made her stomach clench.

"No, that was something I discovered on my own, actually." The deal she stuck with him about speaking honestly reeled in her mind, and she decided it was best to expand on what she had started. Luckily when she looked at him this time, he had licked the apple chunks clean from his tusks. "It was when my mother had an artist come in and do a portrait of myself."

"Who was the artist?"

"Jean Laffite. A local artist. But I sat still the whole time, mesmerized by how he painted. It was an art itself, the way he dipped his brushes into the pallet. I asked for my own set that very afternoon." She smiled at the fond memory.

An awkward silence followed, and her smile faltered. A part of her was disappointed he had not continued to ask more about the subject or to see her art. But, it was enough that he had asked questions about it in the first place. She should be satisfied.

"What of your family, Henri?" she asked, abrupt and a bit too cheery even for her tastes.

He paused mid-bite and chewed slowly like he was avoiding answering the question. It was not the first time she had asked, nor the first time he had evaded the subject altogether. However, she had hoped that he would open up a little more after their conversation last night. After swallowing, he sighed.

"There is not much to say about them."

"Well, do you have any siblings?"

"Three. Half-sisters. They want nothing to do with me."

"Oh." Her face fell, and her hands fidgeted with her fan. No wonder the subject was avoided.

"I don't blame them," he continued, lowering his eyes. "They have every right not to forgive me. I took my father's title and forced them out of their home. I arranged for them to live elsewhere, but it was still inexcusable behavior. I see that now."

The fan stilled in her hands as she stared at him. A heaviness settled over her, and she felt more than one pair of eyes look in his direction. After being forced out of her own home, she understood the despair and shame of it all too well. But, perhaps there was more to the story. Swallowing, she cleared her mind of the initial shock of his statement. "How did this happen?"

"I wanted revenge," he said, his shoulders slumped, the mallet game forgotten. "I was neglected as a child. My stepmother kept me away from everyone except the servants. I wanted her to...feel the pain I did of...of many things. But... my half-sisters didn't deserve it. They were young and listened to their mother's lies. They didn't know better, but I lashed out. And I also lashed out at the Enchanter, which put us all in this miserable mess." A pause followed, and he frowned. "I'm sorry. This is terribly candid of me, isn't it? And dismal at that."

"No, don't be sorry. I want to know you, Henri. All of you. But, I suppose I don't understand what you meant by taking your father's title. Wouldn't that be yours to claim?"

"I'm an illegitimate," he deadpanned.

Her fan could not hide her surprised expression fast enough. Never could she have guessed he was illegitimate.

"Does that concern you?" he asked, breaking her dazed state.

"N-no, not at all," she said, but he eyed her as if he did not believe her. "I promise, Henri...it does not concern me," she attempted again.

"It's fine if it does."

"No," she shook her head. "I was simply surprised, is all. But believe me...I don't care about where you come from or how you entered the world. All that matters to me is the content of your heart."

"I still have much more to repent for," he said. "I know your family was put in a similar situation, and I see how it has affected you. You did not deserve that. Perhaps my sisters didn't deserve it."

"Well, you didn't deserve to be neglected either," she said, and from her peripheral, she swore she could see Isa smile. "Only Kyros may judge you, but you clearly feel remorse over the matter. You made some mistakes, but I see you are trying to rectify this situation the best you can, and that's all that matters."

Claw marks punctured the untouched red skin of the apple as he stared at her. It was an unnerving look of disbelief. The cautious walls she had built around her heart crumbled. His speechlessness spoke volumes of the way he must have been treated in his life.

Finally, he looked away, stiff and uncomfortable, and she took it as her cue to change the subject.

"I believe it's your turn," she said gently, breaking the silence and gesturing to the course.

"That it is," he said, but his lips stretched into a light smile instead of a grimace when reminded of his turn. Despite his lack of interest in the game, she thought it sweet of him to venture out of his comfortable reading routine. It was certainly a much-needed break for her.

There were at least two meters worth in length between himself and the next hoop. He would have to strike a little harder for it to pass.

His cloven feet spread wide in an awkward stance for his lumbering body. He gripped the mallet with his huge hands—more claws than fingers wrapped around the thin end. The cloak of dark, matted fur draped over his broad shoulders revealed his disproportionately lean torso as he swung.

Her eyes widened as the ball arced in the sky. It flew over the several stakes across the grass and landed with a metallic clang against the iron-wrought gates. Her mouth hung open; her fan lowered as he turned to her. His shoulders were hunched, an attempt to appear smaller like a boy caught smashing one of his mother's vases.

"Uh...I did not mean for that—I mean...I-I wasn't hitting it hard enough before, and I—oh, blast—no, I apologize! I shouldn't use such language. Curse it all."

"Well," she said, but a giggle bubbled up within her, and she quickly cleared her throat to kill it. His stuttering made it clear that he was more than ashamed of the action. It would not be appropriate to laugh at him for it.

"Does that count for at least one point?" he asked.

That did it.

A snort escaped her nose, and she pressed her hand over her mouth. His expression was unreadable, and for a moment, she was unsure if she angered him. Worry twisted within her before she heard a low chuffing sound reverberating through his chest. His shoulders were shaking, and she realized he was laughing. She joined him as she lowered her hand and snorted again. It was an unflattering sound that inspired more chuffing from his large form. She looked to the servants behind her and saw many were holding back a smile...all except...

Never mind, Claude. *He* didn't count. Not anymore.

"Yes," she said, her smile stretching to her cheeks. "That can count as one point."

"Good." He smiled back even though the tusks in his mouth protruded when he did so. "I was losing miserably already. The least I could do was lose with one point to my name."

"You are in luck then. I am feeling gracious today."

He bowed to his waist. The gesture was so dramatic that she giggled again. "Thank you, most gracious lady."

"It's my greatest pleasure, Sir Count," she said with a mock curtsey of her own. As their eyes met, a new emotion welled inside her. Despite being together for two months, this was the first time she saw more of who he was. Who knew this awkward, bumbling creature could be so playful and funny? She would never have guessed, even yesterday, that a man like this was lurking behind his books.

Maybe Isa was right. Maybe there was more to him than she had judged him for.

Even so, she glanced toward the man driving pins through her heart. Looking at Claude hurt. It was self-mutilation at this point, but he drew her in despite the pain.

It was not as if they were more than friends or maybe even good acquaintances. Being angry did not make sense to her logically. There were plenty of reasons why her feelings were foolish. One of those glaring reasons was that Claude was a servant performing his duties. He was a prime example of loyalty to his master; she should not have faulted him for it. Even knowing this did not ease the fact that her hurt *was* real and spurned her anger even more.

When his eye met hers, she snapped her gaze away.

"Shall we do another round, or shall we take a break?" Henri asked.

"Let us take a break," she said. She motioned for the wine again, and instead of a sip, she downed the rest of its contents. She would need more liquid confidence if she were to get through another two months of the pain she attempted to squash down. "Would you fancy a walk with me?"

Anything to get away from Claude.

"Of course." He then offered his large, furry arm, as thick as her thigh. Her fingers could not wrap around the circumference of his bicep, but it was warm and soft like Bonbon's fur.

"Let us start around this way." She gestured with her fan and ignored the familiar pair of eyes on her form as she walked.

"As you wish," he said, smiling down at her.

She secured her grip over his arm, anchoring it where it should be, and never looked back.

26

Henri

There was something amiss about Marguerite, Henri decided as he laid a nine of diamonds over her seven clubs. Something he could not place his finger on.

Summer passed like a winded sigh. Muggy, quiet, but not unpleasant. But she had been acting strangely over the past month after their deal. She was friendly, though, and their conversations had fewer lulls. They played more games together and did things she enjoyed, making her more sociable and less stiff.

Despite this, the more he studied her over the weeks, the more he found there was something askew about her smile, her eyes, and the way she talked. It was as if a puppeteer was moving her mouth and acting out the right actions. Sometimes, a spark in her eyes convinced him that her unhappiness was a trick of the lights, but then a dullness would settle in when she would peer at Claude.

Placing a ten of spades, she put down a jack of diamonds and took the pair of cards. She reached for the wine beside her and drank the rest in one gulp.

"Would you like more, miss?" Joseph asked, and she nodded. The dark, crimson liquid splashed into her cup for the sixth time that evening, and although the drink was not potent, he frowned when she drained half of its contents. She had been doing that more lately—drinking, especially in the evenings like the one they shared now.

The parlor was quiet except for the sound of slapping cards on the small, round table between them. A crackling fire warmed the marble fireplace, and orange hues danced over half of her profile. Her eyes were glassy in the light.

The tea at his side was getting cold, but he sipped on it slowly. Wine would have also been his choice of drink, but he knew he would not be able to control his appetite around the tempting substance. Instead, he watched as she finished her cup and asked for another.

"Are you sure that is wise?" he interjected as the lip of the wine bottle touched her empty glass. Joseph's rabbit nose twitched, and he froze, but Marguerite's brows furrowed, and she waved a dismissive hand.

"It's fine," she drawled, but the card she put down was not a higher suit.

"You might make yourself sick if you drink more than you have. Especially for how fast you are drinking it now."

"No, I am fine-fine," she said, indignant, and waved for Joseph. But the man looked at Henri, and he shook his head sternly. Joseph retreated, and Marguerite huffed.

"Do you usually have a habit of drinking?"

"N-not really," she grumbled with folded arms and, in the process, flashed all her remaining cards to him.

"Then I think you will be too sick to play if you keep going at this pace."

"I haven't been drinking much at all, thank you very much."

"I do not believe you have kept count."

"Yes, I have—I've had," she put her cards on the table, lifted both hands and put a few fingers down before lifting them again, "something like this."

He gave her a pointed look, and she giggled. It was clear she was more than tipsy at this point.

"Joseph," he said and motioned to him.

"Yes, sir?"

"Have the cook prepare a hearty stew for the lady—"

"I'm-not—I'm not hungry," she said, slapping a queen down on the table. "There. See if you can-can beat that one."

"And some baguettes, if there are any left from this morning. It'll help with the drunken sickness," he said, and the servant nodded and swiftly exited.

"Oooh, bread sounds lovely," she sighed and slumped in her chair until her shoulders squished up to her neck above the table. She coughed, sputtering since her stays most likely prevented her from slouching.

"Maybe we should end the game and retire for bed after you eat, hm? I do not want you hurting yourself." He set his cards down face-up, and she scowled.

"No." She put one elbow on the table and struggled to compose herself. "I am winning, and I plan on winning. And you, sir," she pointed at him, "have revealed your cards."

Maybe placating this drunk version of Marguerite would be more difficult than he thought. Shame rang through him, along with a new sense of appreciation for those who attempted to appease him while *he* was drunk. He would have to thank Isa and Claude in the future.

"Then you are the winner," he said, pointing to her pile. "You have the most. You win."

He expected her to fight back, but instead, she reached forward, grabbed both massive piles, and gathered them to her lap. "I win," she giggled as the cards fluttered around her.

As she began to stack the cards with clumsy hands, he stared at her fingers and thought of how she had accepted his arm every day since their deal. Although her hands were soft and free of calluses, they did not bring the spark he felt when holding...

Shaking his head, he attempted to get rid of the thought, but it was too late. He was thinking of Isa again—of how her rough palms felt against his cheek. The way she trailed her fingers down to the crevice of his throat, to his chest.

Biting his tongue seemed to do the trick even as he winced.

It was not fair to think of her anymore. It was never fair to begin with, but the old memories persisted to haunt him even as he was enjoying Marguerite's company. He should be thinking of *her* and how her almond eyes crinkled when she laughed or how her tongue peaked when she concentrated on a game they played. More importantly, he should think of how he looked forward to seeing what activity she would think to do for them that day. That feeling, the feeling of anticipation, should be nurtured until it grows into love. That is what he should be pouring his energy into.

So why did a pair of dark, raven eyes still torment his thoughts?

"You look sad."

He looked up and found Marguerite leaning her torso across the table. Her mouth worked into an exaggerated frown. Her face was so close he could see every line around her glassy eyes as they squinted at him.

"It's nothing."

"I don't think that's possible," she slurred, holding a finger up. "I, for one, cannot—not...not? Is that it?" She shrugged and plowed on, "Think of nothing. Can you?"

"Perhaps not," he mused.

"Henri, listen to me. It's very...acceptable." Her face scrunched suddenly as though she were uncomfortable before she let out a small burp. "Excuse me—umm...what was I saying? Oh, yes!" She pointed her finger back toward his face, reaching for his snout. "It's perfectly acceptable to be sad. I have also been quite...melancholy." With that, she tapped him on the nose with a lopsided grin.

His snout scrunched in tandem with a raised brow. "What has been upsetting you?"

"Oh," she said, "it's a secret." She directed her finger toward her lips. "You cannot tell Claude."

"Claude? What has he—"

"Shhhh!" a little spittle flew from her mouth, and she snorted when it landed under his eye.

This was getting out of hand. He planned on waiting for the stew to be finished, but perhaps it was best he send it to her in bed.

"Come on." He stood and waved a hand upward so she would follow the motion. "I think it's time to retire now."

Her pig-like chortles instantly ceased as she looked up at him. "No...please, I do-not wanna go to bed. I-I'm sorry I spit on you. It was an accident, I promise."

"I know," he said, as though appeasing a child, "but I think it's best that we *both* retire now."

She shook her head and pouted.

"Come on, don't act childish," he sighed.

"Childish?" she retorted loudly, "I-I am *not*, I am-am...a lady."

"A drunk lady."

"Hey!" She pointed a finger in his direction. "I...*may* be a little tipsy—"

"*Just* tipsy?"

"Fair point, sir. I may be *drunk*. But I am a...lady drunk. Not drunk lady, thank you very much."

It was his turn to hold back a grin as she said this with as much seriousness as she could while swinging that finger she enjoyed pointing with. "Very well. I am mistaken."

"Good. Now I will go to bed. I am feeling so...sleepy." She yawned, proving her point while slumping over the table.

He exhaled a long, heaving sigh. If he ever acted like this when he was drunk, a double apology would be owed. It was also a good thing he was the only one to witness her drunken behavior. Others within their status might have spurned her from their circles for being so careless with her drink. He himself might have done the same once upon a time, but he also knew from experience that there was a concealed motive for her generous consumption.

Or someone, his thoughts whispered.

"Come on, let's get up."

An incoherent grumble followed before she peeled her cheek from the table and sat up. With all the sluggish movement of a snail, she wobbled to her feet and then stretched out her arms for balance. He offered his arm, and she clung to him, putting all her weight into his side. He might have stumbled at how she leaned into him if he were not two heads higher than she.

"We are walking this way," he said, guiding her away from the table and toward the door.

"Shall I inform the cook to send the meal to her room?" Albert, the greenish turtle man, asked.

"Yes. Find Joseph and tell him as well." He looked to Marguerite's little dog following them. "Also, take care of Bonbon. Make sure he has relieved himself before you put him in her room."

"Very good, sir." He tipped his head, stooped down to pick up the dog, and opened the door for them.

"Thank you very much." Marguerite smiled and waved as they passed.

She stepped over his cloven feet and tripped more than once, but he kept her steady every time, careful of his claws over the delicate material of her sleeves. When they came to the grand stairs, he mentally groaned, wishing he could carry her without the fear of being improper.

The slow way it is, he thought as he helped her up one step.

"Henri?" she asked, the word lethargic on her tongue.

"Yes?" he grunted when he tightened his grip over her arm when she swayed backward.

"Is Claude angry at me?"

It was his turn to pause on the step. This was the second time she had mentioned him that night and the first time she uttered his name in a month. Despite the glances she thought were hidden from his view, he knew she was avoiding his valet. In return, Claude clammed up every time he spoke to him about her. Both actions did not go unnoticed, and he frowned when he looked down at the crown of her head.

"I do not think so. Why do you ask?" Maybe it was wrong to ask such a question while she was inebriated, but his curiosity had been piqued.

"I am...angry with him. And he knows it."

"Is that so?"

"Indeed," she said, drawing out the vowel with her head limp to the side. "Henri?"

"Yes?"

"Why can't we do whatever pleases us?"

"What do you mean?"

"I mean, we cannot-not-do whatever fancies us. My mother, father...people. They will not let me do what I want."

They were not even a quarter of the way up, but Henri did not grow frustrated by their speed but rather intrigued by her topic of choice. "Well, there are plenty of things you are free to choose. But I suppose none of us can do whatever pleases us. There are rules in place for a reason."

"Yes, but-but why? Some rules seem so...silly."

"Which ones are you referring to?"

"The stuffy ones. The ones saying we cannot be with whoever we want. I don't understand why or who made that a rule."

His brows shot up as he adjusted his grip on her. She slumped into his side, but he held her up with ease. "Do you think it's because we are held to a higher standard?"

"Standard?" She looked up at him as he urged her onto the next step.

"Yes. We are born into circles that hold more responsibility for others. We cannot simply marry anyone, especially those beneath our ranks...because they were not bred for that responsibility. Can you expect a farmer to retain any of your father's wealth?"

To his surprise, she pushed from his grip and took four wobbly steps forward. At this level, she was almost as tall as he, and she placed both hands on her hips, swaying.

"Excuse me, sir," she said, and he raised his arms in case she fell forward. "I-I will not see a single copper from my father's wealth. I am his *daughter*, so what is to stop me, or-or *anyone*, from being happy? Hmm?"

"I was not—"

"They are people too, Henri," she sputtered, wavering on one foot before she set both down. "They are people like us, and I do not understand why we treat them so differently."

With that, she turned around and began to climb the stairs one shaky step at a time. He followed, afraid she would tip backward before they made it safely to the top. Grumblings flew from her mouth, but nothing he could make out as they passed through the dimly lit hallways.

Together they walked slowly, turning a corner until they entered her bedroom door. "Your meal should be ready soon. Make sure you don't fall asleep until after you eat and after someone helps you undress."

She mumbled something he could not understand as she opened the door and shuffled in with all the grace of a waddling goose. This time, however, she kept herself upright before placing her hands on the back of a cream, satin chair in the center of the room. His hand was on the doorknob, ready to close it before her shoulders shook.

"Claude is a person too," she hiccupped suddenly.

"What?" he asked, but she turned around and stumbled toward him. Tears welled in her eyes, and before he could register what she was doing, she disregarded the space between them and flung her arms around his torso. Every muscle stiffened as she hooked her fingers into his fur, her tears wetting his chest.

"Why is it that I am forced to live my life for others—for-for my family and I cannot do anything selfish for myself?" she cried, her voice muffled.

Arms spread wide, and he looked down at the mess of pins and curls that was her head with rounded eyes. Words escaped him as she clung to him like a weeping babe. What was he supposed to do? How was he to untangle himself? But as her sobs grew louder, her wet tears sank to his skin and thawed his panic. His frown deepened as his heart twinged for her. He could not stand there and do nothing.

When he could take it no longer, his arms tentatively encircled her, hovering over her shoulders in an awkward, non-touching embrace.

"Shh...it's alright," he said, hoping it was the right thing to say. "Don't cry."

"I-it's not okay," she wailed. "I want to be selfish."

"But you can. You should be selfish occasionally."

"So-so, why can't I have him? I-I don't ask for much. I do what I am told, and-and this is what I get? Why can't I have this one thing, Henri? Why can't I choose my-my happiness?"

Despite her blubbering, her words struck a deep chord in his heart. This ache, her sorrow—it was all too familiar to him and confirmed things he had worked to ignore for the past three months.

Marguerite had feelings for Claude. He was not angry or jealous, as he should have been because...

He still cared for Isa.

And as she clung to him, pouring her drunken despair over his chest, his lips trembled at the revelations piercing him like a well-aimed arrow.

"Why?" she demanded again. "Why, Henri?"

Closing his eyes, he placed one hand on her head. His claws curved around her skull as she cried.

"I do not know, Marguerite. I do not know."

27

Isa

Moonlight poured over the dining room as Isa swept. Cream curtains fluttered as she passed and maneuvered around her cleaning companion at the table. Claude had volunteered himself to polish silverware and relieved chatty Sanson of his duties for the night, and so she found herself in his company.

Not a word was exchanged between them, but she did not mind—the silence was a pleasant change for once. Sanson was a cheery man who could fill her ears with more stories about his childhood than she could keep track of, but his antlers always managed to knock a crystal strand from at least one of the chandeliers hanging above them. She climbed on a stool every night to fix it, but tonight, she counted on leaving it alone.

Hunched over the side of the table, Claude spared her no acknowledgment but shuffled into the table when she needed to get around him. She would peer at him every so often, but then her gaze would stray to the light gleaming from beneath the double doors leading to the kitchen as scurrying footsteps, clinking pots, and sizzling dishes sounded from the other side of the wall. It was unusual to have the kitchen staff up and running at this time of night, but a dish request must have been ordered since Joseph bounded through the doors and out again.

Claude kept his eyes on the silverware, his bulky fingers clumsy in their hold on the metal. Yet, she could not help but take a moment to fully observe her old friend from the corner of her eye.

A stone expression was carved on his face. Brows heavy over round eyes, there was a dark emptiness there, one burning out any trace of happiness. His lips tugged downward under his black nose. He rubbed a cloth over a knife in circular motions and then proceeded to put it down and move onto a fork with all the enthusiasm of an emotionless slab. He might as well have been a moving statue.

Sympathy pulled at her heart, but she resisted the urge to speak. She knew nothing she could say could ease his heartache, for nothing he had said to her had ever eased any of her pain.

She clenched the broom tighter as memories of those foolish times made her cringe and ache. It was a time she had selfishly anticipated when Henri would whisk her away behind his father's stables and kiss her until she was breathless. Hushed laughter and whispers were said against seeking mouths. Claude had not said a word, even as he stumbled upon them one afternoon. Despite their forbidden trysts lasting for two years, their friend never intervened.

A small part of her was grateful to him, and another part of her wished he would have spoken sooner to save them the heartache that inevitably came. Maybe they wouldn't have listened. Maybe they would have. But at least...at least she could taste the sweet innocence of adolescent love before the fantasy soured.

A sigh escaped her as she bent down to sweep the dirt into the dustpan, hoping to sweep those bitter-sweet memories away. Before she could move it into a bin, the door from the hallway leading into the room opened wide as Jeanette rushed in. Her scaly, black hands picked up her skirts as she jogged, her bulbous, black eyes set on the kitchen doors, and her large, papery white wings kissed the ground behind her.

"Oh no, oh dear," the maid said as she pushed through to the kitchen. Isa looked up at Claude, who did not remove his eyes from his task. His focus was so intense that she doubted he would stop even if a fire started in the kitchens.

Isa continued sweeping until Jeanette came out with a trolley and teapot. "Who is this going to?" she asked the moth woman and glanced at the clock. It was nearing ten in the evening. Those enormous, black orbs settled over Isa. The two feathery plumes from her head shook as she wrung her hands over the trolley's handle.

"Oh, to the miss upstairs. The master says she's quite upset. Crying a whole river, he says."

A rattle of sharp clanging echoed in the room, and Isa and Jeanette swiveled their heads toward Claude. The silver spoon in his hand had fallen and sprawled over the 'unpolished' pile of silverware. "Is she alright?" he asked.

It was best Jeanette didn't answer so as not to encourage him. "Do you need help with this?" Isa gestured to the tea, turning the moth woman's attention to her.

Relief was evident in her pinched face. "N-no, it's fine. I've got it. He said he only required me since he didn't want to overwhelm the miss. But I must get going."

"Of course." Isa ran ahead to hold the door open for her, and Jeanette offered her a small 'thanks' as she passed. As soon as the door shut behind her, she turned and stiffened. The pit of emptiness in Claude's eyes vanished into something fiery and dangerous. Never in all the years she had known him had she witnessed such unhinged determination in her friend. He used to be full of smiles and positive words, and now he stood like a man at his breaking point as his fists clenched over the table.

"I have to go to her," he said, and before she could blink, he abandoned his place by the table and marched toward the doors. Instantly, she placed her back there and held her feathery arms out.

"No. You don't."

"Did you not hear her?" He jerked his chin. "Our guest is upset and—"

"And you have no business with her."

His jaw slackened under his extended snout for a moment until he snapped it shut with a growl. "But I have every business ensuring *he* did not upset her."

He made to move around her, but she blocked his path. Their feet scuffled as they danced left and right. "No. That is their business, not ours—not anymore. You, above all people, know that."

"I—" He finally stopped and raked his large, paw-like hands through his golden hair, his ears flattening. "I cannot sit here and do nothing."

Her heart jerked at his raw vulnerability—a side she had rarely seen of him—but continued to bar him from exiting. This was the only way he would learn. "Yes, you can."

"I have done *nothing*, Isa. I have done nothing for a month, and I cannot stand it any longer."

"You must," her voice dropped into a low, firm tone. "You *must*. Or are you that selfish?"

A war of emotions flitted over his face—repressed anger, frustration, hurt—she saw it all until his features relaxed. An eerie, calm mask replaced the torrent of emotions. The shift was unnerving, but she took it as her cue to continue.

"With everything you told me after Henri," she lowered her voice to a heated whisper, conscious of anyone listening from the kitchens. "After everything you said to me, you want to stand there and act like you have any right to do the same?"

Nothing penetrated his mask as he stared at her, but she refused to bow and resumed her lecture. "You gave me your sympathies, but then you told me, *'We all have our place.'* Do you remember that? Because clearly, you don't. If you go marching up there, what will you do? What would you even say to her?"

"I would apologize."

She blinked, lowering her arms. "Pardon?"

"I have already stopped myself. I have told myself I was foolish for even...entertaining *this*." His hand circled in a wide motion toward himself and then upward to where their guest resided. "But

I feel I owe her this. I owe her an apology for betraying her trust and omitting the truth."

She shook her head. Curses, the man was stubborn, but she could not help but admire his sincerity—his unadulterated affection.

Looking into his puppy eyes reminded her of her younger, idiotic self, who believed love could conquer anything, including positions of power. She thought if maybe she had loved Henri enough, they could have run away together, or the Gods could have blessed her and magically bestowed her the status she needed to be with him. Those were foolish notions—stupid yearnings from a girl on the cusp of womanhood. Two years had passed before Henri brought her to the chateau, and although not long, it was more than long enough and painful enough to grow up and realize she could not have the man she wanted.

Claude needed to know it too.

Just as he stepped to reach the door again, she advanced and took a step forward in a challenge. "You don't owe her anything. You never did. And I imagine this would hardly be the time to do so, and if you go marching up there, I swear to you that I'll tell Henri. I'll get Pierre—anyone, and make sure they drag you down those steps before you can even reach her door."

He stiffened, and she watched as his determination flattened out of his eyes. "You would," he whispered, "You would do it."

"I would," she nodded. "I would do what I wished you could have done when our roles were reversed. Not only to save everyone but to save you from the heartache. You will thank me later when the curse is finally broken."

A mirthless chuckle broke from the pinched line of his lips. "I think it's too late for that."

"What do you mean?" Her arms tentatively lowered to her sides.

"My heart is already broken."

Before she could say another word, the double doors from the kitchen burst open, and another trolley was pushed out by a familiar face. Steam rose from a bowl in the center with sliced baguettes, and Anna paused in the doorway. Her triangular ears twitched on top of her wavy, brown hair as her yellow eyes landed on them.

"Am I interrupting something?" she asked.

"No, there is nothing to interrupt," Claude said unconvincingly. He turned from them and resumed his previous position at the side of the table. When Anna made no move to leave, he nodded toward the stew. "It's going to get cold."

"Ah, yes, of course," Anna said, exchanging a look with her, but Isa shook her head with a defeated shrug. Cupping her mouth with her furry hand, Anna whispered, "How is he?"

"He'll be fine," she mouthed back, but as she looked his way, she knew it was a lie.

Isa sat up in her cot, surrounded by darkness and her thoughts. The conversations she had with Claude repeated like a mantra. The sight of his hurt, mirroring her own, made her chest heave with unwanted emotions, and she winced but did not utter a word of discomfort when she plucked the feathers from her hands. It was a habit—a comforting ritual. Her once tan skin dripped crimson as she tore the black plumes by the root. Blood dripped in a curve down her wrists and onto her lap. Drips of it fell over the pile of feathers lying around her blankets.

Anna turned over in her sleep in her bed, and her ears twitched as Isa mechanically plucked herself raw. Her cat friend had already attempted to stop her multiple times for several weeks, but her eyes remained closed in the darkness, and for once, she did not wake to end her mutilation.

Anna must have been exhausted then. They all were. Their transformations were taking a toll on them.

But Isa was beginning to realize it did not matter how much she tore out or how bruised and red her body was. They always grew back with a vengeance. In the beginning, they did not grow for another week. In recent events, however, they returned within the hour, and three more would replace one. It was futile, like how she could not fight off the strange, new urges overwhelming her.

Shiny things—a collection of clear pebbles, a stolen fork, a button—were stowed away under the floorboard beneath her cot. There was no use for them—she understood this logically, but something possessed her to keep them and to keep them for herself. Like a stupid crow.

She was losing her mind.

The only glittering object she refused to stow away with her other "treasures" was the golden locket around her neck—a gift she kept, hung like a shameful token. For all her bluntness and harsh words to Claude, she was aware of how much of a hypocrite she was for keeping the item. She claimed him to be selfish but had selfishly held onto a reminder of sweeter days she still could not part from.

But, if she remained silent and never intervened with Henri and Marguerite, she felt she had every right to keep her gift. On the other hand, Claude was threatening to ruin everything—including the last semblance of happiness she clung to, which was why her friend needed to remain silent.

With those thoughts, she continued her abuse until Pierre, the butler, pounded on their wall on the other side where the men's quarters were.

"Rise and shine, ladies," he yelled despite the darkness still blanketing them. Servants stirred in their beds—all of them more beast than human as they yawned and shuffled into their shoes.

It was time to get up.

"Isa," a voice next to her hissed. "I cannot believe you."

She did not look at her friend even as the woman pawed at her shift. "It's nothing."

"It doesn't look like nothing."

Finally, she looked up to large, yellow eyes glaring at the fresh blood streaking her wrists. Hiding them was pointless, but a wince twisted her features as Anna reached for her hands with her furry ones.

"You must stop this," Anna said to her. "There is no need for this. The curse will be lifted within the month, and we will all return to normal."

Rather than responding, she looked back to the pucker marks on the back of her hands, all the way to her elbows. Some were already tight and hardened, ready to sprout even more feathers. Her friend tutted again before standing to dress, and Isa followed, focusing on getting ready rather than letting doubt erase any hope for them to return to 'normal' as Anna claimed.

As much as she feared Claude ruining what chances they had, a nagging feeling she suppressed told her that maybe it didn't matter if he interfered. Henri and Marguerite were as much of a match as oil and water.

Casting the thought aside, she tied her apron to her skirt and headed outside with the others. Glancing behind her, Claude followed the sleepy crowd, dressed impeccably in a navy, embroidered jacket, but his paw-like feet were bare. When they made eye contact, he nodded sharply to acknowledge her but picked up his pace to pass her.

He was still angry, but she could live with that.

Yet, she worried that he would not heed her word despite their conversation and do something foolish in his anger. She would have to warn someone to keep an eye on him, maybe even warn Henri. Doing so would probably end her friendship with him, but she had to believe it was in everyone's best interest.

And even though her friend would not be fine, not for a long time, it was a price they would both share.

28

Marguerite

S omething wet and slimy pressed against Marguerite's cheek, startling her awake. As soon as her eyes flew open, she groaned, clamping them just as fast as hot, sour breath washed over her. Bonbon nudged her, his nose cold against her temple, and she swatted him away.

"No, please, not now," she mumbled, drawing the heavy duvet over her head. Soft feet climbed over her body, and she curled into herself and rested her cheek against something smooth and cool. Her arms curled around the square object as she attempted to fall back asleep and ignore how her saliva felt thick and scratchy, like a bar of wood in her mouth. A dark haze loomed in her mind, expanding against her skull until it rattled and pounded for an escape.

As she felt herself slipping past the pain into weightless dark-ness, three knocks sounded against the door.

"Miss?" a voice called—one she recognized as Jeanette's. "Are you awake, miss?"

Bonbon barked and then whined, jumping from the bed and jostling her. The pounding in her head grew worse, ebbing and flowing like an icy tidal wave, and she screwed her eyes tighter together. How much did she drink last night? Her cheeks were stiff, and her eyelids were sewn shut with heavy seams. Foggy memories danced out of reach amidst the pain, but she abandoned the effort to grasp any of the broken images.

"Is it morning already?" her voice croaked beneath the duvet.

"I'm afraid it is, miss," Jeanette said, patient and motherly. "We brought a nice cup of tea for you."

Tea would soothe her sticky mouth and sandy throat, but the thought of consuming anything induced an unfriendly flip to churn in her stomach. "I don't feel so well."

"Oh no, miss!"

"I feel as though I have been run over by a carriage. Four carriages—maybe a hundred even. I think I drank too much last night."

"Oh, dearie. Will you be well enough for breakfast?"

Her stomach lurched at the mention of food. It was the last thing she wanted to think of as she struggled to sit up with her head spinning and toppling over. The square mystery object slid to her lap as she peeked from the covers. Her eyes cracked open, peeling past the sleep crust, and she winced at the blinding light. Who opened the curtains?

Her stomach convulsed once, twice, until she placed a hand to her mouth. "I do not know. I feel like I am about to be sick."

"Well, maybe breakfast might not be wise then," Jeanette said with a frown. "I will come back with a bowl. Look after her, Isa."

Wait—Isa? Through her bleary gaze, she spotted the feathered woman, wondering how she had not heard a second pair of footsteps enter the room. Bonbon barked, following Jeanette out of the door, his claws clicking as he scampered off.

The maid's eyes lowered, pouring tea into a porcelain cup. Her sharp, beak nose had grown longer, covering her mouth, and when she looked up to hand her the cup, Marguerite shook her head.

"No, thank you."

"It will make you feel better, trust me."

She hesitated before reaching out to the proffered drink. If it did not smell or look like wine, then perhaps her stomach would settle. She raised the cup to her lips, careful to take the smallest sip lest she vomit, and to her relief, the hot water soothed every parched crevice in her mouth—her throat—even pacifying the cursed headache pounding away against her skull.

"I should trust you more often," she said, smiling despite the tugging cracks in her chapped lips. She went to set it aside before Isa took it from her, and she offered her a hoarse "thank you."

Blinking, the room was half a blur, and she looked at her lap beneath the blankets to see what she had decided to sleep with in her drunken stupor. It was heavier than she thought as she dragged it out, but as soon as her eyes roamed over it, she threw the duvet over it with a fluttering heart.

It was a portrait—Claude's portrait she painted.

When she looked at Isa, memories stormed like a horrid cloud-burst. Flashes of herself laughing obnoxiously, stumbling up the stairs with a firm guide at her arm, bumbling words, tears, and...an embrace.

"Oh no...oh no, oh no, oh no, no, no, no," she groaned, pressing the heels of her palms to her eyes, attempting to stamp the images out. Most of them were hazy pictures, but the worst of them was glaringly clear. Memories like how she clung to Henri, sobbing free as a babe.

"What is it? You look pale."

Dropping her hands, Marguerite bowed her head, not daring to look up at Isa. She could not bear to look at her, nor anyone. For once, she was grateful she had no access to mirrors in her room, for she could not even stomach looking at herself. How could she have thrown herself at Henri? Or better yet, how could she allow herself to lose control of her drink last night?

As wonderful as the wine was in helping her loosen her tongue and forgetting her woes, this never should have happened. Yet, all she could remember was the face of Claude clouding her vision throughout the night. She had to erase him—drown him out—but at what cost?

"Miss? Are you alright?"

Isa's voice was soft and concerned, but it burned more shame through her. "No, I am not."

"Is it about last night?"

Marguerite stiffened; every nerve heightened as she looked up at the maid. Feathers framed Isa's face, leaving her skin only a space above her brows, down the bridge of her nose, and around her mouth, yet concern lay in her fowl-like eyes.

Slowly, she nodded her head. "I don't think I can see him today. Not now and not ever."

"Marguerite." Isa pushed the trolley so there were no objects between them. "What's wrong?"

Marguerite clenched both hands before flopping on her back, and the soft pillows cushioned her fall. "I made a downright fool of myself. I was careless of my drink and lost control of all my sensibilities. I do not remember much, but I know it was humiliating. Henri must think I am horrible."

"I doubt he thinks that low of you. He is not innocent with his drink either."

"You were not there. You did not see how I threw myself at him," she groaned, pulling a pillow to hide her face.

When she could not stand the silence a second longer, she pulled it from her face and peered at the woman. Isa's forehead creased; her mouth pinched as though she bit into something sour. The expression dissolved when they made eye contact, but it did not fool her. She understood the look.

"You think it too," Marguerite said, her frown twisting with her stomach. "You believe me horrible as well."

"No, not at all, miss." Isa shook her head.

"You do not need to spare my feelings. I am already ashamed, as it were," she sighed, gathering the goose-feather pillow to her chest. "But that is not all. It's not even the worst of it. I..." Dare she say it? "I think I might have mentioned Claude as well."

Another spell of silence sliced through her. Large stones of embarrassment splashed in her gut as she hung her head, waiting for judgment to pass from the maid. At last, Isa spoke, controlled and quiet, "What did you say?"

"I-I do not remember," she sputtered, hoping the woman would believe her—hoping it would dull the shame rising to drown her. "All I know is that I said something about him and then..." She blinked as more memories poured seamlessly through her mind. "Oh goodness, Isa. I acted like a fool in front of Henri. Crying like a child! I do not think I have the strength to face him."

"You do not have to this morning if you are truly feeling ill," Isa said, firm and fast. "Take a moment to rest before you see him...to think before approaching him again."

"Do you think I've ruined it? That I've destroyed my chances with Henri?"

"I doubt it would, but it depends."

"On what?"

"On whether you still have feelings for Claude."

Ice filled Marguerite's veins despite the resounding 'no' she wanted to retort. But none came—silence stole her words as she gaped at the maid.

"I—"

Without warning, a feathered hand grabbed the duvet and pulled it downward.

"Wait, no!" Marguerite said, but it was too late. The portrait was exposed, and the face of the man she could not rid her thoughts of stared kindly back at her. Isa studied the painting for a moment until recognition lit her face.

"This resembles Claude."

"I can explain!" Marguerite said.

"It's fine. You don't have to," Isa said, soft and without a hint of venom.

Did she hear correctly? Was she not angry? Marguerite looked to the maid and her brows furrowed in confusion. "No, you must understand because I don't want you telling your master of this. Please, it was painted before the deal."

"Then why do you still have it?"

"Because—" but the words died on her lips as she hung her head. How was she to explain herself? How was she to explain she meant to give it to the man she was never supposed to care for? How he hurt her and then repaid her with cold silence? Cut her deeper than any man had done before.

And yet, she did not have the strength nor heart to rid herself of it.

Let Isa think of her what she would. It did not matter. Even now, she clung to the portrait—to the man who never cared for her.

"You don't need to look so ashamed, you know," Isa said, cutting through her miserable thoughts. "It's perfectly fine to feel what you do."

"But I thought—"

"We cannot help who we are drawn to. But we can choose to either hold onto our emotions or let them go. If you truly are sincere about breaking the curse, then maybe you should confront these feelings inside you once and for all. Admit what they are and then abandon them."

Why was this woman being so kind to her when all she wanted to do was rip herself to shreds for how she felt? Yet, she could not deny the relief swelling in her breast as Isa's words wrapped her in the comfort she needed.

She picked up the portrait and looked at Claude's soft features with a trembling chin. "I am afraid they'll last with me forever."

"I understand." Isa stood but reached for her hand. The feathers tickled her palm, giving her the strength she needed. "Some feelings last for a lifetime. But time heals all things."

There was something wistful about how she spoke—something testifying to memories long ago. "You speak as if you know." Marguerite looked up at her. "As if you have experienced the same. Have you?"

"I..." Isa began but closed her mouth and glanced at their clasped hands, squeezing it once before releasing. "I have loved someone."

"What happened?"

Pain laced through Isa's expression as she reached for the cart. "He disappeared. A long time ago."

Marguerite opened her mouth to ask what she meant, but the doors opened, and Jeanette entered with a bowl. She shoved the portrait under the blankets beside her as the maid approached her bed.

"Are you still feeling sick, miss? I have this if you need it."

"Yes, thank you." She reached for the bowl, and Jeanette handed it to her.

"You weren't sick over the bed while I was gone, I see. Are you feeling better?"

The moth woman looked at her expectantly, and Marguerite gripped the bowl tighter. "I don't think I can join Henri for breakfast."

"Ah, no worries, miss." Jeanette's small lips tugged upward in a smile. "Do what you must to feel better, I say."

"Thank you." She eyed Isa, who left a teacup and saucer on the nightstand next to her. They exchanged a look. An empty, spiritless expression stole over Isa's face before the woman averted her gaze and continued to the fireplace to stoke the fires there.

Despite her encouraging words, whoever this love used to be for Isa, it was clear they never fully left her heart either.

29

Henri

The last rose bush was full of red blooms. The warm, August air wrapped around his fur, making him sweat, but Henri was not bothered by the heat as he scrutinized the other three bushes and frowned. Crisp, brown petals littered the ground, and despite the death that claimed them, their white branches had thorns that would slice through skin if he touched them.

He had walked through the gardens on numerous occasions with his guest, but it had been a long time since he had stood in front of the roses alone to ponder and reflect. The last time he had paused here was three months ago when Marguerite had seen him for what he truly was: a monster. He appeared threatening and beastly with her dog in one hand, ready to throw the runt across the gardens. He would never forget the fear in her eyes—the pure terror in them as she stared at him.

Much had changed since then.

However, despite his change in himself, he still did not feel romantic love for his guest.

Turning away from the roses, he made his way toward the chateau while a pit grew in his stomach at the thought of time slipping from him. With only mere weeks left, panic crawled under his skin at the thought of failing those who depended on him.

To make matters worse, the things Marguerite had said in her drunkenness last night replayed in his mind. Her tears had soaked through his fur, but her words wove spiraling knots in his gut. Surprise, dread, and sympathy combined to drive nails through his heart as she clung to him. Her words about Claude, about being free to love—

He did not need to be drunk to admit he wished the same for himself.

But what did that mean for them both? Were they both still so far from feeling the stirrings of love for one another? Was it all hopeless?

He entered through the dining room door with lumbering steps. Objects blurred together, and his feet felt cumbersome under his weight while he ghosted through the halls, passing faces he vaguely recognized as they bowed their heads in his presence.

Finally, he stopped and recognized where his feet had led him: the music room. It was a small space, with a pair of red velvet chaises and only one instrument occupying the corner of the room. It was large and painted dark forest green with golden detailing. After making his way toward the neglected harpsichord, he lifted the lid. He propped it to reveal a mural of a battle between heavenly beings and hellish creatures—the fight between Erus, the God of the Heavens, and Saleos, the God of the Hells.

The scriptures said that when Ghiana first formed Gallia, Saleos betrayed the Gods to fill the world with his hellish creatures. Erus and his Enchanters swept across Gallia to fight off the monsters and banished them, and Saleos, to a different realm: the three Hells. The story was a perfect reflection of the war raging in his heart.

When he sat down, the keys felt awkward under his elongated, clawed hands. It had been too long since he played, but his fingers began to move of their own volition. The brittle rattle of plucking strings came alive in a sweeping melody as his claws danced over the keys like a torrent rainstorm. It was a fast-paced, trilling song he stumbled through at first, but soon the memory of the notes came to him as he pushed through. All his confusion and forbidden desires came to the surface as he played, pouring his heart over the keys.

In this moment, he imagined a world without magic or curses and without hierarchy and restriction. A world where he did not have to hold back all the things he wanted to say to the woman who still plagued him. The woman who had comforted him supported him and spoken difficult words he needed to hear. The woman he might still...

Suddenly, he jolted when someone tapped him on the shoulder, and he whisked around on the seat. His heart stopped. It was the very woman he could not expel from his mind.

Isa.

Upon seeing his startled expression, she said, "I called your name, but you did not hear me."

"Ah, it's alright," he said after pulling his thoughts together. "Is there something you need?"

"I came to tell you that Marguerite is not feeling well and will not be joining you for breakfast."

"Oh." Although he enjoyed his time with his guest, a niggling feeling in the back of his mind told him he should have felt more disappointed at the statement. "Is she well?"

"She has drunken sickness."

"Ah." He nodded as understanding dawned on him. He had hoped the stew and bread he sent last night could have helped ease some of the inevitable sickness this morning, but it appeared she drank more than she could handle. "That's a shame. Tell her she is free to rest the entire day if she wishes."

Nodding, Isa turned to leave, but something caught his eye, and without thinking, he reached for her hand. Her arm tensed under his claws as he inspected the sizes of black feathers covering her skin, but she did not pull out of his grip. Turning the hand over, though, there were dozens of curious pockmarks littering her palm, and his brow furrowed at the sight. A dark, crusty substance caked the wounds, and she pulled her hand away just as he realized what it was.

Blood.

"Isa..."

"It's nothing," she said like she had rehearsed the statement several times.

"Clearly, it's not."

She clutched her hand to her chest and stepped away as he reached for her again. "And clearly, it's not your place to care," she said pointedly, and his seeking hand shrank back.

He knew perfectly well what she meant, and yet, "You know I cannot just sit idly by while you are injured."

"It doesn't matter."

His brows pinched together. "What do you—"

"It doesn't matter. None of it matters. Just forget what you saw."

"I cannot."

"You will." She jutted her chin out in the familiar way he knew she would not back down. At first, he wanted to counter her stubbornness until his jaw slackened with revelation upon thinking of the shape of her wounds.

She had done it. She plucked the feathers out. There were no other explanations for the bloody pockmarks, and when he looked into her eyes, a bitter sensation washed over him as he realized she was afraid, afraid of becoming a monster like him.

And it was all his fault.

The weight of this realization threatened to flatten his lungs to shreds. Isa was almost unrecognizable, and he was to blame. He had known this all along, yet the truth—the depth of it—sunk deeper in his bones.

Before he could speak, she turned away and walked out the door. This time, however, a fire set flame to his heart as he caught sight of something gold peeking around her neck, something he recognized and thought lost forever. Before he could douse the flames, he shot out of his chair to follow her.

"Stop this," she hissed as she walked ahead of him. "Leave me alone."

Ignoring her request, he pursued her through the halls until she pressed against the white double doors leading outside. They swung back in his face, but he easily pushed them and reached for her feathered hand again.

"Don't!" She whipped around, but he caught it despite her warning.

"Isabelle," he said, and she froze under his grip. The other palm she raised stopped in mid-strike as she stared at him.

He hadn't spoken her name since the day he had denounced her. The day he told her he did not love her and never did. The day he broke her heart.

As a young boy, he teased her relentlessly for how her name meant "beauty" when, in his eyes, she was nothing but a grubby little girl. At the time, he dubbed her the nickname "Isa," and the name stuck despite her chagrin.

It was not until they were teenagers, meeting in secret that he whispered her name like a prayer as he kissed her. She was Isabelle—his beautiful Isabelle, whose tan, rough skin was more alluring to him than the powdered, perfumed hands of women with whom his father attempted to match him. Those women did not want a lowly byblow.

But Isabelle did. She wanted him. She loved him.

And he had thrown it all away for all the things she would have happily lived without.

"I am so sorry," he said, not knowing what else to say to ease the guilt gnawing through him.

Those round, black eyes stared at him with burning severeness. She frowned under her sharp beak, but he refused to let go, and she did not fight him.

"For what, Henri? For this?" She raised the wrist he held and continued with biting sarcasm, "What could you possibly be sorry for?"

"For everything," he breathed, putting all his remorse and shame behind those two simple words. "*Everything.*"

The narrowness of her eyes did not relent, but before she could speak, he continued, "I am sorry for the curse, for bringing you here...for even pursuing a relationship with you. It was unfair, and as a future Count, I should not have sought you as I did. I was selfish and foolish. I was only thinking of myself as I always have. And ending it as I did..."

Henri shook his large head, his cloak of fur shifting over his shoulders. The swell of Isa's throat bobbed, and his brows pinched as he took her in. She stood with her hand clenched by her side, and a slight tremor ran through the one he held.

"It was cruel what I said to you. I should not have said what I did. I'm sorry," he said at last.

She said nothing, but he could feel the pressure of her gaze as he hung his head. For a moment, he thought she would stare at him until she bored holes into his skull, but then, she finally spoke. "Why? Why are you speaking of this now? You have no right to even bring up such things to me when you are promised to another."

Her touch burned now, but he could not retreat when there were too many unsaid words between them. "You are right. I have no 'right,' as you say, to confess these things given our circumstances, but you must know, Isa. When all this is done, I want you to know I lied to you that day."

By the way she tensed, he knew she understood what day he spoke of.

He pressed on. "I lied when I said I did not love you. That I never did and that you meant nothing to me. It was all a lie."

Isa's eyes widened and then tapered. He should stop now. Yet, he could not stop. Not when he had so much more to say.

"As selfish as I was, I do not regret our time together. You...you have always been a good friend to me, and I did not deserve you then as I do not deserve you now. I had never apologized for my actions until now, and all I can do is beg for your forgiveness and hope you do not hold hatred in your heart for me. But, even if you did, I could not blame you for it. I have been...monstrous. And I deserve every ounce of your anger."

Despite his confession, he held his breath, anxious she really did loathe him as he feared. Finally, her wrist slid out of his grasp.

"You do," she said at last. "You do deserve it."

He exhaled, allowing disappointment to escape from his lungs.

"But I don't," she said, avoiding his eyes and lifting a hand to the nape of her neck. Her fingers worked to unclasp the necklace he had given her—one he thought she had disposed of—before she held it out in her palm. "I don't hate you. I can't. Even after everything, even after this horrible curse. And I do not regret the time we shared either."

"You should, though," he said, even though exhilaration flooded every stretch of his veins.

"I know, but I don't, Henri."

"You should hate me for taking advantage of you as I did," he insisted. "I knew better. I should not have pursued you when I had more status over you. I had an unfair advantage over you."

"Do you think that I was seduced by your status?" she asked, and he blinked in surprise. "I'm insulted. I was perfectly in control of myself and old enough to understand what I was choosing. I understand what you are implying, but Henri...I wanted you. I wanted *all* of you, with or without your title. I just hope you loved me for me and not because you were lonely."

His mouth hung open, exposing fangs and tusks. "No, that's not—I loved you for *you*!" He made to reach for her hand, but she stepped back. "You must believe me, Isa."

"I suppose it doesn't matter," she sighed. A strange mix of sadness and relief twisted in her expression. "But I appreciate hearing you say it all the same."

The gold in her fingers glinted against the sun, and she waved for his hand. Confused, he stretched out his arm and opened his palm. She placed her hand in his and held her other hand over hers to prevent him from pulling away.

"I should have done this long ago," she murmured before looking into his eyes. "This is yours. I should have returned it to you the day you left me, but I held on. I am letting go now. You need to as well."

She unfurled her hand, dropping the still-warm chain in his palm, and he curled his claws over it to ensure its place. Metal cut through his skin when he clenched it in a tight fist.

"Do you remember when I gave this to you?" he asked.

"Henri, don't," she warned, but he shook his head.

"Humor me," he said, a desperate plea. "Just allow me this. One last time." Despite the storm brewing beneath her eyes, she said nothing, giving him permission. "Do you remember?"

"Of course, I do," she whispered.

Opening his hand, he untangled the chain and held it in the light. "It was by the oak tree...the one you loved so much? The one we spent hours looking up into those branches?"

"Yes," she said, closing her eyes like she was savoring the memory also.

"Is it still in here?" He gestured to the oval locket, and she opened her eyes and nodded. It was difficult to unlatch it with his claws, but after a moment, it opened, and his eyes softened at what lay inside.

To anyone who might have come across the locket, they might have been confused at seeing the tiny, pressed object. It was the first leaf that fell in her hair as they sat under his father's oak tree for the first time. He kept it as a token and a reminder of the day he knew he loved her.

Instead of touching it, he closed the locket once more, preserving the leaf and memories inside.

"I gave this to you the day I confessed my love for you...and you laughed at me." His smile pained him. "But then you said, '*I know, I have known for a long time.*' You always seemed to know what was in my heart long before I recognized it myself. But...do you know now?" he asked, seeking confirmation. "Can you tell me what I feel now?"

"No," she said, taking a step away from him. "Only you can decide that. But, please, for all our sakes, figure it out before it's too late. Time is running out."

"I know," he said, tension building between his brows. She was right, but this moment between them was ending too soon.

He closed the distance between them in one swift movement, reaching for her hand again before she could flee altogether.

He pressed his papery-thin lips over the back of her hand in a light kiss. Warmth and bitterness clashed—desire and sorrow—shattering his heart. But he could not help but relish how the feathers tickled his skin, and he bowed his head over her fingers, willing the moment to last just a second longer.

Please, he prayed, hoping the Gods could ease the way he ached at her touch. But there was no time. There never was.

He had to let go.

Soft fingers slipped from his claws, and she finally walked away. Only when he looked up, glancing at the third floor, did he see a brief silhouette at the window. Cream curtains fluttered, and he realized he had been watched.

30

Marguerite

Heart racing, Marguerite pressed her back against the wall with both hands clutched up at her sternum. Heavy curtains rippled beside her as she slid to the ground, her heart sinking in tandem.

The scene flashed in her thoughts, burning the memory into her brain.

She should have been content to wallow in her misery rather than be drawn to the familiar voices speaking outside. Undeterred by the little hammers rattling in her skull, she drew closer until she quietly opened her window and peered below.

Most of their conversation was muffled by distance and quiet tones, but the one line she heard dropped like stones to the pit of her stomach.

"*I gave this to you the day I confessed my love for you...*"

Love? Henri had loved Isa? Did he still now?

And that kiss.

Despite his large form, the way he gently held her hand, the way his misshapen lips caressed skin and feathers had made her blush and stare. She should have looked away from the scene, too intimate for her eyes, but could not. Something rooted her to the spot and compelled her to witness the anguished creature who was loath to let the hand go.

Now she sat, heart still warring in her chest like thousands of soldiers trampling on everything she thought she knew. All her thoughts dispersed like the breeze pushing through the curtains she closed in panic. They pulled in different directions, forcing betrayal, anger, and confusion to battle for precedence.

However, the first thought pushing through the foggy aftermath was the image of Isa in her room only twenty minutes prior. The woman had been here, standing only a few paces from where she stood, encouraging her to abandon her feelings for Claude once and for all.

It was shocking. Scandalous. And most of all:

Hypocritical.

Was this the lover—the man—Isa had spoken of? The man who had "disappeared?" If it were true, her love had not gone very far. Living under the same roof as the man hardly counted as "disappearing." How could she have been so foolish as to fall for another horrible lie?

Yet, the Isa she knew was straightforward and true, like an arrow. She did not seem to be a model of deception, and she had walked away from Henri after he kissed her hand. It seemed he wanted her to stay.

But why?

By the way they spoke in hushed tones and exchanged what she could make out as a necklace of some sort, it was evident there had been or was an intimate history between them. She hadn't the foggiest idea about their history and how long ago it happened.

But, if she was forced to give up everything if she desired to make things work between them, so should he.

Lunging up, she stormed from the window as bitter emotions burned under her skin. Her mind whirred, spinning for ideas of what to do or what to say to the man she was fated to love—a man who was supposed to love her in return. Nothing was going as planned despite everything she had put into the relationship. All those days, those hours at his side—did they mean nothing?

As she paced, she stopped in her tracks as she spotted the portrait where it lay across the duvet. Picking it up, she ignored the tug on her heart and allowed the heat in her veins to pool around the lingering hurt.

Her advice remained sound despite her new, conflicting feelings about the bird woman.

She would do what Henri clearly could not: confront these emotions and finally get rid of the portrait once and for all.

Claude

It had been thirty days since Claude had spoken to Marguerite. Thirty days of silence, of stealing glances when he should ignore her.

No matter how much he wished to forget the passing of time, each day counted like a chiseled tally in his heart. He wanted to apologize on several occasions—wanted to explain himself—but Isa continued to intervene and convince him otherwise.

Besides, Isa was right. What good would it do to apologize now Marguerite had Henri to cling to? They were getting along just fine now. She did not need him. She never did.

No, it was best he resumed his duties and pretended his feelings for her were a trick of his imagination. The hurt and despair he felt were nothing. The longing burning in his heart was nothing.

It was nothing.

But, on the evening of the thirty-first day, he saw her from his window.

The frills of lace hanging from her dress glided over the grass as she approached the servants' quarters. The moon was a thin crescent in the sky, and the candle in her hand illuminated her face like a somber, glowing angel. His canine eyes could make out every detail of her figure despite the darkness and noted the large, square object tucked under the other arm.

Heart thundering, he ignored the warnings Isa had given him, all the risks of not breaking this curse, and raced through the quarters to meet her.

Marguerite stopped in her tracks when he shut the door behind himself. The warm breeze tugged at their clothing, and for a moment, he was afraid to breathe a word lest she change her mind and turn the other way.

She nodded to the object under her arm. "This is for you."

With both of her hands occupied, he stepped forward and gently took the item from her. It was a canvas, he realized, as the side he looked at was blank, but the other side—

He studied it before his mouth slackened. Could this be him? The question sat in his eyes as they shot up to hers, but she was already turning to leave. "Wait. Marguerite, wait, *please*."

To his amazement, she stopped and turned to him again. The emptiness of her eyes and her silence should have given him reason to pause, but the words erupted from his mouth.

"I am sorry. Please—I—whatever you heard that day, I want you to know I didn't mean any of it."

His fingers tightened over the canvas while his heartbeat swam up his throat. An increasing shininess glazed over her eyes before she lowered her gaze.

"As you might have heard, I have made a promise with Henri that we would not lie to each other," she said slowly. He was confused, wondering how her statement related to what he said before she continued, "And so I wish you would follow that same promise."

His eyes widened. "Marguerite, no I'm not—"

"Because I cannot stand seeing you lie to my face like this," she interrupted him.

"I swear to you—"

"You do not need to swear. You have proven yourself already. Your silence was enough of a confession," she said. He wished to soothe the sadness from her eyes, but her words fixed him to the spot. "You claimed to be my friend and could have come to me at any time, and you did not. How do you explain yourself?"

He could not. Sharpness gathered at his ribs like he had been trampled and kicked by a stampede of horses. He half wished he had been because it might have been preferable to the pain he was experiencing now.

"You are right," he said after a pause. "You're absolutely right. I've shown you I'm not as trustworthy as I made you believe. I shouldn't have lied to you. And more importantly, I should have apologized much, much sooner. For that, I'm deeply sorry. I didn't mean to hurt you. I never did. But let me explain that day. Henri commanded me to—"

"I don't want to hear your excuses either. I...I have thought about it and refuse to be *duped* again." The words were quiet as she stood taller. "Perhaps you do not know me well enough, but I cannot stand to feel foolish as you have led me to feel. Especially since you put on a show of being my friend and for making me believe—" She stopped suddenly, swallowing down whatever else she was about to admit.

Securing the portrait under his arm, he took a step forward. "Believe what? Tell me, please, so I may know the extent of the pain I have caused you."

The sharpened edge of her stare dissolved, but her lips did not move to speak.

"Marguerite," he said softly. "Please."

"I believed you," she said, a whisper in the dark. "I believed you when you said my passions were noble. That I was talented and...and I was...never mind. This must sound absurd to you anyhow."

"No, it isn't. I understand why you feel hurt and betrayed."

"I do not think you do, not entirely. But it doesn't matter. It never did, and it never should have."

"It matters to me."

She opened her mouth, a denial on her lips, but she looked up into the stars instead. "If it ever did...if it ever mattered to you...it was foolish all the same. We were both foolish."

"I don't believe that," he insisted, as a clawing feeling wound up his throat.

"No?" she said, her head still tilted upward. The two birthmarks near the hollow of her throat he admired so much were on display like pressed kisses to the skin, and the sight undid him.

All the emotions he suppressed about her, all the lies he told himself, were banging against the walls he fortified in his heart. He clutched the object that solidified what he had bottled and denied being true.

"No, I don't believe it. Not for a second, because I want you to know I meant every word I said to you in private. Our conversations, our friendship—all of it still means something to me even after all this time. It wasn't a lie. I care about you more than you know and...more than I should." Her eyes widened as he met hers with unwavering determination. "And that matters to me. It matters because every time I look at you, my heart breaks, knowing fate has brought you here to be with another. And even if it hadn't...I would never be good for you."

"Claude."

"I do not know the extent of what you feel—" Without warning, the word cracked in his throat into a high-pitched bark, like those of her little Bonbon's. He stiffened, covering his mouth with his hairy hand.

Her hand unclenched at her side, and her face slackened with surprise. Another emotion worked its way over her features, one he never thought he would see from her: pity.

He hated it. It was a reminder of what was happening to him—to all of them. Of the control he was losing over his thoughts and body. He tried to open his mouth again, only for another bark to escape.

No, not now, he pleaded to the Gods. Not when he finally had this chance to speak to her.

"Claude," she whispered his name more gently. "It's fine." It was a silent plea for him to stop, to cease whatever else he would confess. But he lived in silence for too long. Lived like a coward.

Blast the curse.

If Henri were stupid enough not to fall in love with her already, then he and everyone would live and die as animals within the month, and he would never forgive himself for stopping now.

Gritting his teeth, he forced the words out.

"And I know it might be foolish even to admit that I care for you here and now, but fine. Let me be foolish. I know what's at stake, I understand my life is forfeit under this curse, but I have lived my whole life on the whims of others. I have never felt more alive and *seen* as I have felt with you. Perhaps it's selfish of me to say all this to you now, but I could not live with myself knowing I never had the chance to stand before you as I am. Not as a *dog* but...as a man falling in love with you."

She stiffened, yet sparkling tears pressed in her eyes. But now, with those words finally free, they gave him the courage to shrink the distance between them. She did not back away. She did not move even as he touched her face for the first time. The tips of his fingers had formed into rough and hardened paw-like pads, but he cradled her cheek with gentleness. To his amazement, she closed her eyes and leaned into his touch. A tear slid down her cheek and looped between his index finger and thumb.

"I love you," he whispered, hardly believing the truth flowing out of his mouth. Her eyes fluttered open. It was crazy, stupid, and downright improper. Yet his heart was nearly bursting.

"I love you, Marguerite. I love when you smile and brighten the whole room with your presence. I love when your tongue peaks out when you concentrate and when you snort when you laugh," he half-chuckled and sighed an aching breath. "But most of all, I love you for your courage, your kindness, and your passions. And I...I wish...I wish I were the one you were meant for."

More tears fell from her hazel eyes as she stared up at him. All the hurt he witnessed there melted away as her hand met his own. She held it there, a clash of slender fingers over his bulky ones before gently removing them from her face. The candle in her other hand flickered in the cold breeze until it was snuffed out. Smoke coiled like a wreath above her head as she held his hand at their sides.

"I..." she began. Even in the darkness, he could see the emotions wrestle over her features.

Realization of what he said—how he had dared touch her—jolted his senses, but he stood, unwavering before her. He understood the weight of his words and accepted the consequences that came with them. If it meant she would never talk to him again, or if it meant Henri's wrath, it did not matter. He only regretted the tears that continued to slip down her cheeks. Adjusting the canvas under his arm, he reached for them, but she evaded his touch.

Barbs hooked around his heart, but he respected her space.

After an eternity of silence, she squeezed his hand before releasing it. "I am sorry," she whispered.

Who knew three words could completely shatter him? Despite the torn pieces of his heart dropping to the bitter bile of his stomach, he smiled—the one mask he perfected for moments like this. "No...no, do not be sorry. Never be sorry for how you feel. I put you in an awkward position. But I am glad to have been fully honest with you."

Her silence only solidified the reality of her rejection. Yet, the smile stretched even higher across his cheeks to the point where they ached and screamed in protest.

"It's late, and perhaps you should retire to bed?" he suggested with false cheeriness. "I do not want Henri to worry about you too much after you have been in bed all day today, right?"

She nodded, still unable to look at him.

"Would you like me to light your candle before you go? I don't want you tripping or bumping into things," he said, keeping his mouth busy.

"It's alright," she said at last. "I know the way."

"Very well." Another piece of his heart dropped when he thought no more could be spared. "I wish you a good evening, and thank you for the painting, Ms. Dupont."

She winced as if he had struck her, but he could not understand why. Clearly, she did not feel the same for him as he had thought and hoped for. All the cues of attraction on her end were just foolish misunderstandings on his part. And, regardless of if he had been correct, it was stupid to assume she would ever return his feelings. She was meant for Henri, and Henri was meant for her. He was not a part of the equation. He never would have been, curse or not.

Even so, he wavered at the sight.

"Thank you," she murmured and had his hearing not been heightened, he would have missed it as she turned to leave.

But he could not go to bed, not now, when everything inside of him threatened to collapse and cease functioning. No, he needed a walk first, away from the quarters...away from the chateau...and her.

With the portrait still under his arm, he walked over wet, cold grass and toward the line of trees. Perhaps he could find solace there. Maybe he could find a nice-looking stump or tree, curl against it, and let his mind float away. That sounded nice.

However, he paused mid-step, his ears perking at the sound of fast, approaching footsteps.

When he turned around, he let out a wheezing *'oomph'* as a body collided with his. Slender arms wrapped around his torso, pressing him against a warm, trembling form. His eyes doubled in size as he looked down at the woman he thought would never speak to him again.

"Marguerite," he whispered.

31

Marguerite

"Marguerite," Claude said again, breathless. "What—I thought—"

"I know," but she could not look up at him. Not yet. If this were all the time they would have, she would hold onto it, memorizing how he felt under her arms—warm and lean. The way his heartbeat thundered under her ear. The way he slowly relaxed in her embrace and wrapped his arm around her in return. The other arm was loose at his side, still holding the portrait she gave him like he could not bear to let such a gift be soiled and touch the ground.

All this time, she thought he used her and then abandoned her when Henri did not need him. Refusing to break again, she had resolved herself to stand strong, building walls of bitterness to protect herself.

But hearing all he confessed cut through her defenses, allowing old emotions to weasel their way in and destroy those walls—her crumbling fortitude. Yet, she refused to fall. She could not abandon her promise to Henri. Determination drove her to ignore all she heard and pretend she felt an inkling for Henri as she did for the man who walked away from her. The curse had to be broken. She must not give in to the pull drawing her to the valet.

Her eyes betrayed her as she glanced at his retreating form.

No.

She must be strong.

Yet, she could not look away. She stared after him in the darkness, watching how he drifted away into the night, an invisible grapple hooked into her heart and...

She knew she was not that strong. The candle thudded to the ground, and she ran.

"I...I thought I could walk away," she said. "I thought I could just go back into my room and forget everything you said." She looked up at him with tears curving around her chin. Warm, light brown eyes met her own with shimmering emotion. Those eyes had transformed into rounded orbs like Bonbon's, but their sincerity was not lost. He was still Claude—the man who stirred feelings she was still too scared to accept and continued to frighten her even now.

"Maybe you should have," he said, brushing a strand of hair from her face. When her face fell, he smiled. "Because now I don't want to let you go."

She leaned her head against his chest, and the buttons on his coat were cold on her cheek. "I cannot bear to let go either."

"Then don't," he whispered and rested his pointed ear against her own. It was soft and tickled her skin, but she did not move away. Rather, her hands moved higher over the brocade material of his coat and fastened themselves over his shoulders. Instinct had taken over, and she refused to let any thoughts of propriety ruin this moment.

Was this what it was supposed to feel like with Henri? Warm like sunshine. Tender and sweet. Freedom.

None of those feelings came to her heart for the Count. They were present here in Claude's arms. But thoughts of her new intended burst the happy moment. This could not last. It should never have.

Every limb screamed at her as she pulled away from him, but his free arm slid down hers and kept her close.

"I was going to walk away without telling you that...that I also wish you were meant for me, I..." she said, and his hand reached for her face to wipe the tears. Another confession lay at the tip of her tongue, but she held it back and hoped she could say what she was too afraid to say in other words. "I also have felt *seen*. I felt it when you told me I could do anything—become anything. I felt it when you said you would buy one of my painted snuff boxes even if it were designed for ladies," she chuckled, but the memory burned her eyes. "I felt it when you brought me your father's tea." At this, her voice cracked, and another wave of tears consumed her. "It was so simple but so kind. I have never received a kinder gift from a man."

"Don't you mean dog?" He smiled sadly.

"No." She shook her head. "A man. A kind, gentle man." Impulse drove her hand toward his face, and she cradled his soft cheek. "A man I must save now."

His hand rested over her own. He then turned his cheek and pressed what little lips he had to her palm. It was soft, like his warm breath ghosting her skin, but it broke her all the same. "I wish you were not burdened with such a task. It's not fair for you."

"There is no other who can," she said. "It has to be me."

"What if it doesn't have to be?"

Her fingers twitched over his cheek. "Who else then but me?"

Silence and a frown met her question. She was seeing more of those on his mouth this evening, and it shot spikes into her stomach.

"I know," he said. "I know, and even if there were another way, I know I would never be suitable for you."

Finally, his grip loosened, but she was too stunned to move her hand away. His wording was familiar to her. Words she had thought she stowed away because she'd been sure she solved its riddle came back with full force:

"*Love is a choice, precious and free, treasure the one who is suitable to thee. Know that all is possible but choose well. Only then can you break the spell.*"

In an instant, the fantasy she allowed herself—the one where it was acceptable to throw her arms around him, holding on for dear life—was shattered. Claude was right. Even if she was not forced into loving Henri, how could she allow herself the freedom to love him? Mother...and Papa...they would never understand. They would think her mad even if her chances with Mr. Bellanger were dismal. And if she did not break this curse, the man before her might never be a man again.

Yet, knowing all this did not make it easier to part from him. All she wanted was to be looked at like how he was looking at her now—like she was spring itself, breathing life into his soul. When would she ever find a man who would gaze at her like that? Was it worth never having again?

Perhaps it did not matter. It was never a choice she could make.

"If it were up to me," she said, "you would be suitable. You would be more than enough for me."

His mouth stretched upward, but it quivered like he couldn't decide whether to smile or cry. It straightened into a hard line in a flash, but his eyes glazed with gratitude and emotion she now recognized as...affection. It was exhilarating but strange to understand what the spark was behind his eyes. She attempted to deny its existence all this time, but now it stared at her, unflinching and unapologetic. Looking down, she followed his gaze to the portrait still in his hand.

"Was it accurate, at the very least?" she asked, sniffing.

Bringing up the portrait, his eyes scanned the painting and a soft grin formed beneath his snout. "Yes," he said at last. "I hardly recognize this man anymore, but if memory serves me right, I cannot believe how accurate you were. Except..."

"Except what?" Worry folded over in her chest.

"I think you made my nose too handsome. Look at how straight it looks." He smiled and turned the picture toward her. It was too dark to make out the details, but she had already memorized it in her heart.

"Is your nose crooked?" she laughed, a pathetic breathy sound.

"Depends."

"Depends?"

"If you would still think me handsome."

It was a jest, but the chuckle in her throat strangled her. When she thought she could not afford more tears, another one slid down her cheek. "I would."

"You say that now, but just wait until the curse is broken. Perhaps you might change your mind."

"I doubt that," she whispered.

"We shall see." He wiped another stray tear near her mouth. "You, on the other hand...you will always be beautiful."

Warmth flooded her chest. He thought her beautiful. No.

She shook her head and attempted to crush the weightless bliss threatening to whisk her away into the stars. How could she stay true to Henri when her thoughts would stray to another? She could not do that to him. It was wrong. It was unfair. It was—

Even if Henri *might be thinking of another?* her thoughts whispered as the image of him kissing Isa's hand surfaced. Just hours ago, she witnessed a secret unfold before her eyes. The man she believed was getting along with her was holding onto something that could ruin everything. Yet, how could she confront him now that she was holding on just the same?

What a hypocrite she was.

A feather-light touch at her chin broke her thoughts. One of Claude's fingers lifted her face so her eyes could meet his. She must have had a somber expression because his thumb swept the edge of her lips upward, coaxing her to smile.

"No more frowns tonight, not with me, at least," he said.

"You say that as though we will not have to part and forget that any of this ever happened."

His thumb by her lip paused and then slid toward the base of her skull. The weight of his hand cradled her neck there, creating sparks to explode in her belly. Her eyes fluttered close as he shrunk the distance to kiss her forehead.

"I understand if you must forget." His words caressed the skin there before he pulled away. "But I shall treasure it forever."

Throat clamping, her breath hitched, but she refused to cry. Too many tears had been spilled—too much grief had poured from her heart. Instead, she allowed the sincerity of his words to wash over her like dripping pearls of water. Even as the August wind blew around her, the tenderness she felt warmed her from the inside out. If she had the choice, she would capture time, rearrange the stars, and hold this moment in her hands forever.

Perhaps she did not need to. Not when she knew her heart had penned it to memory.

Finally, she parted from him, already aching for his touch, and gave him the one thing she knew he wanted that evening.

Her smile.

Despite the pain she felt, it was genuine as she pushed all her gratitude and joy she felt toward him into that one simple action. It was all she would give him before turning away from him for the last time.

32

Marguerite

Marguerite forced a pleasant smile as Henri pulled out a chair for her.

"Are you sure you're feeling well?" he asked after she sat at the small table with a large chessboard set up in the parlor. "I know you have been ill for the past couple of days. Are you sure you don't want to keep resting?"

Nodding, his concern touched her, and her smile was eased of its strain. "No, I'm more than well now. I think it was the change of cold weather."

The lie came out easier than she expected, but it felt wrong on her tongue. Even though she wanted to be honest with him, how could she explain she was both humiliated by her drunken display four nights ago and heartbroken by a man she could never have?

Three days passed since the confrontation with Claude, of pretending to be ill when she was in good health. Yet, no amount of time was enough when images of Henri kissing Isa's hand also swirled around her paralyzing emotions. Every day, she debated whether she should confront him about the matter, but did she have the right to after she threw herself in the arms of another man?

No, she did not. Perhaps it was best they both kept their secrets.

After all, it was not too late. Love would come. She loved him as a friend; more affection was bound to follow. Twenty-six days would be enough.

She could not waste any more time. By the fourth morning, she gathered her courage and finally went out to face Henri.

Now, she stared at a pawn before her, debating whether to sacrifice it to Henri's rook or take his other pawn. It shouldn't have been so difficult to choose, but memories of sweet touches and a bitter goodbye made little room for rational decisions.

Each chess piece was a polished red or cream piece of painted wood with solemn, carved faces, staring up at her to make her choice. Finally, she took his pawn; in turn, his rook took hers. It might have been the wrong choice, but for the first time in months, her competitive spirit did not care.

Joseph came to her side with a bottle of wine, interrupting her thoughts. "Would you like a drink, miss?"

His large whiskers twitched over his protruding mouth, and his morphed fingers held the bottle with both hands clasped over it.

"No," she said as shame and temptation coursed through her. "I think not. Thank you, Joseph."

"Of course," he turned away, and she looked back to the board before a dull *thunk* sounded behind her. The bottle had slipped from Joseph's hands and rolled toward her feet. It was a miracle it didn't shatter, and he stooped to pick it up. Without opposable thumbs, she watched as the bottle slipped out of his hands over and over again.

"I can get it for you." She reached down but was cut off when he lifted a furry-paw-like hand to stop her.

"No, allow me, miss."

A protest sat on her lips, but she held it back when she saw how determined he was to accomplish the small task. After three attempts, he finally picked it up with both hands and smiled at her triumphantly. As he turned the other way, knots twisted in her stomach, and a weight settled over her shoulders.

His life and all the lives here were at stake, yet they did their best to retain their humanity. Her eyes swept over the three servants in the room, and each face inspired guilt to drop in her stomach.

What was she doing?

They depended on her and the choice she would make. If she continued to wallow in her self-pity, for her feelings for Claude, they would be cursed as animals forever.

She could not let that happen.

After she made another careless move with another pawn, her eyes landed on Henri, who sipped his tea with careful, steady claws. For a moment, she pushed aside all the pain, all her emptiness, and tried to imagine what he would look like beneath his large, hairy exterior.

Would he have blond hair? Chestnut? Or dark, ebony locks? Would his eyes be as blue as they were now? Would he be tall and lean? Or short and stout? Whatever he looked like, it was easier imagining herself by his side...

As a Countess.

She imagined attending many events and balls with him by her side. Together, they could combat the whispers of his parentage, and she would hold his hand through all their difficult challenges.

It was not an unpleasant image. In fact, it was a life she secretly dreamed of leading with whoever her parents would match her with. And knowing by the end of all this, they would be married and in love...

Perhaps it was a future worth fighting for.

"What are you thinking about?"

Blinking, her gaze refocused back on the beastly creature before her. For once that afternoon, she had something honest to say. "I was thinking of what you must look like—without the curse, I mean."

"Oh?" He set the cup down and made another move with his rook. "Are you afraid you will be disappointed?" he chuckled darkly.

"No, I'm curious to know what my intended will look like. It's easier to picture our life together if I have a face to go with it. I cannot find any portraits either," she explained.

"It's because none have ever been commissioned."

"Never?"

"I didn't have the choice."

"I don't understand."

He paused and then sighed. "My family did not want any memory of me. If they had their way, I would have been tossed out of my father's home as soon as he died."

"Oh."

"It's of no consequence now." He waved a hand to dispel the awkwardness, but her heart continued to twist. "What would you like to know about my appearance?"

It felt wrong to push something serious aside, but she would comply with his question. "How tall are you?"

"If I recall...I think I'm about this tall," he raised one of his long, thick arms up, down, and up again. "About there. I wrote it down the last time I measured. I was six feet, but who knows what happened in the meantime." He shrugged.

"You are quite tall." She moved her knight. *Taller than Claude*, she thought. "How about hair? What color is it?"

"Black." He claimed her knight with his own.

"Eyes? Are they the same blue?"

"Not quite."

Her brows furrowed. "What do you mean?"

"They don't look so frightening as they do now." The top of his lip stretched upward into what she interpreted to be a smirk. He revealed sharpened teeth, but time had dampened their frightening nature. Smiling in return, her eyes strayed to her pieces, where she made another move.

"This is not like you." Henri nodded at her bishop she had placed next to his pawn. It was another reckless maneuver on her part, and he claimed it between spidery claws, raising it so they could inspect it together. "You are usually more thoughtful with games."

"You think so?" She fluffed her skirts at her side, feigning innocence. "What if I'm executing a new strategy?"

"A losing one?"

"An unconventional one." She tipped her chin up in a mock challenge, feeling her usual competitiveness again.

"I see." He hummed as she made another move. Instead of claiming her piece again, he moved another pawn, leaving himself wide open. "It seems as though you are distracted. Perhaps something is on your mind?" Suddenly his voice deepened, and his eyes narrowed. "Something you are not telling me?"

"N-no, there is nothing to tell." She took his pawn and hoped that denying his accusations would force him to drop whatever he was insinuating.

"Pity, I thought you would be honest with me."

Her skin flushed. "Honest about what?"

For a moment, he was silent as he took her second knight. She only had a few pieces left, and she realized too late that he had won. Every piece surrounded her king, and he looked at her with a pointed stare.

"About Claude."

Checkmate.

The word was written all over his cerulean eyes, but he did not say it out loud. He did not need to, not when she froze like a hare in the jaws of a wolf. Yet, as they held each other's gazes, there was no trace of anger on his face, and his demonic shadows had not appeared either. Suddenly, he snapped his fingers, and the three servants stood at attention.

He did not break his stare as he said, "I would like some privacy with Miss Dupont. You may be dismissed for now. Thank you."

Fear, dread, and anxiety crept up her spine as they shuffled out of the parlor. Its emptiness made the room much bigger, leaving her feeling small under his stare.

"What is this all about?" she ventured cautiously.

"I thought we could talk in private. Servants have ears, you know. And eyes as well."

Marguerite swallowed, her mouth becoming dry like cotton. If Henri was implying what she thought he was implying, she was in trouble.

"Well, what do you wish to speak to me about in private?" Her voice cracked despite herself, and she attempted not to look so stiff across from him.

Sighing, he pushed the chessboard to the side to place his elbows there. "I realize I'm not the best at confrontation," he admitted, and his words relieved her. "I'm not angry, or at least, not in the way you might think I'm angry, but I thought it best to speak to you alone about what a servant informed me of."

"And what did they inform you about?"

"They saw you and Claude. Together. Three nights ago."

"Oh." Her breath flattened out into one syllable. It was more of a squeak as her heartbeat flooded up to her ears.

"Again, I am not upset even though I have every right to be," he continued. "To be honest, I am more frustrated with you avoiding me and not being honest with how you felt. Jeanette told me you were not feverish in the slightest. She suspected the same as I—that you weren't as ill as you pretended to be. You were simply avoiding me."

"I..." What was there to say? He figured it out.

"And I know you also saw me with Isa four days ago. I don't know how much you saw or heard, but I know you saw enough."

Her head snapped up before she nodded in defeat. "Yes."

"I thought so," he sighed, rubbing his fingers over his naked brow. "I wish you had confronted me before you visited Claude."

Understanding dawned on her. "I did not go to him out of spite, if that's what you're implying."

"No?" The question was genuine, and she nodded stiffly. "Well, if what you say is true, I can admit to being wrong about your intentions. Why did you go to him, then?"

Her gut tightened, forcing out her held breath. Speaking about another man to the man she was supposed to be in love with was awkward, to say the least. But he was sitting there, patient, which gave her the courage to explain herself.

"I...I did it because I wanted to give him something." At his confused expression, she continued, "I promised him a painting months ago. I completed it but never gave it to him. It sat in my room, and I couldn't bear to keep it with me any longer, so I thought I would finally give it to him."

"There was more, though, wasn't there?" he said, steepling his claws together.

"Yes," she admitted, cringing.

"Do you have feelings for him? Please be honest."

His voice was surprisingly gentle, coaxing her to be brave. "I do. Do you have feelings for Isa?"

"Yes, but we have made an understanding with one another."

She squeezed her hands over her dress. "What does that mean?"

"It means I am letting go of those old feelings," he said, but a dark weight seemed to pull his features into a frown. "I am focusing on you and you alone now."

"I," she began, and the memories of turning on Claude three nights prior filled her mind. She made her choice. Now she must stand by it. "Claude and I have made a similar understanding."

"So, you will not be sneaking off into the night to meet him anymore?" he asked, with a twinkle in his eye.

"No. Will you still be kissing servant girls on the hand anymore?" she retorted, feeling much more at ease with the conversation, even though she could slice the tension with a butcher's knife.

"No, I will not," he said with a strained smile.

"What is your history with her, if you do not mind me asking?"

Shoulders slumping, he sat back in his chair. "We grew up together. I was always ordered to be out of sight and sound around my stepmother and half-sisters. I had no one to play with or talk to besides the servants." His blue eyes darkened as if the memory brought him pain. "Isa...was my age...and she was always there for me when I needed her the most. We started a secret relationship when we were sixteen. It lasted for two years before I called it off."

All of it was making sense now. The whispers, the necklace...the kiss. Yet, knowing more of the story did not inspire jealousy as she expected. Rather, she felt sympathy inflate within her as the beast heaved a long sigh.

"I hurt her...deeply," he continued, with shame and longing painting his voice. "I said things I shouldn't have because I was afraid of repeating the same mistake my father had with my mother. He, too, had an illicit affair with a servant and...I could not afford to do the same. I could not allow another child to suffer as I had."

Another swell of compassion stole through her emotions. It was admirable of him to relinquish all he wanted for the sake of a child's future. She had not considered the idea of unborn children when she wallowed in her feelings for Claude. But now, she felt selfish for never considering it at all.

"When my father passed away when I was twenty, I was given my title, and I ran with the money." Henri averted his gaze. "I selfishly forced Isa to come with me because...I was still holding onto what could have been. I took her and my personal servants to this chateau here." He gestured to the room. "It was one my great-great-grandfather had built but abandoned for unknown reasons. Some said it was haunted. I should have listened. Otherwise, I would not be here, and neither would Isa...or you...For which, I am very sorry." He hung his head. "It's my fault you are here. I hope you can forgive me for what I have done and for my actions with Isa the other day. Both are inexcusable."

She supposed he expected her to reprimand him, to berate him until he was nothing but a shell of a man, but she would do no such thing. For all his mistakes, her heart warmed upon seeing the new man in front of her. One who admitted his wrongdoings, who felt ashamed of them, and more importantly, one who was willing to amend them.

"It's not entirely your fault," she said instead. "The Gods did not need to curse you."

"Regardless, I am sorry for it," he insisted.

The sincerity of his apology loosened the knots in her chest, and she inhaled a cleansing breath, hoping to dispel the awkwardness. "Well, no matter. All is forgiven, and I appreciate you telling me about the history between yourself and Isa."

"Yes, of course."

She felt an apology was due from her, but it felt wrong to be sorry for how she felt for someone else. It would feel condescending if she did so.

"I should not have avoided you for three days," she said. "I was embarrassed by my actions after drinking too much." She cringed at the memory. "And then sneaking off to see Claude the next evening. I was not sick, as you have correctly assumed, but I did not know how to face you after such...behavior. I apologize and would not blame you if you thought me indecent as a partner."

Head shaking, his stringy, untamed hair followed the motion. "No, if anything, I respect you for being honest when I confronted you. I know you were delaying speaking with me, but I appreciate you not denying the truth. I hope despite what we both know about our...feelings," he said the word like it was a barb in his throat, and she stiffened in her seat at the awkward reality of their situation.

"For others," he continued hoarsely, "I hope we may cultivate feelings between each other within the next few weeks."

Although she had resolved herself with the same hopes, hearing such words gave her pause. Could such a feat be possible? She reached for the image she created in her mind earlier between herself and Henri. All the parties and the title of Countess were attainable if she could forge romantic affection for the beast across from her. More importantly, she would save not only her family but all those who lived in the Chateau d'Alarie.

Including Claude.

A burst of determination eased the sinking of her stomach. "I would like that very much, in fact." A smile played on her lips at a sudden thought, "How about we have an engagement party on the last day of the curse?"

"An engagement party?" He tilted his head. "Is this a new tradition in your time?"

"Oh." She had almost forgotten he was from a different era than she. "Yes, but it's not a traditional party as you might think. It's usually between the immediate families as the couple exchange words of promise. It's to legitimize their engagement before announcing it in the papers publicly."

"I see." He tapped a bony finger to his chin. "So, it's like a wedding ceremony of sorts?"

"In some ways, yes, but without it being an actual wedding. A dance is also held between the couple." She paused as heat flooded her cheeks at the thought. "But we do not have to do any of that if you do not want to."

"No, I would very much like to. I think it would also give the servants something to look forward to as well. Heavens know, they need some...hope."

"Then let us give them some."

A crooked smile flashed over his features, and she returned the favor with a soft grin despite her chest tightening into her lungs. Ignoring the pain, she reached across the table, and he looked at her hand curiously before extending his massive palm. His brows raised in surprise as she laced her fingers between his clawed ones.

"I am looking forward to it," she said.

"As am I." He gently curled his fingers around her own, and for a moment, she could pretend they were soft and warm instead of cold and bony.

This could work, no—it will work, she thought as she compelled her lips to smile. But it brightened when another thought came to her.

"And after this curse is broken," she said, squeezing his hand, "I would be more than happy to paint your first portrait..." The words trailed off as she realized how self-imposing the offer was. Looking down, she continued, "If you would like, that is. You are not obligated to do so if you do not want me to. I suppose I thought having one in our home would be nice."

Oh no, she was rambling and making a fool of herself. Shutting her mouth, she relinquished his hand, reached for her fan, and snapped it open, hoping to cool the fires of her embarrassment.

Something smooth touched her jaw, and her fanning ceased. It gently lifted her face toward his strange one. The long curve of his black claw had turned flat against her cheek to not cut her delicate skin, and a blaze burned her face from the inside out at the intimate gesture. She supposed she was to blame for initiating the intimacy in the first place, but her heart hammered away as he looked at her with a gentleness she had never witnessed before.

"You have no idea how much that means to me," he whispered.

Her jaw slackened at his sincere gratitude and the dip of vulnerability in his voice. Before she could respond, the claw moved upward and tucked a stray hair behind her ear.

Her face lit up like a blasting volcano as awkwardness and bashfulness fought for dominance, but her mind raced to school her conflicting emotions. Henri was not just her friend, he was her fiancé, and she would do well to remember it.

When he pulled away, she reigned control over her voice. "Of course. I want you to be remembered, Henri."

Another gentle smile lifted his odd features, and the sight lifted her heart.

There was still hope yet.

33

Isa

The bucket of water had gone cold as Isa scrubbed the floor. Her coarse knees buckled despite the towel she put underneath to pad them, and her hands ached from her work. In a matter of weeks, her fingers had fused into a club-like appendage, and black feathers covered her body from head to foot. Yet, despite the changes, she pressed on, working without complaint with the others.

Six worked beside her, standing on ladders to string up garland and tidy the abandoned room for tomorrow's engagement party.

"What will you do when the curse is broken?" she heard Joseph say while nudging Sanson.

"Oh, I think I will dance for days." The deer-like man pointed to his large antlers. "And I will be happy to be rid of these."

"Same." Joseph gestured to his long, sloping ears. "I don't know if I will cry or shout, but I cannot wait for this to be over tomorrow."

They laughed, and their excited whispers buzzed around her ears, agitating the jealous thorns around her heart.

Standing, she wobbled on her new feet, which had transformed into four long digits with sharp talons on each end over the past few days. Her teeth clamped together when they scraped across the clean marble.

Leaving the ballroom and excitement behind, she passed through the halls and headed toward the kitchens before hearing a familiar peal of laughter. It was hard to ignore the tinkling sound as she carried the cold bucket at her side and even more difficult when the parlor doors she approached were wide open for anyone to look in.

Her eyes betrayed her, and she glanced inside. To her surprise, Henri stood behind an easel while Marguerite sat on a chair before him. A large bowl of fruit decorated the small table beside her, and she placed her arm unnaturally against it. It appeared she was modeling for him and fought to keep a straight face as he dipped his brush into a paint palette.

Isa had never seen Henri touch a paint set, and the image must have been just as humorous to Marguerite since she sat restless and giggling. His large head looked up from the canvas, and he pointed the paintbrush at his fiancée.

"Ah, ah. You cannot move...not yet," he said, and the thorns around Isa's heart pierced through the sensitive muscle at his teasing tone.

"It cannot be helped!" Marguerite laughed.

"It can. Now stop wiggling, and let me add the finishing touch."

Isa should have walked away; she should have averted her gaze but found she could not. If perhaps she had been her old self, untouched by the curse, she would have left the moment her eyes landed on the engaged couple, but now, all the rationale she had slipped away like crumbling sand. It was as if he were the shiny rocks and trinkets she obsessed over—once she found them, she could not bear to part herself from the items.

But Henri was no pretty trinket. He was worse. As much as she had sworn she had let him go, of all their happy memories, deep down, she knew...

He remained the keeper of her prickly heart.

"I think I am done," he said, smiling in his grotesque way. Behind the tusks and sharp teeth, she recognized the smile she knew before his transformation, the smile once gifted for her and her alone. Warmth flooded her as she latched onto the shiny line of his grin.

A figure crossed her line of sight, and she realized Marguerite had stood and skipped toward Henri to see his painting. She almost forgot the woman was there.

"Oh!" Marguerite raised a hand to her mouth to stifle more laughter.

Henri chuckled. "I am no artist, but I doubt anyone could capture your beauty in a single painting."

A sharp tear jabbed her chest.

Marguerite smiled as she took the painting and turned it toward him. It was crude, with a stick for a body and a disproportionately sized head with curls coming out the top. "You don't think you captured it perfectly here?"

"Never, my darling."

Another stab and cringing followed at the pet name. He never used them with her because he said he was not fond of them. She supposed being in a new relationship had a way of changing someone in more ways than one.

His kindness and genuine romantic gestures had not gone unnoticed. Over the past fortnight, she saw a side of him she thought was long buried. Her resolve weakened as sweet memories between herself and Henri surfaced in her mind. Of chases through the fields, laughter beneath the oak tree, and sly glances across the room. That was the Henri she knew.

At least Marguerite could experience the best of him.

Suddenly, he turned, and their eyes met long enough for her heart to stammer in her chest. She had been spying on them for far too long. Spinning on her heel, she marched away with her head held low and the bucket bumping against her legs.

The kitchen was too far away.

Finally, she made it out of sight and found Claude sitting alone at the dining room table. An array of silverware sat before him, and he began polishing them. Since his hands were also useless, paws more than hands, he placed a fork on the table and rubbed the towel over it as it lay flat. When she approached, he looked up and nodded to her.

"I thought Anna was going to take care of this," she said.

"She is feeling unwell."

"Was it the hairballs again?"

He perked up from his work. "How did you know?"

"She can't stop licking herself. She's been doing it for days now, and it's been making her sick."

"I suppose that would do the trick." He shook his head. "Poor thing."

"Poor thing," she agreed solemnly. The curse prevented some of the servants from doing the required tasks. Their minds were still attached, but their bodies were slowly caging them into uselessness.

"I keep wondering when I'll be completely useless," he said, too nonchalant for the statement, but she spotted his chin trembling as he scooped the knife into the clean pile.

"I think we all do."

A frown etched over his lips, but she turned toward the kitchen doors to fetch hot water. It was best for them both to keep their minds off the subject, but she stopped in her tracks when familiar voices echoed around the corner.

"Where are we going?" the voice laughed. It was Marguerite's.

"Put on a coat. Let's practice our dance beneath the stars tonight."

Henri then passed the open dining room doors with Marguerite in tow. He held her hand and led them toward the foyer with uncanny enthusiasm. Isa held her breath as they passed.

A low growl rumbled from behind, and she glanced toward Claude, who stiffened in his seat. When they made eye contact, he looked down at her form, and she followed his line of sight.

Every feather on her arms had puffed outward. She smoothed the plumes down and ignored his heated stare.

"This is all wrong," he said.

"No, it's right," she said as his lips curled upward in response.

Sharp, canine teeth glimmered in the light as another growl erupted from his chest. "What if it's not? What if we have it all wrong? If they loved each other, wouldn't the curse be broken by now? Wouldn't we—"

"They belong together."

"I cannot believe that. Did you see them? It's a lie. It isn't real." He suddenly barked as he swept his arm across the table. The silverware crashed to the ground like a cacophony of cymbals. "It isn't love—she...I know her smile—it's all wrong!"

He was right. None of the affection between Henri and Marguerite felt genuinely romantic, but she could not allow herself to listen to him. If she did, if she let doubt weasel in, she would break knowing she had let Henri go without telling him how she truly felt.

She would live her last moments with regret.

A stinging rush assaulted the cavity of her chest. The thorns around her heart withered into nothing as the feelings there broke free. For a moment, blood rushed to her face like a swarm of locusts, tempting her to faint. The dizzy spell almost consumed her before she steeled herself, took a deep breath, and suppressed the chaos of emotions deep, deep down.

When she looked back to him, to the fire in his eyes, she knew it was her duty to douse them into ashes, just as she had done within herself.

"You are not thinking," she said, slow and deliberate. "This isn't you. The curse is making you irrational."

"No," he snapped. "It's me. For once, I am making sense, and you do not like it. *You* don't know her...she...she wouldn't look like that!" The words broke in his mouth into another high-pitched bark as he directed one paw toward the doors.

"You should have no concern for her."

"But I do!" His fists came down on the table, jolting her where she stood.

Heavy breathing filled the silence as they stared at one another. The clock on the mantle ticked down the seconds, and his shoulders slumped.

"I love her," he whispered.

The admission did not come as a shock. In fact, she suspected his feelings ran deep for their guest. Yet, the root of it needed to be dug out once and for all.

"And I know you still care for Henri. I can see it in your eyes," he continued softly. "He acted differently around you. It's not the same when he's with Marguerite."

"So?"

"So?" he echoed back, and his frown deepened.

"Do you expect her to choose you? You are a valet. What future could she have with you? What future could Henri have with *me*?"

He stumbled back as hurt extinguished whatever passion lingered within him.

She continued her assault. "Do you think she will give up her wealth? Her status? Run away and live a simple life with you?"

"I...I—"

"Is that what you expect?" she continued and took a step forward while the memories of Henri's rejection and cruel words when they were eighteen fueled her stride.

Throat clamping, she pressed on, "Do you expect a happily ever after despite the difference of status between you two?"

"I thought..." Whatever else he was about to say hung in the air as he looked away.

"Well, you thought foolishly. Love will never be enough, Claude. Do you hear me? It'll never be enough."

"Isa..."

"Put it out of your mind, once and for all. It's not so difficult!" She jabbed him in the chest, hoping her message would strike true.

A softness in his eyes dimmed the pain there as he went around the table and reached for her, but she shrunk away.

"Are you listening to me?" Her voice strained into a shrill squawk. "It'll never work. It'll always end in heartache—"

Warm arms gathered her into an embrace. Her shoulders stiffened, and she squirmed in his grasp, but he held her close. It was then she realized the bullet of tears streaming down her cheeks, dotting his coat like a haphazard constellation.

No. She did not cry. She had not cried in years.

But air refused to enter her lungs. She could not breathe. A sob choked whatever words she wanted to fire at him—to protect him from the pain burning her from the inside out.

"It'll always hurt," she hiccupped, but her arms reached around her friend. "Do you hear me?"

"I know, I hear you," he whispered in her ear.

"Then why won't you listen to me?"

"Because...some things are worth hurting for."

More tears trickled down her feathered face as she closed her eyes. Shudders wracked her body, but he held her like he was attempting to keep them both from falling apart.

"I'm not so sure," she said. "I'm not sure if it's worth it."

His chest rose against her as he exhaled a sigh. "I know it is. Love always is."

For once, she did not wish to argue his point because she knew deep down, despite the years of heartbreak and agony, it was true. She would not trade the memories, the sweet words for anything. Love was worth the pain.

She only hoped it would not shatter her.

34

Marguerite

Tonight was the night—the night the last petal of the last rose would fall.

Her engagement party.

Marguerite stared at the silver talc box with shaking hands at her side and hoped her appearance was decent. It took her an hour to navigate her hair and pin it correctly, even with Jeanette's guidance. Without a mirror, the task was doubly difficult, but she patted around, feeling if there were any stray bumps or pins she needed to correct or ribbons out of place. Satisfied with her work, she swept the remaining long curls to drape over one shoulder.

"You did well, dear," Jeanette said. "I wish I could have helped you more."

Marguerite regarded the woman's thin arms and forced herself not to make a face at their transformation. No fingers, hands, or any resemblance of human flesh remained. Fuzzy, stiff-like hairs covered her thin, arthropod arms in a black and white pattern, and they lay at her side by her silky, white moth wings. The plumes on her head had grown longer, and they twitched as she spoke.

"It's alright," she reassured her and smiled. "But thank you, I trust your word that I won't come out looking like a crow's nest."

"Never, miss. You are radiant."

She reached for the curl on her shoulder. "You are too kind."

"Not at all. I'm just honest. But I wish I could help you dress as well." Jeanette frowned. "I'm sorry I'm no use to you."

"No, don't be sorry. I think getting dressed might be easier than my hair," she teased and approached the magical wardrobe.

An array of frills, lace, and silk dresses hung before her. She picked the dress she thought most beautiful and sighed with relief when it had ties that were easy to manage. The wardrobe must've sensed her predicament, and she placed a hand against its wood in thanks.

With Jeanette's guidance, she tied the right pieces together until she was fully dressed, but her hands continued to tremble as she patted down the silk material. Gold and emerald embroidery decorated the entirety of the cream dress in a floral motif. Delicate lace encircled the tops of her shoulders and around her chest in a scooping, oval neckline. A shining broach stood center upon her sternum, connected by pearls and gold beads down the seam of her bust. She donned a pearl necklace to sit high upon her throat and matching pearl earrings as the finishing touch.

"You look absolutely stunning," Jeanette crooned behind her.

"Thank you." She turned and looked down at herself. It was a gown fit for a princess, something she would have fawned over as a little girl but all the bubbling excitement she should have felt fizzled into a crashing wave of nerves.

"Is something the matter, dear?"

"No." She fixed her posture and put on another smile. "Nothing is the matter."

Jeanette's bulbous eyes took in her appearance, but it was difficult to decipher any emotion behind the black orbs. The small line of her mouth puckered. "It's alright, dearie. You don't have to feel so nervous. We'll all be fine, no matter what happens."

The words snapped through her like a whip. "What?"

Jeanette reached for her shoulder. "I said...everything will be alright. Don't you worry your pretty head, dear. We'll make it through."

The cryptic words gave Marguerite little comfort, and she did not like what Jeanette was insinuating. She would break the curse. She must. She would save them. And she would prove it once and for all. "Yes, everything *will* be alright. I promise."

With one final smile, she took a deep breath and opened the doors. Every step inspired sweat to collect in her hands, but she held her head high as she descended the stairs and into the ballroom.

Beneath the vines of colorful flowers, garland, and twinkling flames of the chandeliers, everyone waited for her, all deformed and more animalistic than ever. Among them, both Claude and Isa kept their backs to the walls and their heads bowed as she entered. It was the first time she had seen him this close since their last encounter. They avoided each other well. But, for a moment, she took in his appearance and tempered the rising emotions from spilling over.

His spine curved, forcing him to hunch, and his paws dangled out of his coat. The face of the man she had grown to care for was no longer recognizable. Sleek, golden fur replaced his shaggy hair, his long snout mixed with his once human lips, and a long tail had grown where none used to be. His transformation was nearly complete.

Her heart squeezed seeing him reduced like this. All the words he said, all his sweet touches, came rushing back to her.

Claude inclined his head a little, and their eyes met. For one brief moment, all her breath rushed from her lungs, and she hesitated in her stride. A small, twisted, pained smile lifted on his snout.

"You'll always be beautiful."

His words battered around the space of her skull, and she shut her eyes for one second to embrace them one last time.

Yet, beneath the chandelier lights, Henri stood, offering a hand. She came to him, forcing her eyes away from Claude, and stretched her hand out to greet her fiancé.

"You look very beautiful," he said and gave her a crooked smile.

"Thank you," she murmured, aware of all the eyes and ears on them. "You look fine yourself." She gestured to his jacket and vest.

"You are too kind. We both know how hideous I am, clothing or not."

"If I squint, I can hardly tell." She grinned, and his hand squeezed over hers gently.

Another chuckle rumbled from his chest before he leaned down to her ear. "Are you ready?" he whispered.

"Are you?"

For a moment, he hesitated but finally nodded. "I believe so. And you?"

She took a deep breath and gathered the remains of her courage. "I believe so too."

With one final nod, he squeezed her hand and turned to address his servants. "Thank you all for being here tonight." He swept his long arm around in gesticulation. Usually, the bride-to-be's father would lead the engagement ceremony, but Henri had agreed to lead it instead. "We are gathered here in celebration of our up-coming union. We have prepared some lines to say to each other as a declaration of love and engagement. But first, a dance."

A knot tightened at her throat as he bowed so low the cape of stringy fur pooled around his cloven feet. She curtsied in return, fanning out her dress before taking his hand. No music played, none of the servants knew how and if they had, their bodies rendered them useless. Without a cue to start, she looked to him to lead, and he began by parting and looping around her just as they practiced. As she mimicked the move and clasped one hand with his, the back of her neck prickled as she felt every pair of eyes on her like a specimen under a magnifying glass.

The clack of her heels and the scrape of his feet echoed across the room, but it was not enough to fill the silence needling its way through her stomach. The flow and push of the dance imitated dancing waves, meeting and pulling apart at the last second to signify young love coming together. Yet, all she could think about was the oppressive silence hovering over them like a dark shadow.

Her heart began to pound, and one foot twisted over the other through her footwork, but she righted herself immediately. Heat crawled up her face, but she attempted to ignore how awkward this dance was, how every soul in this room watched this display of "affection," and how much she could not ignore the banging emotions against her heart.

Instead, she focused her thoughts and feelings on Henri to emerge. Beastly form aside, he had been kind to her. The conversation had flown more freely between them, and she had more fun with him these past few weeks than she ever had in the sum of all the months combined.

He was witty.

A little charming.

A perfect match.

She loved him for that.

She loved him.

Loved him...

"Marguerite."

Her thoughts dissolved as she turned to address the whisper and was startled when she found Henri bowing again. The dance had ended, but she frowned when she realized his horns, fur, and claws were still there. Perhaps she needed to say the words out loud to break the curse.

She curtsied, and a chorus of clapping and excitement reverberated through the room as he took her hand and led them to the center of the floor.

"Thank you. We will now proceed with our words of promise. I will go first," Henri said, pulling out a piece of parchment inside his jacket pocket. She blanched, wishing she had prepared her words on paper, but she put her worries aside as he began to read:

"As all of you know," he began, and she masked her expression, surprised he chose to address everyone. "I have not been the best employer to you. I have not lived up to my title, and worst of all, I fear," his voice grew thick and hoarse, "I have even failed as a man.

"I know I do not deserve forgiveness for what I have done. This curse is my fault, and none of you are to blame, but I wish to stand before you to say I am sorry. I also wish to thank you," the paper shook in his large hand, "for your service and all you continue to do even when the curse has ruined your bodies. When all of this is over, and we can celebrate, I will see to it personally that you are taken care of and compensated even if you wish to leave my service."

Whispers of surprise echoed around the room, and Marguerite's eyes softened on the beast.

"I know many of you may not trust that I have changed," he continued. "But I promise to be true to my word. I hope in time, you may all live happy, satisfying lives after this horrid experience we have endured together." Clearing his throat, he shifted his stance to face her. "And to my fiancée..."

For once, she did not mind all the stares as she swept her thumb across his pale skin.

"From the day you came here, you have changed our very lives. Your presence has sparked not only hope but happiness once more in these dreary halls. I know this has been difficult for you, and the circumstances are more than unfair. However—" He lowered the paper and lifted her hand to his mouth. Thin lips ghosted over her skin, and her gut clenched. "I am so very happy fate chose you. You are kind, patient, and spirited. I have enjoyed your company and your friendship immensely. I do not deserve you, but I will strive to support and cherish you for all my days."

Henri folded the paper and tucked it into his jacket, and Marguerite exhaled a shaky breath. It was her turn.

"I wish I prepared a beautiful speech as you did," she said and chuckled nervously. No one laughed at her joke, and she swallowed the knot in her throat. "All I can say is that...despite our struggles and differences, I have grown to appreciate you and all you have overcome. I am proud of you, truly, and—" She paused, attempting to find the right words. Everything she had practiced disappeared.

The silence rang in her ears as she wet her dry lips. Finally, she pushed through the mental fog and blurted out, "I am happy to call you my fiancé. I promise to be true and faithful to you for all my days."

Heat flushed through her body as she averted her gaze. What a bumbling idiot she was. However, he squeezed her hand, and she looked up to see his soft smile.

"I love you, Marguerite."

"I—" she began but the words halted in her mouth. Everyone was staring at her, waiting with bated breath.

This is all on me now.

Her eyes betrayed her as they glanced toward Claude's. A wave of acceptance and despair washed over his face.

All I need to do is say the right words.

Closing her eyes, she shut out Claude and brought all her focus to the present.

Maybe that will be enough.

"I love you too."

A chorus of exhales filled the room, and heads turned to each other to see if the curse had been lifted, but nothing happened.

Perhaps she did not say it correctly. Clearing her throat, she tried again, "I love you, Henri. I love you."

More waiting. More unsettling silence.

And then every flame extinguished into curling smoke. Darkness consumed them before a bright light flashed like a strobe of sunlight, filling the room with blinding rays.

35

Henri

Henri shielded his eyes, but the light burned against his lids. Potent energy surged forward, forcing unnatural wind to blow against his face, and a cry shrieked by his ear. Marguerite raised her arms out beside him, attempting to ward off the gust, and he stepped in front of her, taking the abrasive flurry in her stead.

Screams echoed before the blast settled into nothing. The light flickered out, and an eerie calm blanketed the room.

Had the curse been broken?

He dared open his eyes, and the question dissolved into horror. The Enchanter floated above them, wearing the same majestic robes as he did the day Henri first met him. Skin blue as hydrangeas and eyes as bright as a firefly's, they burned through him like brimstones.

His heart dropped to the pit of his stomach.

"I see you have not broken the curse," the Enchanter said, and his deep voice sent shivers along his spine.

No, it couldn't be true. They had done everything right—he loved Marguerite. He had to. But all the warmth drained from his face as he looked down and found nothing but his beastly form. Nothing had changed.

The curse had remained.

"What?" he sputtered as his limbs grew weak under the Enchanter's scrutiny. "B-but we have confessed our love for each other."

"Words are just that." A blue hand waved forward like a father explaining a lesson to a child. "They are easy to say but harder to mean. If there were truly love between you, then the curse would have been broken when you said them."

Dread skewered his heart, but he took a step forward. "Please...Just give us time—"

"Will you love her in five minutes? Because that is all the time you have left." The Enchanter pointed to a lopsided clock on the wall, no doubt askew due to his windy entrance, and then gestured to Marguerite behind him. "And you? Will you fall in love with him within that time?"

Despite her palpable shaking, she stepped around him to address the floating figure. "We have been trying, sir. Please, if we were given more time then—"

"You have been given a sufficient amount of time already."

They were doomed. All of them. Henri knew it. He felt it in his very soul. There was nothing he could do, nothing but beg.

His knees hit the ground; his pride vanished under his desperation. Yet, this time, self-preservation did not rear its ugly head. No, he did it for the people behind him—for Claude and Jeanette...for Joseph and Sanson...Pierre, Anna, Paul...

For Isa.

"No, please, wait. I beg of you."

"Ah, have you not learned your lesson? Do you not remember that begging was useless the first time around?"

"Yes, but hear me out." He held out his arms in a placating manner. "I beg you to spare them. Spare all my servants. They do not deserve this. It was my fault. I am the one to blame. I am the one who mistreated you and who moved here knowing I should not have. Punish me. *Please.*"

"Henri," a weak voice said beside him, and a hand warmed his shoulder. He spared Marguerite a glance and met her worried gaze with steel resolve.

"I need to do this." Her frown deepened, and he turned to face the Enchanter once more.

Bright, luminous eyes regarded him with curiosity. "You have changed much since our first meeting."

"I have," he said with more confidence than he felt and was grateful his voice did not crack under the Enchanter's stare. "And I have done so knowing I am responsible for my actions. So please do not deny me this request."

An uneasy hush followed, and every nerve screamed under his skin. Sweat beaded and fell across his temple, but his thoughts strayed to those behind him. He wondered if his servants—his friends—were as terrified as he, how helpless they must feel. And it was all his fault.

Finally, the Enchanter spoke:

"I cannot undo everything that has been done," he said, and Henri's heart plummeted. "But there is a way to grant your request."

An exhilarating relief flooded his chest, and he raised himself from the floor. "I will do it. Anything. I swear it. Just let them go. Let them be free of this curse. I will take it."

"There is a way...but it means placing all their curses—" His staff pointed to his servants behind him. "On you. Doing so will tear your soul to pieces. You will live not as either man or beast but a wraith upon Gallia. Never seen and depleted of all feeling and humanity. You will wish for death, and it will never come."

"No!" a voice behind him screeched. "Henri, no!" Pivoting around, the breath flattened from his lungs as Isa cawed, reaching out to him as her face contorted, shrinking smaller and smaller. Everyone around her moaned, crying in pain as their bodies twisted into beasts while he stood there debating their fates.

Time was nearly up. He must decide.

"I will do it."

"Don't do this!" Marguerite tugged at his arm. "Please don't do this."

Turning to her, he pushed against the fear, the end of his life, threatening to suffocate him. "I have to. I have to do this," he emphasized firmly. "And listen to me. All that I have will be for you and everyone here. Take what you need to rebuild your father's business."

"Except there will be nothing left," the Enchanter said, and his mouth slackened with disbelief. "Everything you owned that made you into the selfish person you had become will vanish with you."

So, he would leave them all with nothing. It was all for nothing.

"I'm so sorry," he whispered to her, reaching for her hand while tears stung his eyes. "I just wanted to do right by you."

"I don't care, Henri!" Marguerite clung to his arm, attempting to pull him away. "Don't do this, please!"

"I have already made my decision," he swallowed thickly. "I pray that chap you were supposed to marry keeps his word—"

"No, don't talk like that. It's not too late! Please," she cried and lifted her chin toward the floating Enchanter. "Do you hear me? I love him. Don't do this to him."

"I do not doubt your affection, Ms. Dupont," the Enchanter said. "But your affection does not run as deep as you have been telling yourself."

"Liar!" she screamed, but Henri gently pulled her back from charging at the being.

"No, stop, Marguerite," he said, tugging her to his chest and smoothing the silk material on her back.

She shuddered against him. "How can you say such things? Look at what you are sacrificing!"

A swell of wailing, growling, and groaning resonated in his ears as he held her. The suffering cries of his friends, their cracking of bones, pierced through his heart like a stinging harpoon.

He could not wait any longer. The time was now.

Wiping the burning tears away, he untangled himself from her grasp and turned to the Enchanter. "Do it. Place their curses on me."

"As you wish."

"No!" a guttural, foul scream sounded, and he glanced behind to see every servant morphing back, losing sharp teeth and fur—transforming back into a human. Among them, Claude's face twisted into disbelief as their eyes met. He reached out as though to stop him from sacrificing himself.

A sad smile ghosted his lips before a green light flashed, and pain ripped through him. It tore under his skin like a club of fire, demolishing everything in its path, eating and clawing its way to the center of his being. Shouting, he fell to the floor and convulsed.

A body fell beside him. Warm hands hovered over him as if lost on where to soothe him. "You idiot!" Through the pain, he peered through hooded lids and surprise wormed through the agony. "You stupid, stupid man!"

"Isabelle," he said through clenched teeth as another wave of fire shot through him. Feathers fell from her face like black pearls of water, and smooth, tan skin pushed through her fowl features. His beautiful Isabelle...

"You can't do this!" Tears fell from her dark eyes, no longer beady and unnatural but glistening with emotion.

"I will," he gritted out and winced. "I have to."

"I will share your burden then. Take me as well," she called upward, and his eyes shot open.

"Isa, don't—"

The blaze receded from his veins, halting in its wrath. Air filled his chest, and he choked on the blessed life filling him once more.

"Do you understand what will happen to you as well?" The Enchanter regarded her carefully. "You will share his fate if you do this. The pain will hardly be lessened. Why would you suffer such a thing?"

"Because I love him!"

The confession was said so firmly, and so suddenly that it knocked the very breath from his lungs. "Isabelle," he rasped.

"I love you, you foolish man." Her tears blunted the harshness of her tone as she turned toward him. "I always have. And I will not let you suffer alone."

"You cannot—"

"But I will."

"I cannot allow you to do that."

A fierce determination settled over her features, a passionate fire he adored. "Watch me, Henri."

"Please," a sob caught in his throat. "I cannot let you do that. I—"

"And you cannot tell me what I can and cannot do," she said and extended a hand, a featherless arm, toward him. He grasped it, and she hauled his lumbering form up with ease. Her strength, inside and out, never ceased to amaze him.

"I cannot," he conceded hoarsely. "But don't throw your life away. Be free. Go live your dreams, sing—perform…just…live. Live for yourself. Live how you always dreamed of living."

Her dark brows furrowed, and her throat bobbed up and down. "I would have. I would have done just that, but…If I go free while you suffer, that would not be living. Not without you."

His spirit soared, but he tethered it back to reality before it could reach beyond the stars. All this time, she had cared for him. All this time.

"Why do you wish to deny her this choice, Henri?" the Enchanter asked, pulling him from the bittersweet emotions.

A tear dripped down his snout, and he grasped her hand. "Because…" he addressed her, "I love you too much. I would rather suffer alone than to ever see you in pain—to ever see you be caged again."

Tears mixed with her wavering smile, and he reached for her face to brush them away. Her eyes widened when he touched her cheek, and a gasp flew from her throat. His mouth slackened while his heart raced at the bright light consuming his hand. It shimmered like warm butterflies on the skin as it danced over his body.

"What is happening?" she asked.

"I don't know." He swiveled to the Enchanter but grew rigid as a burst of light broke from his chest.

"Henri!"

Mouth opening, an invisible force pushed him to his knees with light surging from every pore. A rush of tingles gathered from the top of his head and rushed down the length of his body. There was no pain, only warmth as he fell forward on his palms. Hours, seconds, he did not know how long the light continued to consume him until it vanished without a trace, and his eyes fluttered open, staring at the glittering specks of color on the marble.

Gasping, air shuddered down his throat as he pushed himself up in a sitting position. His eyes widened as he looked down to see pale, bare feet instead of hairy, cloven ones, but before he could assess the rest of himself or collect his thoughts, a weight landed in his lap and wrapped their arms around his neck. Familiar curves and shapely muscles pressed against him, squeezing him until he wheezed.

"What—" he managed before the figure pulled away, and the sight of a sharp nose and broken smile stared back at him.

"You're alright," she breathed a sigh. The softness of Isa's breath tickled his mouth, and her eyes drew him in like sweet air. Raven hair spilled over her shoulders, curtaining his face and shielding them from view. "I was so worried about you," she whispered. "And...I was worried I'd never be able to do this again."

He was unsure who moved first, but it did not matter. They met halfway until their mouths melted upon the other. Her hands sought his untamed hair, and he wrapped his hand to the back of her neck, pulling her impossibly closer. All the pain between them, all the heartache dissolved into a crucial point of desire as he held her like she would be ripped from him at any second.

"I cannot believe it," he said against her mouth.

"But you should," a voice said, and the two snapped toward the Enchanter.

Marguerite also stood, with hands wringing bashfully but otherwise smiling. Claude and the others gave them some distance, but shining relief beamed from their faces. Pushing himself to his feet, he stumbled, but Isa caught him by the arm. "But...I thought—"

"Do you remember what I told you in the woods, Marguerite?" the Enchanter asked her.

"Love is a choice," Marguerite answered. Isa stiffened on his arm but did not let go.

"Indeed, it is." He smiled. "The most suitable for love does not require riches or status. No higher power, including fate, can force two people to love. Marguerite was fated to be here, but only to help you both understand your true desires."

"So, all this time—"

"Love was there all along," the Enchanter finished with a knowing look. "Now, rebuild your lives. You may keep your wealth and precious belongings, Henri. This is a second chance to start over in this new era. But, be warned, never return to this sacred place again, or may the Gods have mercy on your soul."

Another gust of power exploded from where the Enchanter stood. Turning his back, he shielded Isa as another beam of light assaulted them. When all became still, he glanced up, and the Enchanter disappeared.

36

Marguerite

Cheers lifted toward the vaulted ceiling, and Marguerite observed the scene like an invisible spectator while servants embraced each other, weeping and laughing all at once. Their faces, although familiar, were foreign to her without their animalistic features, and upon seeing their unbridled joy, her heart churned like an olive press, squeezing until she thought it might burst.

The curse was broken. They were free. She was free.

And not in the way she had thought she would be free. Curiously though, she searched through her heart and found she was not angry by the outcome.

Perhaps she should be. Perhaps she should have felt cheated by all the work she spent trying to be with Henri. Despite the time and the hours with him, all she could feel was relief and...happiness as she peered at her friend, cradling the woman he loved in his arms.

Yet, the Enchanter's words stuck like tar against her thoughts, mixing confusing emotions together.

"Marguerite was fated to be here, but only to help you both understand your true desires."

She wanted to scream at how stupid the Enchanter's words sounded. What did the Gods want from her? Was this some experiment to toy with her emotions? To give her hope for a happy future, only for reality to set its course and dash it all away? Even now, the end of the curse did not relieve her family's burdens. What was the point in realizing what she wanted if she could never have it?

The questions dissolved as her gaze fastened onto a figure parting through the crowd. The very person her heart soared and broke all at once upon locking eyes.

Claude.

Sandy hair, big ears, and a slightly crooked nose. Just as he said. He was beautiful. More than beautiful.

A tightness clamped her throat as tears pricked her eyes at the sight. Oh, how she wished to run to him and embrace him as Henri and Isa allowed themselves to be beside her. But she stood frozen, cursing her fate as a woman who could not throw herself to her whims again. She had a duty to remember and one Claude could never fulfill as a valet.

However, she would concede with the Enchanter's words.

She did desire him—no, desire was too tame of a word, she realized. She loved him. She loved him with every fiber of her being.

As the servants chattered and danced, she willed herself not to move as the man she knew she could never have ran and wrapped his lean arms around her.

"The curse is broken," he laughed. "Look at us all!" He lifted her, and she suppressed a squeal of surprise as he spun them around. The room became a dizzying spectacle before he set her down and cradled her face with warm, strong hands. Her heart roared in her ears as she took in his face for the very first time. She memorized every freckle, every line around his wide, perfect smile, and when she found his eyes, her mouth grew dry at the softness—the desire there. One hand slid to the base of her neck, toying with a stray curl before he edged forward.

Panic tugged at her sensible side, and she reluctantly pulled against him.

"Marguerite." His beaming smile faltered. His eyes scanned over her face, one she schooled into stoic features. "What's wrong?"

"It's..." she paused and swallowed her thoughts down. She could not ruin this joyful moment when there had been so much at stake. "I am happy for you," she settled on with a cheery tone and plastered a grin. "It's incredible—I cannot believe it!"

His hands dropped from her face, from that delicious spot behind her neck, like he could sense her discomfort. Everything within her screamed at the loss of his touch.

Brows furrowing, he opened his mouth to speak before Henri clapped him on the back. Marguerite jumped in surprise and re-garded his new appearance in awe. Black hair settled in fine waves above his shoulders, and blue eyes brightened with his smile. He was thinner than she imagined, with a pale, narrow face and small lips. He no longer towered over her but stood taller than Claude by a hand's width.

If things had turned out differently, she would not have been upset had they been married. He was fair in appearance, even if her physical tastes in men were different, but she no longer had to worry about such things when he had a raven-haired beauty by his side. Isa's tan complexion clashed with his own, but their hands laced together by their sides like a complete puzzle piece.

"We did it, Claude! We are free," Henri laughed, and it rang bright and true. However, his expression sobered upon meeting her gaze. "Marguerite...I..." He glanced between her and Isa like he was unsure of how she felt about the new outcome.

"I'm happy for you, Henri," she said, and she meant it, even if her heart broke thinking she could not claim the same happiness. "I'm glad you found each other again. But I'm sorry," she said and reached for an excuse—any reason to leave the room immediately. "I must excuse myself. I think the Enchanter's appearance made me a little dizzy."

Bowing her head, she turned and swiftly exited before anyone could say a word. She had no destination in mind, but when the excitement became nothing but a distant echo, she stopped, and the emptiness of the hallway swallowed her whole.

Clenching her fists, salty tears rolled down her cheeks.

"What was it all for?" she whispered.

"There you are," a deep voice said, startling her. She jumped and whirled on the intruder.

"Henri?" her voice pitched as she wiped a tear from her jaw. "What are you—"

"Doing here?" he finished for her. "I came to find you, silly."

"But why?"

"Because you're a terrible liar." His lips tilted into a smirk. "I *have* spent all these months with you. You would think I would notice when you were upset."

"But you shouldn't worry about me," she insisted, feeling heat sear her neck at how selfish she must look standing out here, crying. "You should be inside celebrating with the others—with Isa. This is a huge moment for you all. Enjoy it, please."

"And so should you," he said. "You can be honest with me. Is it about Isa and me?"

She shook her head. "No, it's not."

"What's wrong, then?"

Perhaps it was the gentle way he said it or the safety she felt in her friend's presence, but the tears fell loose as she choked on a sob.

"I—I'm sorry," she hiccupped.

"No, don't be. It's alright," he said soothingly, spurring more tears to fall.

"I don't want to take away from this. From-from this moment. Everyone is so happy, and I hate to ruin it all."

"You're not, I promise," he said, offering her a reassuring smile.

"You should be with Isa and not me. It's okay, Henri."

"I will have a lifetime with Isa if she will have me. I can spare a moment with you. Here." He looked around him before gesturing forward. "How about we sit and talk about this somewhere more private."

Nodding, she followed his lead, and he opened the door to their left down the hall. Despite the tears blurring her vision, following his human form rather than his large, lumbering one felt odd. No scuffing feet or clawed hands at the doorknob—he gestured inside the music room with pale fingers. She sat at the chair near the harpsichord, and he took a seat at the instrument, facing her.

"I believe this should be private enough," he began, propping his elbows on his knees and interlacing his fingers. "Now, tell me, what's wrong?"

"I..." she bit back the words, unsure how to start. Her throat tightened as she spoke. "I suppose I am unsure why I was needed here at all."

His dark brows—no longer naked and broad—pinched together. "What do you mean?"

There was no use wasting more time. All her feelings, pent up for months, bubbled to the surface and rushed out like a surging geyser. "Why was I summoned here? What was the point? I don't understand," she cried. "Th-the Enchanter said it was for both of us...to realize our desires but..." Another wave of tears consumed her. "Why would the Gods show me what I wanted only for it to be taken away from me? I want him, Henri. I want Claude, but I still can't have him. I must think of my family."

Every limb trembled as she leaned forward to cover her face. The shame of it all, her tears, sitting in this room made her feel so very small.

"I feel selfish for even—" She swallowed. "For even feeling this way. For wanting more."

"Oh, Marguerite," Henri said and reached to pat her knee over the expensive silk. "You are the least selfish person I know."

Relief and sorrow stirred within her at his confirmation.

"In fact," he continued, "you are so selfless, I believe it's a shortcoming of yours."

"What?" She perked up, sniffling. "What do you mean?"

He relinquished her knee and sat back to regard her with gentle eyes. "Everything you have done, you have done for others. For your family, for my servants, for me, and for Claude. Am I correct?"

She nodded, not trusting her voice.

"Let me ask you this: if your family did not need you, would you consider a life with him regardless of his class? Would you give up your life of luxury to be with him?"

The question was not difficult for her to answer. "I would. I would give up everything if it meant I could be happy with him."

"I see." He hummed in approval. "Maybe it's time for you to do something for yourself then."

"But..." Her brow crinkled. "How? I still cannot ignore my family's financial burdens."

"No," he agreed. "You shouldn't. But why must it cost you your happiness?" She made a face and opened her mouth, but Henri beat her to it. "Look, I'm saying that perhaps you can do both."

By his tone, hope budded within her. "What do you mean?"

"I meant it when I said you can still have what you need to save your family. I plan to help you and hope your father can accept me as a new business partner."

Her eyes widened. "What about your title—?"

"We shall see where that stands in your time." He shrugged. "Besides, I am quite passionate about..." He rolled his hand and lowered his voice to a whisper, "What was it your father traded?"

"Linen," she provided as warmth blossomed in her chest.

"Yes, linen. I am very fond of the fabric. It breathes quite nicely on the skin, don't you think? I believe such a business must be revived at once!"

"You..." A watery smile broke over her lips. "You would do that for me? For my family?"

"Of course, I would. For you and Claude. I believe you two deserve the same happiness." He smiled. "And, of course, I'll have to keep myself busy in this new world."

Her grin widened until a thought spoiled it. "My mother would never approve, though. Of Claude."

"Would that still matter?" he asked in a reminder. "Her approval?"

A soft breath exhaled from her lips in a half-chuckle. "No, I suppose it wouldn't. As I said, I would give up everything to be with him."

"Ah, well, that would be quite a lot to sacrifice," he tutted.

"I think it would be worth it," she said, determination filling her like a hopeful beacon.

"Of course. But I don't believe you will have to give up so much. I do not think your mother will mind if she learns Claude and I are related."

Her head snapped up. "What?"

"Cousins," he said with a soft smile. "On my mother's side, but he's also my right-hand man. I would not be where I am without him. If we can keep his valet history a secret, no one would be the wiser. The Enchanter said to rebuild our lives. If I can move on in this world without being an illegitimate, then he can remake himself, too. I also think he deserves a part of my wealth whether he wants it or not."

A new wave of emotions consumed her as tears welled in her eyes. "I...I don't know what to say."

"You don't need to say anything," he said and paused for a moment. "I was too selfish for my own good, but perhaps you should learn a little from my weakness. You have lived way too long on the whims of others. It may seem noble, but I'm afraid if you live your life solely for them, you will waste your life wondering what you could have done for yourself. Maybe this new start the Enchanter spoke of could be a good way to start living for you for once."

Standing from the stool, he did not give her a chance to process his words as he strode toward the door and opened it.

"Are you ready to start?" he asked.

Wiping her eyes, a turmoil of knots sat heavy in her gut. "I don't know where to start."

"How about starting with choosing who you want to love?" He smiled.

Another tear looped down her chin, but she returned his smile. "I think I can start there."

Heart drumming, Marguerite stepped out of the music room with Henri by her side. His presence gave her the support and courage to take each step forward.

Instead of turning right toward the ballroom, he steered her left. "I told him to wait in the gardens," Henri explained. "He doesn't know for what purpose, but I wanted him to wait for you there."

"Wait for what? What does he expect?"

"Nothing," he said, stopping before the wide, double doors. "He expects nothing. However, I do believe he wants a moment with you."

Her thoughts strayed to when she had pulled away from Claude, the confusion in his eyes. The hurt. Guilt stabbed where anxious butterflies swarmed her belly. "I don't know. I'm not sure he would want to see me anymore."

"Trust me," he said and opened the door for her. "I know he does."

With a gentle hand on her shoulder, she allowed him to guide her forward before he shut the doors behind her. Under the pale moonlight, the garden had transformed into a lush landscape. Gone were the crackling gray branches and withered leaves. In its stead, the hedges blossomed with full, green leaves. Even the stone path shone with bright hues as she walked with her mouth gaping. Clear water burst from the fountain in the center, and on its ledge sat the man she was looking for.

37

Claude

What a foolish man he was.

The Enchanter's words had given Claude hope to submit his desires for the first time in his life. In a moment of swept-up joy, he'd shamelessly reached for Marguerite, touched her as a lover could. As if they were lovers at all. How could he assume so much? He cradled his face with his hands and cursed his stupidity.

Isa was right all along. He'd forgotten who he was. Who she was. And all her family obligations she'd burdened herself with. Even if Isa could have Henri, it didn't mean he could be with Marguerite.

Another wave of humiliation swept like a prickly wave at the memory of her pulling from his embrace, of the panic in her eyes, the false cheeriness in her voice, and the way she fled the room. She must be disgusted.

"Claude?"

Launching to his feet, his heart stopped. He hadn't heard her approach without his heightened dog senses. Moonlight lit her skin aglow as she stepped hesitantly toward him. The pearls at her throat glimmered in the light, bobbing with her throat when she swallowed. Her dress swayed in her footsteps, and he could not help but linger on the exposed skin of her collarbones.

She was radiant. Perfection. And nervous. But she was not supposed to be here; Henri was to meet him.

"Marguerite? I thought..."

She averted her eyes and wrung her hands together. "I believe Henri fooled you. He sent me here in his stead."

Understanding lit his face. "Ah well..." How was he to voice how he felt? Where were the words? Silence ate the twittering sounds of the night, and he avoided her gaze.

"I wanted to—"

"I'm sorry—"

Their voices clashed before they both gestured to each other.

"You go," he insisted.

"No, please. What were you apologizing for?" She stepped closer, but he could not fathom why she'd want to be near him.

He shook his head, and shame ran its bitter course again. "I shouldn't have made you so uncomfortable. I assumed too much."

"What do you mean?"

He raked his uncursed hand through his hair. No floppy ears or dog fur in sight. It should have relieved him to be human again, but there were too many emotions clawing for his attention.

Now he was unsure if he should be candid with her. After a beat of silence, he figured he owed her his honesty.

"I thought with the curse broken, we could finally be together," he said and sighed at how stupid it sounded. How much had he been in denial about who they were? "I've been selfish. I realized that after I saw you walk away. I thought of Henri and what he was willing to sacrifice, and all I could think of was how selfish I've been with wanting you. All this time, I wanted to right the injustice and give in to my emotions, but I put you in an awkward position. I know...even now, I still can't have you. I am sorry. Please forgive me."

"No." To his surprise, she took another step and reached for his hand, a hand with slender fingers instead of a fused hairy paw. Yet, the size of them still engulfed her own, and he peered into her face, unsure if she meant to touch him. She squeezed it as if to answer his silent question. "No, don't be sorry. I was afraid, but I know I have nothing to fear now."

"What do you mean?"

A soft smile graced her pretty lips. "I would give everything up for you, Claude. All of it if it meant being with you."

"What?" The word came out like a gasp, and it took all his inner strength to squash his happiness at her words. Such sweet words. He shook his head and gently removed her hand. The cold air stung where the warmth of her hand used to be, but he could no longer tempt himself.

"No," he continued firmly despite the cracks around his resolve. "You shouldn't do that. Not for me. I'm not worth your life. I'm a valet."

The smile disappeared, and he was loathed to see a frown replace it. "You are worth it to me," she said. "You are not just a valet; you are much more than that."

"Not in this world, I'm not." He looked away and sighed. "Isa was right. I do not belong in your world. I..." he paused and felt his pride deflate further. "I won't be able to support you. Financially."

A touch at his cheek guided his face to look at hers. "We can make our own world," she whispered. "If you will have me."

Warmth, radiant and pure, swelled beneath his chest, and in a moment of weakness, he placed his hand over hers, where it rested over his cheek. Skin over skin, he relished how soft and delicate her fingers felt beneath his. Throat tightening, the autumn chill stung his watering eyes. "Of course, I would. A thousand times over but—"

"But nothing. For once in our lives, we can be selfish," she said, determination and hope lighting her voice—a hope he felt stretching through his veins. Could he dare to dream? His selfishness had already deluded him into thinking he could be with her. Before he could convince her of the reality of their situation, she told him everything Henri discussed with her. When she finished, he stared at the ground with his head reeling.

"He would do that?" he asked.

"Yes," she breathed and reached for his hand again.

This time he did not pull away, but his head throbbed with confusion. It made sense for Henri to help Marguerite and her family financially, but what would he do with the wealth? How was he to pretend he was not a valet but a free man? The thought terrified and thrilled him all at once.

"By Erus, I never thought he would ever do something like this," he said, breaking the silence. "I don't know what to think of it."

"What do you mean?"

Too many warring thoughts and emotions filled his head. He couldn't answer her, not right away. Instead, he led her around the fountain with their hands still intertwined. He would allow himself the gesture, even when fear and shame clawed at his gut. The fear of not being good enough. Not good enough for her. Not good enough for freedom. Not good enough to want and feel.

These should have been the thoughts to stop him from falling for her months ago. Now they stormed through him, beating his brain to make up for all the time he'd been selfish enough to dream. A dream made from desperation in their dire circumstances.

But his feelings for her were real. That much he was certain of.

The flowers perked bright and full in the moonlight when they came across the rose bushes. The September chill began seeping through his clothes, too light for autumn, and he felt a shiver run through Marguerite's hand.

"Oh, my apologies. It's probably warmer inside," he said.

"Claude." She stopped and resisted his gentle tugs. "Please, just tell me what's on your mind."

His mouth opened and shut again. The temptation to pull her close, to chase away his fears, overpowered his sensibilities. Knowing it might be the last time he could do so, he gave in and wrapped his arms around her to keep her warm. The beads of her dress pressed into his vest, and he breathed in her comforting lavender perfume.

"Truthfully, I hadn't thought I would live long enough to become human again." He tightened his grip and shuddered against her. The last moments of transforming into a dog had been the most painful and terrifying seconds of his life. Flashes of agony and twisting bones filled his mind, and he winced. "I thought if I died without telling you how I felt, I would never be able to live with myself. I allowed myself that selfishness. And when the curse was broken, I was swept under the joy of it all and had not thought about the aftermath. But now that there is a solution...I find myself very afraid."

"Afraid of what?" She craned her face to meet his.

"Afraid I am inadequate for you and your world. All I know is how to serve."

"I understand your fears, and I hear you. But we will figure it out together," she said, resting her cheek against his coat.

She made it sound so simple. So obtainable. "What will your family think? Even with Henri's plan, they will see right through me."

"No, my father and brother will love you when they see the man you are. They will love you for loving me. It's more than they could ask for."

"What of your mother and sister?" They, of all people, would see right through him. He was sure of it.

She scoffed. "I don't care what they think anymore." His eyes widened, but before he could say another word, she continued, "I think they, too, will see how happy I am in time. That's all I could hope for."

Pride filled his heart at how she looked up at him with fearlessness. He knew it took a lot of courage for her to break the shackles of her mother's opinions, and yet, he could not help his own creeping doubts fill his head once more. "I hope I'll be good enough for *you*."

She stared into his eyes and smiled. "You are. You are more than enough. I love you. I love you so much it hurts, but I will respect your decision if you want to end this now. However, know I would do anything to make this work for us. I don't care what others may think now. I am making my path, and I choose you."

Claude could not tell if his heart would burst out of his chest, but he would die happy right here and now. She'd never said the words before. He was sure she hadn't felt the same. He placed a finger to coax her chin upward and met her earnest, sweet eyes. "What did you say?"

"I choose you." She smiled.

"No, the other part, the part about love," he said. He must be sure of it.

"I love you dearly and most fervently—"

He swooped down to claim her lips before she could finish her sentence. She loved him. Loved him. Loved him. Loved him!

The words rang through his bloodstream, singing their way to his heart as the heat of her body pressed against his, igniting sparks to explode in his belly. He parted only to capture her lips twice and thrice more until their breaths mingled in the bitter cold. Her fingers clung to him, reaching past his coat and curling around his vest. Groaning at her taste, his hands cradled both cheeks to draw her impossibly closer.

Something wet dripped onto his finger, and he broke the kiss to bring the tear to her attention. Had he hurt her?

"Marguerite?" He gasped. "I'm sorry, did I—?"

Faster than he thought possible, she grabbed him by the lapels and tugged him down again. This time, she deepened their kiss, parting her lips, and led them into a tangled, sweet dance.

"I love you," she murmured against his lips. "I love you so much."

His hand grazed leisurely upward from her neck and relished her softness, the realness of this moment. Goosebumps pebbled across where his warm fingers touched her, and her eyes fluttered when he rested his forehead against hers.

"I love you too. By the Gods, I may still be afraid of what is to come, but I know it'll be manageable by your side. As long as you love me, I know I can do anything."

"We can do it together," she said, and no doubts came to dissuade him.

He pressed a soft kiss to her forehead. "Together," he whispered.

"Are you ready?"

His gaze softened as he lowered his mouth to hers in a gentle kiss. "I am now." A playful grin spread across his mouth, and she giggled.

"Come, let's go!" She grasped his hand and tugged him forward.

Together, they laughed and walked hand in hand toward their new future.

EPILOGUE

Marguerite

Three Years Later

"This is absolutely beautiful. It was a pleasure doing business with you," Miss Blanchett said and reached for Marguerite's hand.

"It was a pleasure doing business with you as well." She nodded toward the paper bag. "I hope your intended will approve."

"I know he will." The bag crinkled as her client reached inside and took out the small, gold locket. Unlatching it, she placed one hand over her heart. "You made me more beautiful than I deserve."

"I only paint what is already there." Marguerite reached for Miss Blanchett's thin shoulder with a soft grin.

"Oh, you are too kind, Madam, too kind!"

They exchanged pleasantries, giggling until Marguerite bid her farewell and ushered her out the door. As soon as she shut it, she put a hand on her swollen belly and sighed.

"You're an active little one," she said under her breath, and the babe kicked her ribcage as if to prove her point. Wincing, she picked up her shawl hanging by the fireplace and wrapped it around her shoulders. A figure walked down the cobbled path from the window toward her home. Sandy hair and a familiar crooked nose came into sight, and she waved to her husband before dashing to the door to greet him.

Warm arms wrapped around her, and her large belly clashed against his lean form. Claude bent to peck her on the lips and smoothed the stray hairs from her face.

"How was business today?" he asked. "I saw Miss Blanchett pass by me on the road. She looked rather happy."

"I was a little nervous about how she would like it," she admitted. "But I am glad she liked the finished product."

"How could she not? You are very talented," he said, leading her toward their home.

"There is always room to improve," she countered, shutting the door behind them.

"I wonder when you will accept how good you are. Maybe another ten years?" He chuckled.

Putting a hand on her hips, she stuck her tongue out as he hung his coat on the hook by the door. "More like twenty." She liked the sound of his laugh as he pulled her in for another kiss.

"How was managing business today?" she asked.

"Excellent, actually. Your father's shop is thriving, and the linen is especially popular."

"I'm glad," she said, reluctantly pulling away from his warm arms. "The carriage should be here any second. We should get ready."

He nodded, and they helped each other dress in their best clothes. Claude ensured her stays were loose and comfortable around her stomach and headed toward the door when the footman knocked.

Once inside the carriage, Marguerite breathed in the spring air, damp with rain, and watched the countryside pass her in waves of greens and golden grass.

It had been three years since they came out of the forest. When she found her parents, her family wept for joy, and Henri struck a deal with her father. At first, her mother was skeptical of Claude, but upon Henri's insistence and good word, her parents gave her their blessing to marry.

Unfortunately for Henri, upon searching for his family, his title had been passed on to a cousin who lived outside of Avilon. His stepmother had married Mr. Jacques and passed away years ago. Henri admitted to being glad that his remaining half-sisters married well despite the shame he had put them through. Henri had said they nearly fainted at seeing him, and although they exchanged apologies, they wished to have no contact with him. Agreeing with the terms, he was happy to make peace and never see them again.

Without his title, however, Henri revived her father's business with the wealth he kept within the chateau. Together, they built stronger trades and expanded across the globe of Gallia.

Claude reunited with his aging father before his passing. Many servants, including Isa, could find their loved ones or discover what happened to them.

Mr. Bellanger could care less about her marriage to Claude and married the eldest Paquet daughter upon his return from the navy.

And, of course, little Bonbon, she thought fondly, had been happy to reunite with her sister. Luckily, Rosalie did not marry that disgusting Mr. Laroux and married a jolly merchant who loved nothing more than to bow to her sister's whims. Phillipe also found happiness with the second Paquet daughter.

Much had changed since then. Hardships had come and gone, but Claude was always by her side as he was now, holding her hand in his own.

Two hours passed until the busy roads of Avilon came into view. The sun set over the horizon as the carriage clacked over uneven streets until they stopped at their destination. When the door opened, she jumped upon seeing a familiar face.

"Henri!"

"Surprise!" Her friend grinned and helped her down, clapping Claude on the back as they alighted.

"You did not have to greet us so personally," Claude said.

"You are my dearest friends and family," Henri said pointedly. "How could I not? I gather my footman treated you well?"

"Of course. Joseph is always a pleasure to see." Marguerite glanced behind and nodded toward the young man, who dipped his hat in return.

"Are you all ready? I believe the show is about to begin," Henri said, gesturing toward the milling crowd. The theater glowed gold under the chandelier lights as they took their seats in a private box.

"The best seats in the house," Henri explained, proud as a peacock, and she could not help but laugh. Some things never changed.

"Ladies and gentlemen," an announcer spoke. "We are proud to present our Opera: The Tale of Rumpelstiltskin."

When the lights extinguished, the red curtains swung open. A few singers dressed in peasant costumes and heavy rouge makeup strolled across the stage in front of a painted village backdrop. A woman with gleaming dark hair braided down her back entered and began the song in a pure, soprano voice.

"There she is!" Henri pointed to the lead. "That's Isabelle. Isn't she stunning?"

Marguerite nodded in agreement. Isa was certainly beautiful and the most radiant she had ever seen. They were both able to see their dreams come true. And, as she looked around at her husband and dear friend, her heart warmed at being brought together and finding happiness at last.

THANK YOU

Thank you for reading *Enchanting Fate*!

Thank you for reading *Enchanting Fate.* If you enjoyed this story, I hope you will read more books from the Fairy Tales of Gallia.

To learn more about my books and stay connected, join my newsletter and claim a FREE Cinderella short story. A Charming Dance is a prequel to A Charming Hope. Visit my website, check out my author pages on Amazon and Goodreads, and follow me on all my social media platforms like Instagram and Facebook @ashleyevercott.

I hope you will kindly consider leaving a review. Reviews not only help authors find new readers, but they also help readers find new books to enjoy. Thank you so much!

Acknowledgments

This book wouldn't be possible without the support of many friends, and a loving husband who encouraged me to chase after my dreams. Thank you, Sydney, Keilah, and Sarah for helping me through this writing journey from the very beginning. I wouldn't have gone far without you. Thank you to my beta readers, my editor, and my ARC readers. Thank you to Miblart for the beautiful cover design, you were a pleasure to work with. And thank you dear readers for taking a chance on this book.

You are all superstars.

ALSO BY

Fairy Tales of Gallia Series

Enchanting Fate: A Beauty and the Beast Retelling
A Charming Hope: A Frog Prince Retelling

About Author

Ashley Evercott was born and raised where it's mostly sunny and there's always traffic on the 91. From a young age, she has dreamed of far-off worlds and star-crossed lovers. She is proud to pen these stories to life and combine fantasy and tension-filled romance. When she is not writing, she is consuming as many books as she can and daydreaming at home with her cat and supportive husband.

www.ashleyevercott.wordpress.com

www.ingramcontent.com/pod-product-compliance
Lightning Source LLC
Chambersburg PA
CBHW020552260626
47157CB00003B/665